THERE ARE THI[NGS]
HORRORS THAT MAKE YOU WISH YOU
   COULD DIE.
STORIES THAT LINGER LONG AFTER THE
   FINAL SHOCK.

THE CHANGELING

Kenneth McKenney

Author of
THE MOONCIIILD

"A tale of horror and satanic possession for
mature readers"

Booklist

"A real old-fashioned gripper—a dark and
heady brew"

Frank De Felitta,
author of
The Entity and
For Love of Audrey Rose

Other Avon Books by
Kenneth McKenney

THE MOONCHILD

Kenneth McKenney

THE CHANGELING

AVON
PUBLISHERS OF BARD, CAMELOT, DISCUS AND FLARE BOOKS

THE CHANGELING is an original publication of Avon
Books. This work has never before appeared in book form.
This work is a novel. Any similarity to actual persons or
events is purely coincidental.

AVON BOOKS
A division of
The Hearst Corporation
1790 Broadway
New York, New York 10019

Copyright © 1985 by Kenneth McKenney
Published by arrangement with the author
Library of Congress Catalog Card Number: 84-091257
ISBN: 0-380-89686-9

First Avon Printing, May 1985

AVON TRADEMARK REG. U. S. PAT. OFF.
AND IN OTHER COUNTRIES, MARCA
REGISTRADA, HECHO EN U. S. A.

Printed in the U. S. A.

WFH 10   9   8   7   6   5   4   3   2   1

For my assistant, Bluebottle, whose sole
contribution was to sleep on the typewriter.

THE CHANGELING

Opening

IT WAS COLD and dark and beginning to rain as the bulldozer driver reversed his earth-moving machine and lifted its blade clear of the mud. The heavy vehicle slid in the damp soil, and with a gesture both impatient and weary, the driver slammed the gears into neutral. He'd had enough for one day; if the site engineer wanted the foundations any deeper he could come out and dig them himself. All the driver would do tonight was a final sweep along the soft, muddy edge of the trench he was clearing, and that would be that.

He hadn't intended to work late. None of the others in the gang had remained, but at the last minute, the foreman had taken him aside and asked if he'd mind putting in an extra hour or two, explaining that the foundations for the holding wall of the building they were about to begin needed to be dug a little deeper. And the site engineer wanted it done tonight. They were already behind schedule. Reluctantly, one eye on the lowering sky, the driver had agreed. There was nothing much to go home for, anyway, he told himself. Janet had gone, and the house was empty without her, but as cold dampness began to rise about him and river mist slid along the trench and crept into his bones, the driver regretted his decision to stay. The rain was becoming heavier; through the headlights of the bulldozer, thick droplets drifted and swirled like snow.

Grumbling to himself, the driver shifted into gear again, lowered the blade, and began to cut the final slice of rain-soaked earth. It was a real shame, the driver thought as he watched the soil slide, a backward step. Once it had been beautiful down here by the river. There'd been those nice old Victorian cottages with their tiled roofs and their brickwork. Some of them had been pulled down to make way for the railway marshaling yards; the subsequent gleaming steel and the green-painted buildings looked a great deal better than this new monstrosity would—a multistory carpark blotting out the landscape. The driver shook his head sadly; he had no desire to see the change.

But everything was changing now; he didn't know what this nice old town was turning into—supermarkets in the High Street and garages everywhere. There was a time when Tonbridge had been one of the beauties of Kent, with its winding river and its pale sandstone castle. Now the river was full of garbage and plastic bottles, and the castle grounds were littered with paper and soft drink cans. It was a pity, he told himself, as the bulldozer approached the end of its run, but no one seemed to care anymore; no one was interested in what things looked like. All they wanted was an ugly concrete building to park their cars in.

Not that it would make much difference to him. He wouldn't be here to see it. Now that Janet was gone, there was nothing to keep him in Tonbridge;

he'd go somewhere else—Australia perhaps, Canada—anywhere to get away from this. The driver shivered and rubbed his gloved hands together. Australia'd suit him nicely, he'd had enough of the cold and the damp; he badly needed a change.

The driver shifted gears, and the bulldozer moved forward slowly, its blade pushing the wet earth into a pile on one side of the trench. He grunted: Well, it was over for him tonight. The driver swung his machine, and the headlights cut through the floating drizzle to the wall of sliced earth. The driver nodded; it looked deep enough. He was about to take the bulldozer out of the trench when his eye caught sight of something strange in the rich, brown soil.

For a moment the driver was uncertain of what he'd seen. It looked like broken foundation, part of some earlier structure, but he couldn't be sure. Then his eye noticed a glint of metal, and he rubbed away the faint mist that had formed on the windshield and tried to make out exactly what it was he'd uncovered.

It appeared to be a cabinet of some sort, a piece of antique furniture, something left behind when those neat Victorian houses were removed years ago. Still uncertain of what he was looking at, the driver put the bulldozer into neutral, lowered the blade onto the earth, and leaned out of the cab to get a better view.

But he could see nothing distinctly from where he was. He'd have to get out and stumble over the soggy ground and examine the box closely. For the briefest second, he decided to leave it until morning when he returned. Then a sudden, sharp greed overcame him. It was unlikely he'd be first on the site, and someone else would get the opportunity to poke through the rubbish and take what it contained. God knows, it might be anything, silverware, gold perhaps—those Victorians had everything, and antiques were worth a fortune these days. *He'd* worked late, *he'd* uncovered it, so it was his to examine first.

3

The driver shivered and climbed from the relative warmth of the cab. He lowered himself into the mud carefully, trying to wet his boots as little as possible. He breathed deeply and felt the cold air cut into his lungs. He'd have a quick look and go home. It was miserable out here.

Peering through the drizzle, he approached the cabinetlike structure and, in the closer light of the headlights, suddenly saw it clearly. It was a wooden casket whose entire surface was deeply engraved with an elaborate leaf design. There were small patches where semiprecious stones must have been set into the scrollwork, although most of them had come loose as the wood had rotted. The casket had obviously once been worth a lot of money.

The driver's eyes went over it greedily. With his hands in his jacket pockets he bent over, looking for the glint of metal he'd noticed earlier. It was a heavy clasp of some hand-beaten metal. A bright scar shone where the bulldozer blade had cut into it.

Silver, he thought as he peered. Be worth a mint these days. Just what he needed to get out of here, to get away.

The driver reached eagerly for the clasp and took hold of it. It was heavy and cold in his grasp. He pulled at it, but it held firm. He'd have to break it out of the rotting wood. Through the thickness of his glove he could feel its weight and value.

The driver moved closer. Settling his feet in the mud, he reached forward with his other hand, took a second grip on the clasp, and tugged at it savagely. It came away at once, bringing with it the whole side of the casket, exposing to his startled eyes what lay within.

For a few moments he remained still. He stared at the inside of the casket, not believing what he saw; it was totally untouched by the process of decay.

The casket was lined with purple velvet, which appeared as fresh as the day it had been laid in place.

Amidst the soft, enveloping cloth reposed what first appeared to be a magnificent porcelain figure of a small, beautiful boy. The alabaster skin was smooth, and glowed with health; the hair, a gorgeous crown of copper-gold ringlets, was so wonderfully lifelike; the rose-pink lips and the soft blue tint of the closed eyelids were as real and as perfect as they could possibly have been. Even the material of the little Victorian sailor suit the immaculate figure wore looked as if it had been made from true wool.

Breath caught in the driver's throat. He had never seen anything so finely wrought, never been as close to a work of art so delicately made. As he allowed his eyes to move from the figure to the corners of the interior, his spine grew cold. He saw the white, skeletal bones of a human hand clinging to one edge of the velvet, as if desperately reaching for the figure of the boy.

The driver blinked. He shivered and leaned away from the porcelain figure, the heavy silver clasp hanging forgotten from one of his gloved hands. He wondered if he dare lift the exquisite form from its rotting woodwork and carry it away from the site. It seemed so utterly fragile, it gave the impression it would break at a touch and shatter immediately in his workman's hands. He hunched forward again and slowly began to edge toward the lifelike figure when its head turned on the velvet pillow, its pale blue lids opened; it stared at him vividly.

The driver gasped. Everything within him stopped. His heart stopped beating; blood ceased flowing in his veins; saliva dried in his throat. He could not move. Terror held him like a vise.

This is a coffin, he realized, a coffin that contained a corpse that had escaped the clawing hand of death.

He managed to begin to turn, dropping the heavy clasp into the oozing mud, and to move away from the thing in the casket. He was about to take his first step when a grotesquely distorted hand took him by the throat and began to pull him down into the heavy, wet earth.

He hauled at the terrible fingers as they dug into the flesh of his neck. It was like the claw of an animal but more powerful than any the driver had ever seen. Its nails were spinelike, the knuckles gnarled and coarse, swollen with the power that drove them.

The driver tore at the hand as it bit into his windpipe. He felt his breath thicken. He lifted one hand free of the claw and saw to his horror that his gloved fingers were covered with coarse black hair.

My God, he thought, as his knees weakened. *It's a devil.*

He lurched forward helplessly into the mud as the blood ran from his torn flesh and mixed with the dark soil that enveloped him. He died in the trench he had dug for himself. Behind him the heavy motor of the bulldozer thudded steadily in the wet and misty night.

Slowly the claw-hand withdrew from the remains of its destruction into the rotting casket. It became once more the hand of the beautiful little boy.

But as this occurred, the face of the child began to alter. The eyes closed, and the fine lines that ran beneath them deepened, the rose-pink lips thickened and matured, a small cleft appeared in the chin, and the cheekbones grew prominent as the flesh below them thinned and hollowed. The face, which a moment ago had been that of a child, was developing into that of a small but fully grown man. Its beauty remained, the copper-gold hair was as thick and delicately curled, but what had been infantile had aged a full twenty years.

As the face altered, the body grew. The legs and the arms became longer, and the delicate torso thickened with developing muscle. It soon became too large for the casket and the sailor suit it wore. With its eyes still closed, it curled gently into a fetal position.

Soon the body, fully grown now, had burst free of

6

its clothing. Alone and exposed in the mud on the windswept, cold, and drizzling night, it slept easily, untouched by its bleak surroundings.

Suddenly there was a break in the clouds, and the moon slid clear, near the end of its cycle. For a moment its light shone brightly on the two forms below: the drenched body of the bulldozer driver and the naked body of the newborn male. Then the clouds closed over the moon's bright surface and once more darkness prevailed.

The Release

One

~~

SIMON BLACKSTONE realized he was running. The cold, night air stung his naked body, numbing him, clouding his already confused mind. Try as he might, he could not recall what caused him to be running in this ice-encrusted landscape, fleeing a danger that had neither voice nor shape. He could not even clearly picture what had happened to him. A figure had stood before him briefly; there had been a burst of frightful light, a blackness, the pounding of an unseen drum, and now he was running, naked in the night. But why and in what direction, he had no idea.

Simon Blackstone shivered and wrapped his arms about himself as the cold cut through his exposed skin like small, sharp knives. He ran beneath a streetlight and saw the plume his breath made in the freezing air. He glanced upward at the electric light and its hood of shaped metal and realized there was something alien about it, something he could neither place nor recognize. He was lost.

11

A gust of wind tugged at him, urging him on; small scurries of wet snow swirled about him as he fled past houses that were unfamiliar, up and away from the town. At the top of a hill he paused and glanced back over his shoulder. Street lamps defined the avenues, here and there a lighted window indicated that someone was still awake; but in the main the town was quiet. Only the occasional howl of the wind gave it any voice at all.

Simon shuddered and hurried away. When he came to a signpost that pointed to London, he followed it, not sure if he should, uncertain as to why he was running at all, aware only of a demanding need to escape.

Simon knew he must find clothing, something to cover him, otherwise he would perish. He pressed on and came to a dip in the road; there he halted once more, in the shelter of an oak. Beside the tree was a driveway leading to a large and lightless farmhouse. Simon peered at the vague shape of the building but saw no sign of life. Cautiously he made his way closer, moving under the beam-and-mason wall until the thatch of the roofing seemed to swallow him. Everything was still. A fox barked on a hillside and Simon jumped.

He rounded the building and came to a small cottage. It, too, was unlit, but even in the half-dark he could see that the door was ajar. Simon approached it, ready to run at the slightest sign of movement. He placed a hand against the door, and it swung inward easily; from the interior came the gentle sound of snoring, and a smell of wine.

Simon entered to find himself in a tiny sitting room, where on a sofa lay a man covered with a blanket, breathing loudly. Beside him, untidily heaped on the floor, was a pile of clothing. Quickly Simon scooped it up. He found a woolen sweater and a jacket, a pair of trousers and shoes. There was a heavier coat and a cloth cap hanging over a chair, but Simon left them where they were. To cover himself would be enough; he felt sufficient guilt in taking what was necessary. Pausing for a moment, he stared down at the sleeping face of the man on the sofa and wondered how he might make amends, but a feeling of sudden panic overtook him and he ran silently out into the cold, cloud-covered night.

In the shelter of the oak Simon dressed quickly, although he found the cut of the garments unfamiliar. The trousers were made of a cotton weave he did not recognize. The shoes were of cloth and leather, and were light and strangely comfortable. Only the woolen sweater was familiar; he pulled it over his head and it fit perfectly. The jacket was bulky, was made of some padded cloth, and although it seemed unnecessarily large, it kept the cold night wind away from his body.

When he had dressed, without a further glance at the cottage, Simon hurried away in the direction of London.

Ray Clark knew he should have been home and in bed hours ago, and he would have been if he hadn't seen that little blond in the transparent trousers in the bar at The Vicar of Kent. He'd fancied her something rotten, and after he'd bought her two lager and limes, he thought he was getting somewhere. But it hadn't turned out that way. She'd giggled and made him promises, and then she'd gone off with her girl friend to the ladies' room, and that's the last he'd seen of her. He'd waited for her to return until closing time, and after that, he'd hung about in his van until everyone else had gone, but there was no sign of her. She'd stood him up. He'd known that from the moment she'd disappeared giggling, but he hadn't wanted to believe it. So he'd waited until the pub was silent and empty, and even then he didn't give up. He drove round town for hours trying to catch sight of her, the bicycle chain ready on the seat beside him. One look at her, just one—it wouldn't matter who she was with this time—and he'd show her no one stood Ray Clark up and got away with it. Not and have their face stay the same. His mates didn't call him Mad Ray for nothing. He knew how to give it out.

Never mind, he told himself as he drove up the hill, there'd be another chance. He was down this way often enough, delivering to his uncle's hardware shop the other side of Tonbridge, and he only needed a couple of minutes with the girl to make sure she'd never forget him. Ray grinned tightly and touched the bicycle chain. It was nothing to what he had at home, he thought. There was stuff there he wouldn't even tell his mates about. One look at it from the fuzz and he'd be right back in Borstal. But when the time came even that wouldn't make any difference; the little bitch had stood him up and she'd laughed about it. Next time he'd give her something to think about until the day she died.

He was beginning to grin at the idea when he saw the figure by the side of the road, peering back at his headlights. Looked like a young feller who'd lost his way, Ray reckoned, as he spotted the anorak and the jeans; perhaps he'd give him a lift. He could use the company after all this time on his own.

He pulled the van to a halt beside the figure and said, "London? You want a lift then?" He slid open the door.

The feller in the anorak blinked; he didn't seem to understand. He's a good-looking bugger, Ray thought. They wouldn't have left *him* and gone off to the ladies' room. "Come on," he added impatiently. "You want a lift or don't you?"

"In the ... coach?"

"Yeah, that's right." Ray laughed; the feller had a sense of humor. "In the coach. Hop in."

Gingerly, the young man climbed into the van. Looking about uncertainly, he eased himself into the

14

passenger's seat. Ray leaned across and closed the door with a slam. Funny one this, he thought, perhaps I should've left him where he was.

"Ray Clark," he said, introducing himself. "What's your name?"

"Oh, Simon, Simon Blackstone," the young man said. "I...I must thank you for your kindness."

"That's all right." Ray put the van into gear. "Where're you from?"

"I..." Simon recalled the road sign he'd passed. "I'm going to London."

"You been down visiting or something?"

Simon hesitated. "I've been with my parents," he said finally.

"Should've stayed. Hitching's not much good this time of night. You're lucky I stopped when I did."

"I must thank you again."

"Yeah, well." Ray wondered who this geezer thought he was; he reached for a packet of cigarettes in the glove compartment. "Smoke?" He waved the packet in Simon's face.

Simon shook his head.

"Should try it." Ray pushed the dashboard lighter. "Don't know what you're missing."

Simon was silent as he watched the short, wiry youth light his cigarette; in the soft glow of the lighter the face appeared hard and determined; there was a scar that ran across one cheek. It reminded Simon of someone he had seen somewhere before. He recalled the bitter face above a white collar and a frayed black tie, but he could not remember where. Suddenly other faces flitted across the screen of Simon's mind: he saw his mother clearly, saw the dark wings of her hair and the richness of her smile. His father was beside her, but the image was fainter and less distinct. And then, from somewhere unknown, a large man with a dark handlebar mustache came into view. Simon shivered.

In the same moment he realized that the driver was speaking to him.

"You know The Vicar of Kent then?" Ray Clark was asking.

Simon blinked. "I'm afraid I have not had the pleasure," he replied.

Ray laughed. "You're a funny feller," he said, glancing at the handsome youth beside him. "Have I seen you on the telly or something?"

Simon did not reply.

"One of them pop groups?" Ray clicked his fingers. "The other night, wasn't it? One of them New Romantics." He looked at the jeans Simon was wearing, at the running shoes. Ray felt better now that he'd placed his passenger. "You wasn't wearing that gear then," he went on. "And there was makeup all over your face, but I know what it's like with you lot. Go out looking the way you do on the telly and you've got birds all over you." Ray drew on his cigarette. "That's right, isn't it? You've got fellers what keep 'em away?"

Simon shook his head. "I'm afraid you've confused me with someone else," he murmured apologetically.

"That's all right." Ray's smile was conspiratorial. "I know what it's like. Pulled a bird tonight you wouldn't have said no to. Lovely she was. Knockers like..." Ray held a cupped hand in front of his chest. "Know what I mean?"

Simon moved uncomfortably in the van's bucket seat. He watched the road unwind and longed to break his shell of ignorance, but there was nothing he knew, nor could recall, that might enable him to relate to the youth who conducted the vehicle. What was more, he realized, it was unusual for him to be alone with a stranger such as this; normally when he was out of doors, one of his parents was present, or if not, then Edith Harris, his governess, accompanied him. Poor Edith. Simon's musings became tinged with a heavy sadness he was unable to define.

He sighed deeply, trying again to unravel his tangled remembrances.

Ray Clark glanced at him sharply. "You all right?" he asked, suspicion in his voice. "I haven't said anything to offend your Lordship?"

Simon shook his head.

"I mean, you do go with girls and all?" Ray unwound his window and flicked his cigarette onto the roadway. "You're not one of them poufters?"

Simon sighed. "I'm afraid I may be fatigued," he said quietly. "Forgive me."

Ray laughed again. "Got to hand it to you," he said with some respect. "You don't give nothing away. Now, I like that, I do. That's something I really admire."

"Thank you," Simon replied, not knowing how the conversation had turned in his favor. "I am most obliged."

"Live and let live, I always say." Ray swung the van round a long, sweeping curve. "Don't tell no one nothing you don't want them to know. Now, if I was to mention certain things about me, well, you wouldn't believe it."

Simon did not reply; there was no need to. A contact had been established, and their positions were accepted. He sank deeper into his seat, watching the dark, unfamiliar stretch of road unwind before him, willing his memory to return, seeking in the corners of his mind some fact that might tell him more about himself, some clue that might tell him where he was headed. But nothing came to him; nothing returned as the van drove on toward London.

At Victoria Station Ray brought the vehicle to a halt. "Here you are," he said, "I live with me mum in the Council Flats down by the river. I'll drop you here, if it's all right with your Lordship."

"Thank you," Simon replied politely, looking around him. There was something familiar about the dark stone facade, the huge, well-lit interior. "Is this a station?"

"Get off with you," Ray said lightly. He leaned across and slid open the door. "I won't say a word to no one."

"You are most kind." Unfamiliarly, Simon climbed down from the van.

"There's a taxi rank round the corner if you need one." Ray put the van into gear. "Meanwhile, I haven't seen you and you've not set an eye on me." Pleased with his posturing, Ray Clark drove off.

Simon Blackstone watched the van turn past the vast black shape of Victoria Station and disappear from sight. His eyes returned to the main entrance of the station, and he saw lights and the movements of solitary people through open arches. Automatically his footsteps took him into the station hall where he paused and gazed about in undisguised wonder.

Somehow he had expected an atmosphere more intimate than the formidable space in which he found himself. The expanse of forecourt, the high indicator boards, the relative emptiness of the area gave him the impression he had stepped into another world. Book stalls were shuttered and kiosks locked; nowhere could he see an open bar with its small group of bustling men; there was neither the hustle of porters nor the movement of flower sellers.

Simon stared at the hollowness. The only activity he could see was in a waiting room on the far side of the forecourt, and he made his way toward it. He was becoming aware of a need now, the need for someone to take care of him. The journey to London had made him realize how little he understood of this world in which he found himself, and how much he required time and the protection of someone innocent until he was able fend for himself.

He entered the waiting room to see a young couple, whose clothing was similar to his own, huddled on a bench. The girl was crying, and the youth stared

18

dumbly at the top of her sobbing head; they took no notice of Simon. Still seeking, Simon moved on; he came to the inert form of a middle-aged man lying asleep on a bench and was about to pass it when the sleeping man urinated, through his clothing, onto the floor. Immediately Simon stepped away, his face disgusted and openly confused. The world he had come from was nothing like this.

"Drunks," a voice beside Simon said contemptuously. "Real rubbish, aren't they?"

Simon turned to peer into the soft, fat face of a young porter.

"Expect you to clean it up, they do. Get up and walk away in a bit as though nothing's happened."

Simon nodded uncertainly.

"We get them in here like that all the time." The porter curled his lip and jerked his thumb to a group outside the waiting room bickering over a bottle wrapped in brown paper. "On the whole I prefer that lot, myself. At least you know where you are with them."

"I . . . see." Simon put a hand to his forehead. "I mean . . ."

"Here." The porter stared sharply at Simon's pale countenance. "You all right? You look all in to me. Feel like a cup of char or something?"

Simon nodded. "That would be most kind," he murmured, wondering if this was the sort of person he was looking for.

"Come along then." The porter placed a soft white hand on Simon's arm. "Got a kettle going out the back."

"Thank you." Simon began to smile when the face before him gradually appeared to soften, to lose its definition, to be replaced by yet another that he knew. "No," he whispered in sudden, startling fear. "You have died."

"What's that?" The porter visibly paled.

Simon stared as the porter's face transformed: the

19

cheeks hung in heavy folds; the little eyes became lost in rolls of lard; even the porter's baggy uniform seemed to be replaced by one of a more elegant cut. Simon's throat tightened; he was invaded by a sense of dread so powerful that he was forced to cover his face with trembling hands. Memory, sharp as a nail, harsh as the snarl of a wolf, swept over him; for a moment he felt he might faint.

The porter watched Simon with growing concern. "Here," he said, "I didn't mean nothing." His arm came out again helpfully. "Let me..."

Simon backed away.

"I mean..." The porter looked about for help. "I was...a cup of tea, that's all I was talking about. What's got into you all of a sudden? You sick or something?"

"No," Simon whispered. He saw a heavy face bending toward him in the lamplight of a railway carriage; sensed pudgy hands reaching down into darkness; saw the whiteness of a greedy, dewlapped throat burst suddenly with red spilled blood; and he turned and ran from the inferno of the waiting room. "Leave me alone," he cried as he crashed through the door.

The porter watched openmouthed as Simon sped away; he turned to the young couple in alarm. "What you think got into him?" he asked, his voice cracking. "I didn't do nothing."

The youth shrugged and didn't reply; the girl with him began to sob anew.

"I don't know." The porter walked off quickly. "The things that happen. I've had it with this, if you really want to know. I'd rather be in the bloody army."

Simon's feet carried him through the great hall of the station, underneath the archways, and out into the street; a voice behind him called once, but nothing halted his flight. He ran round the corner Ray Clark's van had taken, away from a fear he neither understood nor could control, knowing only that it was part of him, and would be, until he was strong enough to face it alone.

All he was certain of, at the moment, was the desperate need to escape, to find a sanctuary where he could rest and reassemble himself, where he could learn more of what he was, where he had come from, and what he had to do. The face that had replaced that of the young porter, the familiarity he had sensed when staring at the features of Ray Clark, the bleak misery that filled him when he'd thought of Edith Harris, the confused images of his parents and the man with the handlebar mustache were all part of the horror of his past, a past that reached out toward him whenever it was given the chance. There were ghosts in his memory, evils that crawled beneath the surface of his skin. He must overcome them; he knew that now. He must defeat them before they, in turn, destroyed him.

But he would never do it alone, that was becoming absolutely clear; he needed the strength and guidance of someone else, someone young and strong and innocent who could care for him for however long was necessary. He needed protection and somewhere to hide.

These thoughts tumbled through Simon's head as he ran along a narrow street. He ran past vehicles parked for the night, past closed and shuttered shops without lights in their windows. There was nothing he recognized, and yet he felt familiar with it all; there was no place he knew of to go, and yet he felt as if he were capable of journeying to every corner of the universe.

Simon ran until his legs would carry him no longer, until the fire in his chest threatened to consume him. Then, breathless, pain-racked, exhausted, he came to a halt beside a brick wall in a corner of a twisted street. He placed his head against the cool stonework and dragged damp London air down into his tortured lungs. His knees slumped with weakness, and he hung, threatening to drop, against the brick wall.

After a while his breathing eased and some of his strength began to return. Slowly he lifted his head and wiped sweat from his face, then, with a shock that froze his weary body, he became aware that someone was staring at him. For a broken second Simon could do nothing; he closed his eyes, denying the presence of any other being, wanting neither intrusion nor release. He felt himself begin to tremble. Suddenly it seemed that whoever it was who watched him was too close and too demanding, forcing him to make a decision before he was ready, bringing this alien world closer than he would be able to bear.

Simon Blackstone began to shake.

Another had stared at him this way before. He'd been a child, a boy in a sailor suit, standing on a summer platform in a railway station in Bavaria, waiting for his parents to join him. As he'd watched their twin figures walk toward him, his mother laughing, leaning her head against his tall father's shoulder, he'd been proud of them. And then, feeling so full of life, he'd become aware that someone was watching him, and although he'd tried not to look, although he'd attempted to deny the demanding eyes, they'd tugged at him until he could resist no longer. He'd turned to stare into the face of a woman so old, there seemed to be no feature left intact—apart from those piercing, burning eyes.

Simon had wanted to cry out but could not; he'd wanted to tear himself away from the hideous old woman who crouched beside him, wrapped in what appeared to be nothing but a heap of rags, but he'd been unable even to look away.

Then the crone had spoken to him.

"You are he, child," she whispered in a voice as thin as dust. "You have come."

"W-w-what?" Simon managed.

"Do not speak. Listen." The crone's dirty white face came closer. "I must talk to you before they... interrupt us." The old woman glanced at Simon's parents; they had paused for a moment on the platform to purchase a bunch of edelweiss. "I am here to warn you... of yourself."

"I—I don't..."

"Shhh... I will tell you. You..." The witch's voice faltered; for a brief second there was something like compassion in her ancient eyes. "You cannot escape; the time will soon come for your... reckoning. You must be prepared to be taken."

Fighting his fear, Simon forced himself to breathe deeply, some of his courage returned. He lifted himself to his full height and said as bravely as he was able, "I ask you to leave me alone, madam. I am not used to speaking with strangers." In spite of his manliness, his voice cracked with alarm.

At Simon's words a faint smile passed over the crone's dirty, white features. "You are worthy," she whispered. "They have chosen well."

"Excuse me..."

"Quiet." The crone's voice was suddenly crisp; she looked across the platform to see Simon's father paying the flower seller; soon they would arrive. "You have no choice. Your future was decided the day you were born. You came into this world on the lost day of an antique calendar." The old eyes clouded. "I would save you, little one, if I could," the crone continued, "but I cannot. I am too old and too frail and ... already I have been touched." The windy voice began to fade.

Simon stared at her in cold horror, terrified by what his unformed mind had heard, dismayed by the wretched bundle of rags the words had come from. He opened his mouth to speak, but the crone raised a withered hand, silencing him.

"No," she whispered, "say nothing. Listen, there is not much more to tell you. It is not your fault, you are not to blame, you are lost, that is all. You can only be patient and hope...."

"Hope...?" Simon's voice was a squeak.

"Hope that I am able to convince them...your parents, after it has...begun, to do what has to be done."

"*After*...after what has begun?"

"Shhh." The crone's words grew even fainter. "They are coming." Simon heard his parents' footsteps but was incapable of turning toward them. He stared, transfixed, at the wretched old woman. "You are a ...Moonchild, my little one," she whispered, "and you must say nothing of this to anyone. You must remain quiet and hold your secret and tell no one of what you have learned today. Because, if you tell them, they, too, will be doomed."

"I..." Simon could not speak; his throat was tight and dry. He swallowed as the old woman's bony hand reached out and grasped his own. "Swear," she hissed. "Swear you will not breathe a word of this."

"I..."

"Swear. *To save them.*"

"I...swear."

"Good." The old hand moved away; the crone stared into Simon's face searchingly, then, with a shuffling, crippled movement, she stumbled away: a heap of dirty rags, a bundle of soiled clothing sweeping along the summer platform. "Good." The word from the ancient lips drifted back to Simon's startled ears. "Good."

Simon had closed his eyes; when he opened them again, his mother was bending over him, her expression concerned. She'd inquired if there was anything wrong, and he'd denied it and smiled bravely, and the incident had passed. He'd not spoken to anyone about it, not even to the good, kind Edith Harris. He was far too afraid.

For a year he held the secret in his heart; for a year he tried to erase it from his memory but to no avail. Then, when they'd returned to Bavaria in the following winter to ski, he'd become desperately ill. He'd fallen into a fever and had lain for days, burning, tossing in his uncomfortable bed, fighting something he only partly understood until, finally, he'd just gone to sleep. And that was all he remembered. Until now, this evening, these past few hours. When he found himself running naked in the night and had been brought to London only to run again, to arrive here, by this cold brick wall, where other eyes watched him. Eyes that would not be denied.

Slowly, filled with dread and the knowledge that escape was beyond him, he turned to see who stared at him now.

Simon Blackstone saw a girl, a curious, elfin slip of a girl, who appeared to be in her early twenties. She had long dark hair, and her cheekbones were prominent; in the heavy cloak she wore she looked like a gypsy.

As she watched him intently, Simon swallowed hard. He moved his lips to form a word, but his mouth was too dry and his tongue did not seem to function. He shook his head slowly, unable to speak, but he was aware of an overpowering sense of relief. There was no evil in this girl; she was good, she was kind, and she was innocent.

Two

FROM THE MOMENT she set eyes on him, Sally Lawrence thought he was drugged, had taken something that had distorted his sense of reality. He seemed to be in a world of his own, and physically he was wasted. His face was so white, it made the copper-gold of his hair shine by comparison, almost caused it to glow. He was having trouble with his breathing; his legs were shaking, and the sweat on his face was a silver sheet in the light from the street lamp. When he opened his mouth to speak, he mumbled like an addict.

She'd seen her brother like this before he died, seen him sweat and tremble and lose touch with his surroundings. She remembered a similar, lost movement of his mouth, a mixture of destruction and defiance as he slid a needle into his arm. Toward the end he was incapable of anything at all and lay, like a dog, whimpering on the floor.

Now, as she watched this stricken young man try

to speak, her first instinct was to walk away, to leave him in his vacuum, not to become involved. She'd waited long enough, she told herself. She'd remained while he regained his breath, to see if he needed any help, and now he was recovering. It was time to go, time to leave him to sort out his own problems by himself. Come on, she urged, you don't want to go through all that again. Get out while you can.

But she wasn't able to. Perhaps it was because he seemed so vulnerable; perhaps it was because he contained so much of her brother's anguish that she had to wait. Whatever the cause, she stayed until he had calmed down enough to approach. Then she took a gentle step forward and asked softly, "Are you all right?" knowing, even before the words were uttered, how much she was committing herself.

Slowly Simon nodded.

"Is there anything I can get you?"

Simon shook his head. "Forgive me," he managed, "my...breath."

"Your breath?" Sally peered into the wan and handsome face. "Is that all?"

"I have been...running. Farther than I should."

"My God." Sally smiled briefly. "Don't tell me you've been jogging this time of night." She felt a little easier; whatever it was he'd been taking was losing its effect. She shrugged. Anyway, he was trying to make sense. "You've got to be really keen," she added, "running at midnight."

"I...ah..."

"You live round here someplace?"

Simon took a deep breath.

"You don't have to tell me if you don't want to," Sally said carefully. "It's just that...well, if we're going in the same direction we could walk together."

Simon blinked, then stared at the friendly girl. He watched a hesitant smile waver on her lips, saw her head tilt in question, and the dark wing of her hair fall away from her delicate face. He was suddenly aware of the depth of sympathy in her eyes and knew he could trust her. She was exactly what he needed.

"I don't want to pry or anything," Sally went on. "It's just that you seemed so bad a moment ago and, well, I thought I might be able to help."

"You...you are very kind." Simon's breath was almost even; he had stopped shaking. "The truth of the matter is that...I suffered a fright and started to run. But...but now I am almost fully recovered." He bowed very slightly. "Thank you."

Sally Lawrence shook her head in wonder. He was being so damned English; she hadn't heard anyone talk this way since she'd come over. The carefully balanced sentences, the clipped, well-modulated accent were things she'd been seeking ever since she'd left New York almost a year ago. In the time she'd been in London, many details of this great and ancient city had filled her with joy, but no one had spoken to her the way this guy with the white face and the copper-gold hair did. No one had really sounded English until now. And, curiously, this Englishness made him seem familiar; his polished voice and his manners softened the harshness of his condition, gave him a gentleness she felt secure with.

"If you're really feeling better," she said easily, "why don't you let me make you a cup of coffee. I live just around the block."

"You...have rooms close at hand?"

"Well, there's a bedsitter with kitchen and bathroom you can't turn around in, but I call it home."

Simon extended a hand. "Allow me to introduce myself," he said. "My name is Simon Blackstone."

Sally took the outstretched hand and shook it. "I'm Sally Lawrence," she replied. "American, or is that too obvious?" She smiled. "Will you join me for coffee, Simon?"

"I should be delighted."

"Great."

Quite casually, Sally took Simon by the arm and led him around the corner into an open, tree-filled square; she unlocked the front door of a house, and they walked up four flights of narrow wooden stairs to her apartment. There she ushered him in, turned on lights, and plugged in a two-bar electric heater, smiling all the while.

"It's not much," she said, lifting a bundle of clothes off one chair, hesitating, then putting it on another. "And, my God, isn't it a mess!"

"I find it very cozy." Simon began to relax for the first time that night; she was so easy to be with, this elfin creature who had found him, and so pretty. She belonged to no memory he could recall. "Do you live here all alone?"

Sally nodded. "You couldn't fit anyone else in." She indicated the smallness of the room; it contained several chairs laden with clothing, a bed in one corner, a divan in another. One small door led off to a tiny bathroom, another to an equally small kitchen. "I don't even have room for a cat."

"Do you like cats?"

Sally shrugged. "Not really," she confessed. "Although I was always finding them in the street and bringing them home when I was a kid. I couldn't ever leave them out on their own."

"Like me?"

Sally laughed, surprised how much at ease she felt. "I guess so," she admitted. Then she rubbed her hands together briskly. "Say, what about that coffee?"

"I should like a cup very much."

Simon followed Sally into the tiny kitchen where he sat on the edge of a wooden chair and, with a growing sense of security, watched her light the gas under a kettle. For the first time since he could remember he felt calm and unafraid.

"Tell me, Simon," Sally asked, as she spooned instant coffee into brown pottery mugs, "where are you from? What part of London?"

"I..." Simon began, then paused.

Sally waited.

"I...I have only just arrived in London," Simon continued. "I was with my parents, in the country, as a matter of fact." Association, he found, could teach him; by listening he was able to learn. "I hardly know the city at all, to tell you the truth. I am quite a stranger here."

"Well, now." Sally smiled. "You mean, I know it better than you do?"

"Of that I have no doubt."

"Maybe I could show you around?"

Simon nodded.

"I'm getting to know it well," Sally went on, keeping the conversation going. She was aware of his reserve, but that didn't seem important at the moment; later, when he came down completely, she could find out more about him. In the meantime she knew how to be patient. It occurred to her that if he had nowhere else to go he could stay here for the night; she felt safe enough with him. There was the divan in the corner; it had been used as a bed before, and he could sleep there if he wanted to. "Fact is, I just love this place, and there's nothing I'd like better than to introduce you to my favorite parts. Pubs and parks and walks by the river." Sally put her head to one side. "What do you say, Simon? Put yourself in my hands?"

Simon smiled. She was so vital, so enormously alive. He sensed a barrier being withdrawn. She turned from him and poured boiling water into the mugs, added milk and sugar, and handed one to him. He took it with both hands, feeling it warm his palms.

"Well?" Sally sipped from her own mug.

"I...I'd like that very much."

"Right, but remember, you get any false information from me, I'm not responsible. I'm a stranger here, too, you know."

"I'll remember that."

Sally laughed lightly.

Simon sipped from his mug. The coffee was warm and sweet; it filled him with content. The exotic girl, with her gypsy appearance, was like a bright and friendly bird beside him. For the moment he wanted nothing more than to remain in her tiny kitchen, seated on an old-fashioned chair, feeling warmth inside him and listening to her shining voice.

Sally watched him. The strain was going from his face; soon he would sleep. It was good to see him coming through it, and she was suddenly very glad she'd stopped and talked to him. If he'd never been in London before, God knows what he'd have done on his own.

"Maybe tomorrow we could go to Kew Gardens," she went on easily. "I could show you some corners that'd take your breath away."

"Tomorrow?"

"Sure, why not?"

Simon looked down at his mug, some of the warmth inside him beginning to fade. He'd not thought about tomorrow, nor of any other future time. He'd run from his fears, and now he was safe; all that mattered was to remain here with this bright, protective girl for as long as he needed. His eyes returned to Sally, uneasily.

"Well, you don't have to make any decisions to-night," Sally added, seeing the change in his expression. "Say," she said as if the thought had just occurred to her. "You can stay here if you want. There's that divan in the corner."

"Here?"

"Sure."

"With you?"

Sally nodded.

"You..." Simon suddenly had difficulty in form-

31

ing the words. "You are extremely kind. I do not know quite how to thank you."

"That's okay." Sally shrugged. "I've been in spots myself. I know what it's like."

"Yes, I believe you do," Simon replied solemnly.

"You'll stay then." Sally put her mug on the kitchen bench. "I'll get a couple of blankets. You're going to need them. It's really cold tonight." She'd make it clear, she thought, what the arrangements were. "Then tomorrow maybe we could go to Kew Gardens, or if that's too far I could take you up to St. James's Park. We could walk from here. It's fabulous. I was up there today and there was ice on the pond. I tell you, it's really beautiful." Sally felt her tongue running away with her, but it didn't matter. Simon was at ease again; he listened, he sipped coffee, the concern gone from his eyes. It was so good to see him responding. Sally laughed. "I saw a duck come in and land on the ice. I don't think he realized it was frozen and he skidded about fifty yards before he got his brakes together. It was really something to see."

Simon smiled. "Have you many friends?" he asked a moment later.

"Sure, I've got friends," Sally replied, her voice not quite as animated. "I was with one of them tonight as a matter of fact." She looked away. "Not that it was what you'd call friendly. That's why I was walking home on my own. Sometimes friends don't turn out the way you want them to. Don't you find that, Simon?"

"My father used to say that friends were rather like umbrellas. You never had one when you needed one."

"Hey, I like that. What's he do, your father?"

"Oh..." Hesitation crossed Simon's features. "My father is a gentleman. He...he lives in the country."

"Right, you told me." Sally had no wish to break the mood. She glanced at a clock hanging on the kitchen wall. "It's getting late," she said. "I'll fix the blankets for you."

"Thank you." Simon closed his eyes wearily. "I am rather fatigued."

While Sally arranged his bed, Simon remained on the kitchen chair. He drank the last of his coffee and carefully placed the mug on the bench; he waited until Sally returned and then he stood, smiling politely.

"There you are," she said. "In the corner." She pointed to the divan. "Go ahead, get into it. I'll just rinse these mugs, then I'm going to bed, too."

"Thank you." Simon stood by the door, his hands held before him, his face still. "I really do not know what I would have done without you," he said simply. "You have been..."

"Don't even think about it," Sally said. "Go to bed; you look like you're asleep already."

Simon reached out and gently touched Sally's long dark hair. "You're nice," he said softly, "I like you. You're so innocent."

Sally's mouth dried. She could not account for the feeling that suddenly overcame her; she felt tenderness and something else, a strange, confused compassion. Quickly she looked away.

Simon turned from her and went over to the divan. He paused beside it as if uncertain what to do, as if he might have been waiting for someone to come to his aid, then he undressed slowly, crawled in between the blankets, and was asleep almost immediately.

A few moments later Sally switched off the light in the kitchen, walked over to where Simon lay, and stared down at his face, smooth now, unlined by either fatigue or fear. She studied it and was surprised again by its perfection; in the soft glow of the room he was nobly handsome; his hair seemed to shine like a halo, his features classically beautiful.

My God, she said to herself. You're pretty. What-

33

ever you're on, it certainly hasn't touched you yet. You're as pretty as anyone I've ever seen. For a moment she was tempted to bend and kiss the sleeping lips, but abruptly she turned away, went to the window, and looked out across the square at the skeletons of black trees in its center and the spire of a small church on its farther side.

My God, he *was* so English, she thought as she stared across the square. My father's a gentleman, he'd said, and, *You're nice.*

He was like something out of an old movie, almost unreal.

Then Sally shivered. Abruptly, out of nowhere, a chill that had nothing to do with the outside cold passed her. She felt it begin behind and go through her as if something colder than ice was making its way from the room out into the tree-lined square. Sally closed her eyes for a moment, allowing the bleakness to pass, then she turned and stared back at the dimly lit figure of Simon Blackstone sleeping on the divan.

My God, she wondered half-seriously, half in jest. What have I gotten myself into this time?

Three

DETECTIVE SERGEANT ALBERT SCOT picked up the pack of cigarettes and put it down again. It was the seventh time he had done so that morning. He kept the open pack on his desk to remind himself he didn't smoke, but this morning the device didn't seem to be working. Putting the pack down each time was a little harder. Once he'd actually taken out a cigarette, rolled it in his fingers, and stared at it hungrily, before standing and abruptly walking away from his desk.

It wasn't the death of the bulldozer driver that worried him exactly, he kept telling himself. As a detective sergeant in the London Murder Squad, New Scotland Yard, and with half the city to cover, he wasn't entirely unused to murder. But the fact that the death had occurred in Tonbridge, and the Tonbridge Police had called London for assistance, specifically naming him, contained something distinctly odd, quite outside his control. And, before he'd known anything about it, the process of attaching him to the Tonbridge Force had already begun. Very soon he'd be on his way back to the town he knew so well and, if he wasn't very careful, he'd be smoking again.

Apart from anything else, his mother would get him going—she always did. Albert Scot came from Tonbridge, his mother lived there permanently, and once he saw her again, she'd begin. If it wasn't his weight, it'd be his clothes. And if she couldn't find anything there she'd ask him why he wasn't married or at least living with someone.

You're thirty, Albert, she'd say. It's time you did something about it.

Albert would listen and bite his fingernails. He'd sit staring out of the cottage window at the leaf-strewn garden and the uncut grass, and finally he'd take up the pack of cigarettes, remove one, light it, and he'd be smoking again. He knew it would happen, it had happened before. There was nothing to stop it happening again.

Albert sighed and scratched his thinning hair. He picked up the notes he'd made about the Tonbridge murder, the newspaper clippings reporting the event, and left his office. He walked through the bullpen, the outer room with the sergeants and the clerks and the women constables, nodded, grunted a greeting or two, then went down several flights of cold, tiled stairs to the canteen in the basement.

As he waited in the queue for a bacon sandwich and a cup of tea he was joined by Chris Wilkinson, a lean, healthy colleague who ordered two yogurts and a glass of milk. Albert was sure Chris had never smoked a cigarette in his life, not even at school.

They sat down at the same table without exchanging greetings. Albert stirred sugar into his tea and watched Chris take the top off the first of the yogurts. A pretty woman constable approached, lifted the cup she held to indicate that she'd like to join them, but Albert shook his head and she went away.

"You want to watch it, son," Chris said. "They'll start talking about you and me."

Albert whistled at the woman constable, and when she turned, he blew her a kiss; she smiled and continued on.

"That'll only add to the rumors," Chris continued, spooning apricot yogurt into his mouth. "They'll say you're a tease as well."

Albert grunted and bit into his bacon sandwich.

"Still giving up smoking then?" Chris asked cheerfully.

Albert nodded.

"Tough, is it?"

"Murder," replied Detective Sergeant Scot. "Absolute, bloody murder."

Chris laughed. "You'll get over it," he said. He finished one yogurt and reached for the next.

"Not at home I won't," Albert said dolefully. "Be down there this afternoon listening to my mother listing the shortcomings of her pride and joy. Take about twelve and a half minutes and I'll be on them again." Albert looked at Chris. "You wouldn't like to go down for me?" he asked without hope.

"Sorry," Chris replied. "Far too much to do up here." He grinned knowingly. "What takes you back to Tonbridge? That lorry driver?"

"Bulldozer," Albert corrected. "You hear about it?"

Chris nodded. "Nasty." He reached for his glass of milk. "They need help?"

"That's right. Asked for me direct. Seemed to think I'd jump at it coming from there."

"Didn't you have an uncle who was with Tonbridge for a time?"

"Grandfather," Albert corrected. "The pride of the force. Or became so the day he retired." He sighed and swallowed the last of his bacon sandwich; it was cold, and the fat was beginning to congeal. "I don't suppose I'd be in this business if it wasn't for him and the rubbish he fed me at an impressionable age. Who knows, I could have been driving a train."

"Or a bulldozer."

"Sod off." Albert took a mouthful of tea. "I suppose you've got something cushy that'll keep you by the fire all day."

"As a matter of fact," Chris Wilkinson said with a smile, "I have."

Albert grunted. The curious thing about being attached to Tonbridge now, he thought, was that on no other occasion had he ever worked with the local constabulary. This was the first time they'd ever called on him, and to tell the truth, he didn't really know any of the staff down there at all. He'd always been occupied elsewhere.

After leaving school he'd found a place at Reading University and had taken an unremarkable degree in history, knowing all the time he was only avoiding the inevitable, pretending to go in one direction while his true interest lay in following his grandfather's career. Whatever he said about his grandfather, he'd adored him.

After graduating, Albert joined the London Metropolitan Police and some time later had been transferred to New Scotland Yard. Since then he'd been back to Tonbridge as infrequently as possible. It wasn't that he had any dislike for the place or that he didn't exactly love his mother; it was merely that he found life, and work, a great deal easier and more interesting in London.

Damn it, he told himself forcefully and banged his cup on the table, she's not going to get me smoking again. No matter what she says.

Chris Wilkinson grinned. "Just solved something important?" he asked blandly.

"I have," Albert replied firmly.

"Anything to do with that lot?" Chris indicated the notes and newspaper clippings Albert had been studying.

"Not a thing." Albert re-sorted the papers with his long and slender fingers. "I shouldn't think there was much to this, anyway. I don't even know why they've asked for special assistance."

Chris looked surprised. "Haven't you read the *Sun*?" he asked.

"Do you mind. I can't even take the nudes they print."

Chris smiled cleverly. "*They* say there's some kind of Ripper about. Throats torn out. Hands of death. You'll have a lovely time, even if you don't see your mother."

Albert glanced back at the clippings. "None of the others says anything like that," he muttered. "The *Times* mentions skeletal remains, and there's some speculation that the driver was attacked by wild dogs."

"Wild dogs? In Tonbridge?" Chris laughed. "I'd change to the *Sun* myself, old lad. Everything's a lot more interesting the way they put it."

"Sod off." Albert eyed the healthy face before him. "I suppose this assignment by the fire of yours includes brandy."

Chris nodded. "Be wasted on me though, won't it?"

Albert Scot grunted. He stood and, without a further word, walked out of the canteen.

There'd be nothing to this, he was sure. When they got to the bottom of it, they'd find the bulldozer driver had been drunk and had fallen under his machine. And yet, Albert paused, a foot on the tiled stairs leading up to his office, what was it his grandfather had said one day in the kitchen when no one else appeared to be listening—something about being unable to escape once family blood was involved?

Albert had never really understood what the old man was talking about. When he'd questioned him, his grandfather had half-closed an eye and tapped the side of his nose secretively. "That's why your father went off to Korea," he said. "He knew. I told him and he knew. Joined the army. Went as far away as he could. And died there. That got him out of it. You'd better do the same."

Albert recalled the way the old man's eyes had held him. He couldn't have been more than ten at the time, but he never forgot the look of sanity and certainty on his grandfather's face.

Later, when he was older, he'd tried to probe further but had discovered nothing more. Albert suspected that his mother might have known what the old man referred to, but he was never sure; whenever he approached the subject, her replies were impatient and crisp.

Albert knew little about his father. He was a man who had died before Albert could remember him. All that remained was a handful of snapshots taken when a half-smiling face was turned expectantly toward a camera, or caught in a pensive moment glancing away.

"He left me," his mother said abruptly on one occasion. "He didn't like being married, so he went away. He volunteered for Korea, he didn't have to, and he never came back."

"Difficult when you're dead," Albert had replied. He'd been a teenager then and had no idea how to handle her. "Why didn't he go into the police?"

"The police?" Albert's mother had snorted. "He wouldn't have done that for love nor money." But she never said why.

Now, as Albert paused on the tiled stairs outside the canteen recalling his grandfather, he wondered why, at this moment, the old man should come so strongly to mind. There was nothing to prompt the memory as there was nothing abnormal about being attached to the Tonbridge Force, but the image of his grandfather, with his half-closed secretive eye and his furtive manner, was alarmingly clear. He'd not really thought of the old man for years. It was ages since any reflection of his grandfather, or his father for that matter, had been with him in any way at all.

Albert shrugged and continued up the stairs.

It must be because the old devil would have been over the moon to have me on his stamping ground, he told himself. He'd have been chuffed to have me back where he had been. But even so, he thought, it was curious that the old man's words should come back now.

Simon Blackstone slept until early afternoon. All gray, cold morning he lay curled in his blankets like a child, only the copper of his hair showing to the world. He barely moved in his sleep.

Sally Lawrence had approached the divan several times during the course of the morning, but he had not responded. She'd woken up late herself, decided not to go to work, and had snuggled deeper into bed, pulling the covers up about her. Later she'd risen, made herself coffee, washed and dressed, but in spite of her movements, Simon remained buried in his bedclothes.

Finally Sally had gone down to a shop on the corner of the square and purchased bacon and eggs and a pack of tea. She'd returned and laid out plates and put a frying pan on the gas ring as if hoping that these simple acts of preparation would cause her visitor to wake and join her. But it wasn't until past two in the afternoon, when pale sun had begun to filter through the windowpanes that Simon lifted his head, looked at her, and smiled a slow, delightful smile.

"Hello," he said apologetically. "I do seem to have slept most soundly."

"You have." The Englishness of his clear voice was charming, the precision of his words so *old-fashioned*, it made Sally want to laugh. He seemed completely in control of himself today; his eyes were clear and his hands were steady. "You almost missed lunch," she added teasingly.

"I do hope not. I am famished."

"It's nearly ready. You want to eat in bed?"

"Good Heavens, no." Simon got off the divan, a blanket wrapped around him; he moved toward the tiny bathroom. "I shall be with you in no time at all."

While Simon prepared himself Sally remade the divan. She picked up his trousers where they'd been thrown in a heap on the floor and laid them out; she collected his sneakers from beneath the divan and placed them neatly together. It was only then that she noticed he had no socks. That's funny, she thought, searching further. His feet must've been freezing.

She shrugged and went into the kitchen, turned up the gas, and placed rashers of bacon in the frying pan; soon its busy sizzling and rich, tangy odor filled the apartment. Hearing a sound behind her, she looked over her shoulder to see Simon almost fully dressed, pulling shoes onto his bare feet.

"Hey," Sally called cheerfully, keeping her voice light, "don't tell me you don't wear socks in this weather?"

"I..." Simon paused uncertainly. He remembered the deep, stentorian breathing of the man on the sofa and the smell of wine. There was a sense of claustrophobia. "I... seem to have mislaid them," he replied carefully.

"You want some? I've got plenty."

"Well, yes, please. That would be most kind."

"No problem." Sally went to a pinewood chest of drawers, opened one, and produced a pair of thick red socks. "Hope you don't mind the color."

"Thank you. I think they are most attractive."

Sally smiled, her head on one side, her dark hair floating away from the fine bones of her face. "Nothing else you want?" she asked easily.

"Well..." Simon began; he could not explain. "I do not seem to have any underclothing. I know it must sound quite odd, but...I am without it."

Sally laughed. "Boy, you certainly left home in a hurry," she said, prepared to humor him. "You must've run."

"I did," Simon replied with relief. It was positioned now; the straightforward reaction of this honest girl had provided him with the element that had been missing. "The truth of the matter is that I *have* run away from home. I do apologize. I should have made it clear from the beginning, but that is exactly what happened. I have run away from home."

"Without your underwear and socks?"

"I am afraid that is the case."

Sally shook her head, shrugged, and turned back to the pinewood chest of drawers. "I don't know how I'm going to fit you out with underwear," she said. "It's not something I've got lots of in spite of the fact that I'm a liberated girl." She paused. "I don't suppose you'd want a pair of mine?"

"It would not trouble me in the least," Simon replied without any trace of embarrassment.

"Okay..." There was a vaguely quizzical note Sally could not keep out of her voice. "If you're certain you don't mind."

"Why should I mind?"

"Well, you know. It's not exactly macho...."

Simon looked at Sally, an expression of complete innocence on his handsome features. "I'm sorry," he said simply. "I have no idea what you're talking about."

"Well, who am I to quibble with equality." Sally found a dark blue pair, which she handed to Simon. "By the time you've got them on the bacon and eggs should be ready."

"Bacon and eggs, one of my favorites." Simon's voice was enthusiastic. "Do you think we could manage fried bread while we're at it?"

"You'd like that?"

"I'd love it."

"Sure." Sally moved slowly back toward the kitchen. "I must say you're not hung-up about anything. That's great."

Later, as they sat on either side of the small kitchen table, Sally watched Simon wipe his plate clean with a piece of bread and eat it with obvious relish. There was a freshness about him she'd not seen in anyone for as long as she could remember; there was an eagerness about his movements that infected her with a similar response. She found herself smiling as she watched him, laughing aloud when he glanced up to catch her eye. Whatever his problem, today he was pure pleasure. Whether he had told her the truth or not didn't matter; whatever he was taking appeared to have no hold over him.

"You really enjoyed that," Sally said as Simon leaned back in his chair. "You ate twice as much as I did."

"It was delicious," Simon replied contentedly. "Is there any more tea?"

"Sure." Sally poured it. "Say," she began casually, "do you want to tell me *why* you ran away from home? I mean, you don't have to if you don't want, but, well, I did the same sort of thing once, and you know, maybe we've got something in common."

"Did you?"

"Yes, a few years back."

"Why?" Simon asked quickly. "Where did you go?"

"Oh..." Sally began, then paused and smiled. "I asked first," she said. "Tell me your story." She watched, curious in a different way now, wanting to get beneath his skin. "Why did *you* run away?"

"Well..." Simon studied the surface of his tea; he did not know where to begin. There were doors that must remain forever closed; there were words that could not be spoken between them. And yet he needed her now, needed her with him; he must tell her some-

44

thing and, at the same time, say nothing that might alienate her warmth and friendship. He looked up at her; her eyes were blue-gray with little flecks of dancing amber. He had not noticed how bright they were or how incredibly pretty she was. He turned from her and glanced about the tiny kitchen; there was no item here that contained any memory. He *was* secure in these rooms and must remain so. "I ...I merely had to leave," he said finally, softly. "I was not able to stay any longer."

"That's awful. Why?"

"I had not been happy for a very long time." Simon smiled suddenly, disarmingly. "Is that what happened to you?"

"Well, yes, I guess it was," Sally replied; she felt slightly dismayed by his lack of information but was determined not to push him. Later, when he came to trust her, he would speak more freely. "In a way, it was the same with me."

"But, there was something else?"

"Yes," Sally admitted. "There was." She felt an urge to move. She left the table and walked to the kitchen bench. She looked over the sink, through a small-paned window, out into the winter square. Pale afternoon sun slanted through the bare arms of the plane trees; a child and a dachshund were playing on the leaf-littered grass. Sally could hear the child's delighted cries; they came up like old memories. "I had a brother," she began to explain in a low voice. "He died. After that I didn't want to stay."

"How very sad." Simon was beside her, he put a hand on her arm. "What happened to him?"

"He OD'd."

"I beg your pardon?"

"He ...you know." Sally turned to look at Simon and was surprised by the innocence of his expression. She mimed the action of an injection in her arm. "He took too much of what he was taking. I thought you might have known about that sort of thing."

Simon shook his head.

"You don't..." Sally found herself in difficulties with her own question. "You don't have any sort of problem?"

"What do you mean?"

"With...with anything like that?"

"No." Simon shook his head again. None of this touched him; none of this was any part of the fear he had fled, the faces that menaced, nor the words that threatened. "I am not familiar with...anything like that."

"Sure?"

"Of course." Simon smiled easily. He put a hand on his chest. "Cross my heart and hope to die."

Sally stared. They were often like this, denying any part of what they needed until the demand was overwhelming, and by then they were usually wrecks, dependent, hopeless, and lost. Yet Simon appeared to be none of these; he looked as if he were in the bloom of health. Sally turned away and let her eyes drift once more out over the gardens in the center of the square. She sighed, then turned back to Simon. "Listen. How about we go out for a while? Take a walk in a park someplace."

"Oh." Simon put his hands together in disappointment; he had no desire to leave his newfound safety. "We talked about that last night, didn't we?"

"Sure." Sally nodded. "I was going to show you London."

"I'd love that, only it's..." Simon hesitated.

"What?"

"Well, it's so nice here, with you."

"Wow." Sally laughed at the guile. "You English really know how to lay it on."

"But, you like it here, don't you?"

"Come on, Simon." Sally was flattered but determined; he'd have her round his little finger if she wasn't careful. "Grab your anorak and let's go get some fresh air."

"My what?"

"Your jacket, dummy. The one you left on the back of the chair."

"Oh, of course."

Simon went over and picked up the garment. Sally watched him. You're a funny one, she thought. With all your charm, I wonder where you think you're coming from. "I went back, though," she said abruptly, returning to the earlier conversation. "I stayed away a couple of years, and then I went home again."

"Did you?" Simon sounded only vaguely interested.

Sally nodded. "I wanted to be friends again. With my parents, I mean. I didn't want to stay away forever."

"Well, that's quite understandable."

"You'll do the same," Sally put in quickly. "After a while you'll think the way I did, then you'll go back again." She would have added more, but there was suddenly something in Simon's face that silenced her. It was exactly as if he had closed himself off, shut her out completely. "Don't you..." she began again uncertainly. "Don't you think...so?"

"No." Simon's voice was almost a whisper. "Not if I can help it."

Sally looked away. The chill was back; it seemed to surround them both. She shook it off. "Come on," she said. "Let's go out."

Four

DETECTIVE SERGEANT ALBERT SCOT traveled from London to Tonbridge by train. He watched the winter landscape rattle past his second-class compartment, and his mind filled with conflicting impressions. As a flock of rooks, black sweeps against the turned brown earth, lifted and scattered, he wondered again why the Tonbridge Police should have applied for him personally. There were half a dozen other detective sergeants they could have asked for, all of them more than ready to go. It was a nice little assignment, this loan to Kent. The town was pretty, and the work would not prove to be strenuous. But the call had come for him alone, and he found its precision disturbing. What's more, the request had been granted immediately, with neither question nor delay.

Albert's departmental chief had cleared it, and others down the line had issued warrants and approved expenses. A section of the bullpen was involved for less than an hour transcribing his attachment to the Tonbridge Force. But none of this gave the impression of adding more than a finishing touch to a process already in motion. Try as he might, Albert was unable to shed the notion that he was being manipulated by something, something that had begun a long time ago.

It's my sodding grandfather, he told himself again as the train shuttled past hedgerows and clusters of houses, him and his bloody mutterings. Closing an eye and tapping his nose. What'd he expect, acting like that? Me at the age I was. I still don't understand him.

Albert sighed. He pulled the pack of cigarettes from a pocket of his raincoat, looked at it, and put it back. He wasn't going to smoke, that was decided clearly. He'd taken a nonsmoking compartment to make sure, and who was he to break the law?

The train pulled into Tonbridge. On either side hills lifted slatelike and bleak in the cold afternoon air; in the station yard piles of building materials for the new car park ran away from the sidings. Already the area had the raw-concrete appearance that would be the car park's final facade. Building blocks stood like uninspired architectural leftovers, piles of sand and gravel rose like mountains on the moon, and heavy machinery moved slowly in the gray light as if of its own accord. Everything conspired to give the winter's day an air of drab unreality.

Albert peered beyond the building materials. Somewhere over there, where slender steelwork came up like dry reeds in marshland, was the site on which the bulldozer driver had died; somewhere in this raw landscape a man had come out of his machine and had been killed.

Albert picked up his nylon grip and the brown leather case that contained his papers and disembarked on the southbound platform. He glanced up toward the shape of the yellow sandstone castle, bulking out of the dimming afternoon, and knew he was home. Walking briskly, he left the railway and headed toward the police station. He thought of stopping to see his mother but decided that could wait. After all, he was here on business.

Once inside the station he was shown into the Chief Constable's office. He barely had the opportunity to greet the desk sergeant and refuse a cigarette before a young constable approached and led him into a warm office whose walls were covered with photographs of cricketers standing in tight, white-garbed groups, looking steadfastly at the camera. The Chief Constable, at various stages of his life, was in most of them. He was a stout man with clear, baby-blue eyes, and he gripped Albert's hand firmly as he greeted him, indicated a chair, and dismissed the constable in what appeared to be one continuous gesture.

"So very glad you could make it, Detective Sergeant," he said warmly. "We look forward to working with a man of your proven ability."

"Nice of you to say so, sir."

"We've kept an eye on you, you know. It's not often a local lad does as well as you have."

Albert sat stiffly, his hands deep in his raincoat pockets. He'd anticipated this small talk and could afford to be patient, but the sooner they got down to business, the better. It would be satisfying if he were told exactly what they expected him to do.

"The case of the girl from Chelsea? And the swine responsible? All your work, eh?" The Chief Constable went on cheerfully. "You can't deny it. We know who the credit belongs to, and we're very glad to have you with us for a while. Believe me, our chaps'll learn a thing or two just by watching."

"I'd like just one constable, if that's all right, sir," Albert said clearly. "Just someone to ... assist."

"Eh? Oh, of course. Playing it close to the chest. I understand completely."

"Thank you." Albert turned to the wall beside him and stared at a county side dated 1952. The Chief Constable, hardly changed at all, smiled out at him. "Tell me, sir," he asked, "what actually was the cause of death?"

The Chief Constable cleared his throat. "To tell you the truth, Detective Sergeant, we're not quite sure. Dreadful wound in the throat. Bled to death almost instantly." He tapped a folder on his desk. "All here, in the medical reports, but what actually caused it is awfully difficult to say." He turned his bright blue eyes toward Albert. "That's why you're here, of course."

Albert nodded. "What else should I know, sir?" he asked.

"Well..." The Chief Constable smiled brightly again. "A lot of funny stuff turned up beside the corpse. An old trunk. Some torn clothing. Human bones. A whole adult skeleton to be exact." Again he tapped the folder. "All of that's in here as well. A strange collection, really."

"Any footprints?"

"Not a sausage. Poured all night, you know."

"Was it a grave?"

"What's that?"

"The...the bones and things the bulldozer driver uncovered. Was it an old grave?"

"You know, the same thing crossed my mind. Exactly that. But there's no sign of a coffin. Apart from the trunk I was telling you about. Mind you"—the blue eyes twinkled—"it could have been an old murder site."

"Why do you say that, sir?"

"Ah..." The Chief Constable raised a significant finger. "That's for you to find out. Don't want to start putting ideas in your head." He slid the folder across the desk. "Here, take that. I'll assign you a constable.

The chap who showed you in's a good lad. We've everything that turned up waiting for you out in the storeroom. Have a look at it and then we'll talk." He smiled confidently. "What'd you say to that? Get all the facts together and we'll compare notes."

"Very good." Albert stood. "Why was he on his own?"

"What?"

"The bulldozer driver? Didn't he have a mate?"

"No." The Chief Constable shook his head. "Singular fellow. Liked to work alone."

"No one minded? The union...?"

"He'd done it regularly." The Chief Constable's blue eyes were knowing. "We're not too bloody-minded down here," he said, as if that explained everything. "Break a few rules every now and then, no one suffers."

"I see." Albert reached for the folder. It did not contain very much. "Well, then, if you'd call the constable I could perhaps... begin."

"Of course." The smiling blue eyes continued their appraisal. "I knew your grandfather," the Chief Constable said suddenly. "He was in his sixties when I first met him. Wonderful old chap. You'd have been proud of him."

"I am."

"Of course. You must be. But I was thinking of then, really. When he was in his prime."

Albert Scot waited; something was close to the surface.

"That business..." The Chief Constable shook his head slowly. "Came out of it awfully well, you know. Really stood up for himself."

"What business was that, sir?"

"I thought you'd have known." The elderly policeman seemed vaguely caught out. "I'd have imagined you'd have heard about the inquiry."

"To tell you the truth..."

"It *was* a long time ago, mind you. Keep forgetting

just how quickly time does go by." The Chief Constable tapped his stomach as if to prove it; his figure was no longer trim. "He'd have been younger then, much younger. Don't suppose I'd have heard anything myself if he'd not been still going strong when I arrived. Talked about it on his retirement, they did. Well..." He spread a hand that seemed to comprehend everything. "You know how it is. The way people are. Skeletons in cupboards, that sort of thing. Just can't leave well enough alone. Pity, but that's human nature, I suppose."

Albert Scot listened with respect, partly due to the Chief Constable's seniority, partly due to the older man's ability to say so much and divulge so little. Albert had heard nothing of any inquiry in which his grandfather was involved.

"Grand old man," the Chief Constable continued. "Not a spot on his character. Record as clean as a whistle." He smiled an engaging smile. "They don't make them like that these days."

"No, sir."

"Well, then..." The Chief Constable pressed a button and almost immediately the policeman who had shown Albert into the office entered. He was tall and hollow-chested; his nose was long and hooked. "Constable Hooper"—the Chief Constable waved an introductory hand—"you'll be assigned to Detective Sergeant Scot while he's with us. Please give him all the help you can."

"Yes, sir."

"In that case..." The Chief Constable's hand moved on, dismissing them both. "If there's anything you want"—he smiled at Albert—"anything at all, don't hesitate to ask. Door's always open, you know. Pop in at any time and have a chat. I'm usually here."

"Thank you, sir."

Outside the warm office, away from the bright blue eyes of the elderly policeman, Albert turned to Constable Hooper. "What's your name?" he asked.

"Hooper, sir."

Albert's expression didn't alter.

"Ah, Tony, sir."

"Right, Tony, I'm Albert. You'll find I'll want very little. If there's anything, I'll ask. In the meantime is there a room I could use to go through this?" He indicated the thin folder the Chief Constable had given him. "After that we'll take a look at the strange collection the Chief was talking about."

"Very good." Constable Hooper opened a plywood-lined door to let Albert into a bare office. It contained a small desk, a straight-backed chair, and an ashtray. On one wall there was a calendar from the local garage showing a big-breasted girl, and a narrow window looking out onto the police parking area. "This is for visitors," Hooper said with the faintest trace of apology. "I'll get a phone run in if you like."

"There's no need." Albert looked at the cell-like room. "Who are your visitors? Gestapo?"

Constable Hooper's nose seemed to lengthen, and he snickered. "Accountants, sir, I mean, Albert. TV license checking, people like that." His face resumed its normal expression. "Would you like a cup of tea?"

Albert nodded. He took off his raincoat and hung it on the back of the chair; he removed the pack of cigarettes and placed it on the desk beside the folder; he pushed the ashtray to one side, sat down, and very carefully read the folder's contents. He didn't look up when Constable Hooper placed a cup of strong, milky tea beside him but continued until he'd covered each typewritten page, then he went back to the beginning and read everything again.

Ray Clark didn't see a copy of the *Sun* until well into the afternoon.

After dropping Simon Blackstone at Victoria Station the night before, he'd driven to the Thames Embankment and the tall block of council flats where he lived with his mother; there he'd parked the van and taken the gray, scratched lift with its graffiti and its faint odor of urine up to the eighth floor.

The flat had been dark; his mother was asleep. She left each morning before six for Westminster Hospital, where she worked as a cleaner until four in the afternoon; sometimes Ray didn't see her for days. It didn't really matter. He lived his life and she hers.

By the time Ray Clark got to his room he was tired. He kicked off his boots, removed his jacket, and lay in bed, looking at the crossed bayonets, the commando dagger with the knuckle-duster handle, the German helmet, and the half a dozen other articles of violence with which he'd decorated his walls.

His eyes came to the bicycle chain he'd brought from the van and placed on the floor beside him. He recalled the girl and her fat, giggling friend, and all his anger came rushing back. He reached out and grasped it. The cool of the metal, the sharpness of the links was gratifying. He lifted it and looked at it more closely and could almost see it cutting into her smooth young flesh; he could almost hear her cry. The thought aroused him, and with his other hand he unzippered his jeans and felt for himself. He masturbated, not taking his eyes off the bicycle chain, not losing sight of the girl's face splitting, nor the sound of her voice calling for mercy. Her cries joined his own, and then he lay back on the stale bed fingering the cool links of the ugly chain.

He woke up late the following day and wandered into the kitchen where he found the remains of his mother's breakfast and a copy of the *Sun*. He made himself tea, flicked through the pages of the tabloid, and was about to bite into a piece of cold toast and jam when he came to the item dealing with the Tonbridge murder. Immediately he was interested. He must have been in Tonbridge at the time of the killing.

Ray read the item slowly, moving his mouth with

the words. He knew the building site; it wasn't far from his uncle's hardware shop. He could even have been driving past when it happened. He could almost have seen the killer.

The thought stopped him. That feller he'd picked up, the one with the snotty accent. His Lordship. He'd acted queer, hadn't he—hadn't answered any of Ray's questions, hadn't said anything about himself. He could easily have had something to do with the death.

Ray read on, the piece of toast and jam forgotten in his hand. There was something about an old box of silver the police were investigating. There was a description of the driver's torn throat, which made Ray feel he was watching one of those films on late-night telly and there was something else, a hand, a skeleton's hand in the box with the silver. The bones were right there like they were trying to reach for something. God Almighty, it made the hair at the back of Ray's neck shrink and prickle.

He lifted his head, stared at the kitchen wall, and let the paper fall to the table. It was possible that his Lordship mightn't have had anything to do with it. But you didn't clear out of a town like that in the middle of the night unless you had a reason. What was it he'd said? Been visiting his parents? What a load of cod's wallop. Who'd he think he was trying to fool? Not Ray. Not Mad Ray.

Ray Clark scratched his head thoughtfully. He'd just have to find that feller again. There were a few questions he'd like to ask. Jesus, when you came to think of it, that ponce, passing himself off as a rock star, could actually have been the killer. Could actually have been the one who topped the driver. And the way he'd done it...a shiver went down Ray's spine. God knows what he'd used, but whatever it was, he was good with it. They weren't going to forget him again in a hurry.

Ray fumbled for a cigarette and lit it thoughtfully.

Now where would a feller like that go? Where would you catch up with him again? Maybe he lived close by; maybe that's why he didn't want anyone to know too much about him. There were a lot of expensive flats in the squares between here and the station. He could be in any of them.

Ray drew on his cigarette. He'd bet his Lordship wasn't all that far away right now. The thing to do was to chat up a few barmaids, ask them if they knew his Lordship because his old mate Ray wanted to talk to him again, to settle some business. And then—Ray blew a long plume of smoke across the kitchen table—well, maybe he could squeeze off enough to quit the bloody run to the country.

Five

SIMON BLACKSTONE, hands deep in his anorak pockets, walked through the thickening twilight by the side of Sally Lawrence. His face glowed with pleasure as the cold evening air rubbed against his features. He glanced at Sally and saw that she, too, was smiling; the soft roundness of her cheeks was as rosy and fresh as country apples, and her hair hung back like a scarf.

They'd come from Sally's flat through wide and narrow streets, past lighted shop windows with remnants of bunting and Christmas decoration still on display. They'd passed pedestrians, some hurrying bundled against the cold with coat collars buttoned up to their chins, others with their gloved hands pressed tightly together—all bore the stamp of a winter evening. As they'd walked, Simon and Sally had come closer to each other, had responded to each other's enjoyment. They'd discovered things they had in common, laughter they were able to share; each felt at ease in the other's company. They began to believe they knew each other well.

In St. James's Park they'd trudged around the ice-lipped lake and watched ducks approach for crusts. They'd counted the different species of water birds. They'd jumped over stacked deck chairs and run around a closed kiosk, and they'd felt together and at ease and content with each other. Hardly a word had been spoken to indicate the growing intimacy, but both were aware of it.

Once Sally asked, "Are you warm enough?" And Simon replied "Oh, yes, thanks. Your socks have been especially helpful."

Sally laughed. "Last time I used them was in Upper New York State. I haven't been skiing for years."

"Skiing?" The word caught Simon's attention. "That was something we were going to do once. Only it was far too... cold."

"Who's we?"

"My parents and I."

"Where? I hear there's only someplace in Scotland. And that's bleak."

"Oh, it wasn't in this country. It was in Bavaria. We went there especially." Simon paused, listening intently, testing himself, but nothing intruded, no words came. "I was only a child then."

"But you had socks?"

"Of course." Simon smiled at her impishness. "I'm quite sure I had socks."

"You... Simon." Sally's smile was wide. "You're something, you know that. You're really something."

"And so are you," Simon replied sincerely.

He looked at her fondly, at the elfin face and the honest eyes. He needed her now, more than ever; she was his guide, she was his shield. Even out here, away from her rooms, he seemed safe with her. And, with her, he knew, he must be gentle.

But there was more to it than that.

Not only were the words of the rag-bound, dirty-faced crone and the faces that flitted across the screen of his developing mind beginning to make him understand and, in a sense, come to grips with, the horrors that dwelt in the twilight of his past, but they were also trying to warn him, to tell him that somewhere a deeper, darker, more deadly force lay waiting to confront him.

Soon its shape would be made known, soon he would be shown more of himself than he might wish to see—and then he must be careful. Especially with her. He must save her from knowing too much about him; he must hold her free from any contamination. No matter what it cost, he must keep her safe.

"You are very special." Simon smiled, hiding his thoughts, his face smooth and easy. "And I thank you for being what you are."

"Simon..." Sally shook her head, vaguely embarrassed. "Oh, come on," she said loudly to cover herself. "Let's go. It's getting dark."

They started back to Sally's square. Suddenly Simon lifted his head, sniffing the air. "Chestnuts," he said with boyish delight. "I can smell them, can't you?"

"Yes." Sally pointed toward a corner on the far side of the road. "There's a guy with a stand over there."

"Can we have some? I simply love chestnuts."

"Let's go." Sally crossed the street; Simon followed closely. "You want a whole bag for yourself?" she asked as they arrived.

"Yes, please."

Sally picked up two white paper bags; she handed one to Simon, who took it eagerly. The chestnut seller, a middle-aged man wearing a long scarf and a cloth cap, watched the process without comment, his eyes going from one to the other. Simon took a chestnut, juggled its warmth in his fingers, peeled the outer shell, then began to walk away.

"Hey," Sally called, "you've forgotten something."

Simon turned, his expression curious.

"I think he'd like some money." Sally indicated the chestnut seller, who sniffed once and said nothing.

"I have no money," Simon said with childish simplicity. "None at all."

Concern filled Sally's eyes; she was shamed by her own insensitivity. He had nothing; they never did. "That's okay," she said quickly, handing the chestnut seller a note. "I've got it."

The chestnut seller smiled a wintery smile. "You picked a right one there," he said, handing Sally the change.

Sally turned and caught up with Simon. She glanced at him, expecting to see something of guilt on his clear features but instead found a wide, innocent, gratified smile.

"Aren't they lovely?" he said, breaking open another chestnut. "Aren't they absolutely delicious?"

"Sure." Sally held the unopened bag in her hand. "They're great."

"Don't you want yours?" Simon asked a moment later; he rolled his empty bag into a ball and threw it into the gutter.

Sally shook her head. "I'm not that hungry." She looked at him. "You want them?"

"I'd love them."

"Be my guest."

"Thank you." Simon peeled a chestnut and put it into his mouth. He smiled, and the smile faltered. "You're not cross with me, are you?" he asked carefully, suddenly aware of her change of mood.

Sally shook her head silently, unable to do otherwise.

"I don't want you to...I mean..." Simon became a little more upright; some of the delight went out of his eyes. "What I mean to say is, if I have offended you I do apologize." His accent was pronounced. "I know a gentleman is obliged to pay, but I do assure you I have no money at all."

"That's okay." For reasons she didn't fully understand Sally was suddenly afraid of losing him. "Like I said, I'm liberated. I don't give a damn who picks up the tab."

"I don't know what could have happened to my money," Simon continued as if Sally had not spoken. "Perhaps I mislaid it on the way here. It may even have been stolen."

"Stop it." There was pain in Sally's voice. "It's no big deal."

"I want you to understand...."

"I do understand." Sally moved closer; she took Simon's arm and felt an unexpected tension running through him. "Forget it, will you? It's nothing. I mean it, nothing at all."

"Are you sure?"

"Sure I'm sure." Sally squeezed his arm. They began walking again. "Hey," she said lightly, "you going to give me one of those, or you going to eat them all yourself?"

Simon's eyes came round quickly. "Would you like one?" he asked with relief.

Sally nodded.

"You said you weren't hungry."

"I am now."

Simon searched the bag and took out the biggest nut he could find. "Shall I peel it for you?" he asked.

"Yes, please."

"There." Simon handed her the peeled, pale gold chestnut. "They really are delicious."

"I know." Sally chewed. For a while she said nothing, and when she spoke, her voice was casual. "If you like, I could lend you some money. It'd only be a loan, but it might get you through."

"That would be most kind." Simon's tone was formal again.

"Don't be like that. There's nothing wrong with borrowing from a friend."

"No, I suppose not."

"Here." From her purse Sally extracted a five-pound note. "That'll keep you going for a while."

Simon took the note and examined it carefully, his eyes round with surprise. "Five pounds," he whispered. "You must be very rich."

Sally shrugged. "Not so you'd notice," she replied.

"But... well, thank you," he said simply. "Thank you very much indeed."

"That's okay." Sally took his arm again. "Now you can buy me a drink." She looked at her watch. "It's almost opening time."

They walked slowly back toward the square, the serene center, the small apartment on the fourth floor where there were neither images nor voices, only peace. As they came to a tiny street near the square Sally stopped and pointed through mews houses to an old-fashioned public house half-hidden in a bend of the alley.

"Let's go in there," she said. "It's the nicest pub around."

"Oh..." Simon hesitated. "An inn?"

"You'll like it. It's really cute."

"Very well." Simon turned into the alleyway. "What's it called?"

"The Half Moon." Sally indicated the swinging sign above the door.

Simon's step faltered. For a moment he stared at the yellow crescent against a blue-black sky, the name lettered in rubric. Involuntarily he shivered.

"What's up?" Sally glanced at his strained face. "Don't you want to go in?"

"Yes... yes, of course."

"You sure? We could go someplace else. Or back home if you'd rather?"

"No." His voice was firm. Something told him he was destined to enter this public house, that there was no avoiding what lay within. "I assure you, this will do us very nicely."

Sally turned to him quickly; her mouth opened, but she said nothing. Simon Blackstone was already halfway down the mews, striding. He walked upright, his eyes fixed on the painted shape of The Half Moon sign.

Frowning uncertainly, Sally hurried after him.

With great care and concentration, Albert Scot examined the rotting woodwork of the casket the bulldozer driver had unearthed before he died. He fingered the purple velvet, still damp from the rain, and frowned thoughtfully. "Not common, quality like this these days, is it, Tony?" he said to Constable Hooper. "Nor work like this." He pointed to the carving on the casket.

"That's what the Chief Constable said, sir."

"Albert."

"Albert. He makes a hobby of antiques." Hooper's nose lengthened. "Bit of a one himself, if you know what I mean."

"He put a date on it?"

"Couple of hundred years was all he said. And Spanish. Too far gone to tell more." Hooper came closer. "He said there was something funny about it, though, something he found puzzling."

"What's that?"

"Well, he said the woodwork's gone. Poke your finger through it if you'd a mind to. And the clasp." Hooper picked up the heavy silver lock. "Been in the ground for years. Look at it. Black as..." He grimaced.

"Go on."

"And everything else, cloth, leather, all that sort of thing, rotted away. But this here"—Hooper's long finger pointed to the purple velvet Albert held—"and that." He indicated the remains of a child's sailor suit. "Good as new, almost. Wet but shows no sign of decay. Been protected somehow, though he can't think how."

"It was inside the chest until the bulldozer ripped it open."

"Maybe." Hooper's voice echoed the Chief Constable's doubt. "But everything else's gone. That skeleton, the feller that went in with the box, there's nothing left of his clothing but the belt buckle. Soaking, that soil is, down by the river." Hooper's voice was reflective. "Full of worms."

"Let me see it."

"The soil, sir?"

"The belt buckle."

"Over here." Hooper picked up a solid brass object and handed it to Albert. "Got some sort of bird on it. An eagle, I think."

"It's German." Albert turned the buckle over in his hands. "What about the skeleton?"

"A big man, sir." Hooper's eyes were steady. "Do you want to go through the bones?"

"Not really. The doctor's done that. There's nothing in the medical report about serious injury. The skull's intact, and the neck hasn't been broken. A couple of the ribs were cracked, but that could have happened at any time." He looked at Hooper. "One hand was in the box, though, wasn't it? Some of the papers said something like that."

Constable Hooper almost snickered. He put fingers to his lips to steady himself. "I think that idea came from a local reporter, sir... Albert. You know what they're like, always looking for something."

"None of you saw anything like that?"

Hooper shook his head. "The bones were a bit scattered. A hand here, something else there. Be hard to say what exactly was where before the 'dozer got amongst them."

Albert Scot nodded. He stared at the rotting woodwork. It was mud-caked and moldy. Then his eyes went to the untouched material; it appeared almost

65

new. "What about the driver's gloves?" he asked. "Covered with hair, weren't they?"

"They were, that's true. There's a report about that...."

"I read it."

"He's got a dog, you know." Constable Hooper shrugged. "Or did have. The animal's with neighbors now. I think that's where the hair came from. Mind you, by the time we found him there wasn't a lot of anything. He'd been out all night in the rain."

"You had it checked? The hair?"

Constable Hooper looked surprised.

"Collect some off a glove. Send it up to London. See what they say about it. Some of the dog's as well. In a different envelope."

"Very good, sir." Constable Hooper's tone was slightly more respectful. "Is there anything else you'd like done?"

"Not for the moment," Albert replied. He looked at his watch and sighed. "It's about time I went to see my mother." He turned his eyes once more to the remains of the carved chest, the cloth, and the buckle laid out on this bench. None of it told him a great deal.

"What do you think killed him?" he asked, almost idly. "The reports don't mention a weapon."

Constable Hooper cleared his throat. "Hard to say," he replied noncommittally.

"What's the gossip?"

"Well..." Hooper's voice became confidential. "The lads are a bit puzzled, but he was a funny one, the driver. He could've had it out with anyone."

"Funny in what way?"

"His missus'd left him, and he'd been hard to get along with since then. Picky, if you know what I mean. Take anything the wrong way."

"Don't usually end up with your throat torn out for that."

"I know, but... well it mightn't have begun as

66

something serious. Then, a few drinks and...before you know it, they're at it."

"Down on the building site."

"It's quiet there. And it wasn't any secret he worked alone."

"Any idea who it might have been?"

"Not a clue."

Albert studied the lean face of Constable Hooper; like the display on the storeroom bench, it gave nothing away. "Why do you think they asked me to come down?" he said quietly.

Hooper's face relaxed; the fleeting grin came and went. "The Chief's been trying to get you down for years," he replied easily. "Very proud of you, he is."

"He hardly knows me."

"It's not that." Hooper leaned closer. "You're tradition, don't you see? Your grandad was here. You're history, Albert, and the Chief likes that. He's a bit of history himself. That's why he studies those antiques."

"You seem to know a lot about me."

"We've been talked to, sir." Hooper leaned away. "Ever since you were coming we've been talked to. You're bright and shining, you are. We're going to learn from you."

"Do you mind?"

"Not me, personally..."

"Some of the others?"

"You never know." Hooper actually smiled. "But we'll handle that when we come to it, won't we, Albert?"

Albert nodded. He turned away from Hooper, from the display on the bench. "Why was the wound so savage?" he asked on his way to the storeroom door.

"Rats."

"What?" Albert turned and stared. There was no smile on Hooper's face.

"Thick they are down by the river. Like flies on

67

a rubbish dump. I'd say someone cracked him across the throat and rats did the rest."

"There's nothing like that in the medical report."

Hooper shrugged. "You've not met Dr. Wilson, have you, sir?" he said quietly.

Albert shook his head.

"Half-blind or..." Hooper made drinking motions with a boney hand. "Either way he wouldn't know if someone was up him, if you'll excuse the expression."

"The report's competent."

"Ah, that's not my point, is it, sir? Routine work; you can't fault him. Do it in his sleep he could, and very often does. But something new, something different, where you've got to use your head...well, he's lost there, isn't he?" Hooper sighed a false sigh. "Nice enough old sod he is, but should've been retired years ago."

Albert Scot looked at Constable Hooper for a long moment. "Is there anything else you think I should know, Tony?" he asked pleasantly.

"Well, no...not at the moment."

"Think about it."

"I will, sir." Hooper straightened his shoulders. "And, I'd like you to know you'll get all the help from me you can. I don't hold any resentment. None at all."

"But you don't think there's any need for me to be here?"

"Frankly, I can't see a reason. Professional, that is."

"Just a drunken brawl down by the river?"

"Something like that. Between the rats and the rain and the feller that ran off with his missus, it's not very complicated."

"No." Albert Scot went out of the storeroom and into the box that served as his office. "It doesn't seem to be."

"Would you like to have a look at the building site?" Hooper asked, following closely.

"Later." Albert glanced once more at his watch.

"Be dark later." Hooper looked pointedly out the window to the deepening dusk, the almost visible swirl of cold, misty winter air. "Dark enough now."

"Then we'll do it in the morning." There would be nothing to see now on the building site. The mud and the workmen and passage of feet, no matter what attempts had been made to rope off the area, would have obliterated any clue. "Good night" he said abruptly, "I'll be here at eight in the morning. Don't forget the dog hairs."

"Very good, sir." Hooper opened his mouth pointedly. "There's another small matter...."

"What's that?" Albert was putting on his raincoat.

"The Chief, he was rather hoping to have a further word with you."

"I've nothing to tell him." Albert picked up the pack of cigarettes he'd laid on his desk and slipped it into his pocket. "Should he ask, I'll report tomorrow."

"Very good, sir."

Albert Scot left the small brick-faced police station with its blue light above the entrance and trudged through the rising river mist. He went along the main street, past Boots the Chemist, a betting shop, and a Wimpey Bar; nothing seemed to have changed. He turned in to the narrowness of Brick Lane and walked its length, passing two-storied cottages until he came to his mother's; there he paused by the green wooden gate. It needed mending. He pushed it open and walked through the collection of blown leaves toward the front door with its wrought-iron lamp stand and the globe that never worked. He pressed the bell and heard the double-toned echo ring at the back of the house.

He waited, his hands in his raincoat pockets, one

holding the packet of cigarettes. Soon he heard his mother's footsteps, and he wondered what she'd have to say when she saw him. He hadn't told her he was coming.

Six

SIMON BLACKSTONE went steadily up the three stone steps to the front door of The Half Moon. He lifted a hand as if to grasp the shiny, brass door handle, push open the old wooden door with its pane of frosted glass, and enter alone, when he paused and looked over his shoulder to Sally Lawrence.

"I *am* sorry," he said as if suddenly remembering her. "How very rude of me to rush ahead like that."

"That's okay." Sally stared at him. His manner had altered considerably since he'd seen the yellow half-moon sign hanging over the door of the public house. He had become more determined, alone; the simple innocence of the youth with the paper bag of chestnuts had gone from him completely. "You go on in."

"Allow me." Simon swung open the door and ushered Sally in. "It seems very pleasant," he remarked politely as he followed her into the bar.

"Well, it is kind of snug."

The Half Moon was small and cozy. A single curved wooden bar faced the door, its surface covered with zinc. The pump handles were ceramic, the walls a deeply stained walnut; red satin curtains framed the windows, and wherever there was space, an unending display of old photographs filled the walls. Sepia prints, misty landscapes, formal arrangements of people were arrayed in blacks and whites and shades of gray on every side. To walk into The Half Moon was to turn the clock back almost a century.

"See what I mean?" Sally said as she took a seat at a polished wooden table. "There's nothing else like this around."

"It *is* ... quaint." Simon's eyes moved through the memorabilia. He was beginning to realize, even more vividly, that for him there was no escape. Perhaps in Sally's rooms there might still be some refuge, but it would only be temporary; sooner or later even that would have to be abandoned. He breathed deeply and turned to her, seated upright in her chair. Her hands were quietly together on the table before her, but her eyes were vaguely concerned. "What may I offer you?" he asked, quite formally.

Sally smiled a little; he was being English again, and she was unable to resist it. "I'd like a glass of Guinness," she replied.

"I'll take a little Scotch with water." Simon recalled his father, such a drink in hand, standing before an open fireplace. "Should I order over there?" He indicated the zinc-topped bar and a woman who stood behind it. She gave no impression of having seen them enter; she was reading the evening paper and smoking a cigarette. "Is that the thing to do?"

"Sure is." Sally kept the smile on her face. "You *have* been in a pub before?"

"Of course," Simon replied easily. "But in the country things are quite different."

"Oh, right... but if you're going to drink Scotch all night you'll need that five pounds I gave you."

"Will we be here all night?"

"Who knows." Sally sat back, visibly relaxing. "Go get the drinks."

Simon nodded. "I shan't be a moment," he said, and moved away.

Sally watched him cross the bare wood floor, then her eyes went round the bar. There were only two other customers present. A very old man, with a drip on the end of his nose, sat in one corner holding a pint of bitter close to his chest. The drink appeared oversize in his thin, heavily veined hands. A woman, with a small brown dog at her feet, sat opposite. Obviously the old man's daughter. She drank sweet sherry from a tall glass and repaired her lipstick. Sally looked back at Simon as he turned from the bar, the drinks in his hands. He approached carefully and laid the dark, creamy-topped Guinness before her. He lifted his whiskey in a silent toast and sipped it cautiously. Immediately he made a face.

"You don't like it?" Sally asked curiously.

"I assure you, it's very good."

"You turned your nose up."

"Perhaps I added too much water." Simon stared at Sally defiantly. "I prefer it with less."

Sally nodded and looked away. She was beginning to wonder if she wouldn't be wise to consult someone about him, someone who might help her understand his abrupt changes of mood, his strange unworldliness. One moment he was a laughing child, the next as stiff and distant as an old man. At times his eyes were clear, at others clouded with concern. She was certain he'd taken nothing since he'd been with her. And yet there were so many changes of personality, so much below the surface she couldn't touch. It would help to share her concern, if she could find the right person.

She took another mouthful of her rich, slightly bitter drink, then looked back to Simon. Now he was smiling. The planes of his face were smooth and balanced and beautiful, his eyes deep and full. In the pale light of the bar his hair glowed with health.

By God, she realized, whatever you are, you've got me. We might all be a little funny at times, but we don't all come back the way you do. As the thought crossed her mind, she was aware that she was being drawn more and more deeply into his world. She'd been captured the moment her eyes caught him, exhausted and gasping for breath, in the street the night before; now she was totally involved.

"Are you enjoying your drink?" he asked.

"Yes," she replied quietly, touching her glass. "Do you like Guinness?"

Simon paused. "It looks delicious," he said evenly.

"Like to try some?"

"No, thank you." He lifted his whiskey. "It's unwise to mix your drinks. My father was quite strict about that."

"Simon," Sally began gently, trying to penetrate. "You're awfully old-fashioned. Did you know that?"

"Am I?" Simon blinked. "Perhaps it's because ...because I have led a very sheltered life. I have, you know, been terribly protected."

"Is that why you ran away?"

"Ran away? From home, you mean?"

"That's what you told me."

"Yes, that was one of the reasons."

"You want to talk about them?"

Simon lifted his head. "I lost someone," he replied. "Someone who was very dear to me."

"Like my brother?"

"Exactly." Simon's expression clouded. "My governess, Edith Harris. She disappeared and then... then I didn't want to stay there any longer."

"But...?" Sally frowned. The story was touching, but somewhere it failed. "What about your parents? I mean, they were there. Didn't they...?"

"They did everything they could."

"But wasn't...?"

74

"No, it wasn't." Simon reached out with both hands and took one of Sally's; he held it cupped in his own. "It wasn't nearly enough."

Sally looked at her hand in his. "Why did you come to London?" she whispered.

"For you to find me."

Gently Sally took her hand away. "How old are you, Simon?" she asked.

"I am..." Simon began, then the corners of his eyes crinkled, his lips twitched mischievously. "I am quite old. Older than you."

"I'm twenty-two."

"There. I *said* I was older."

"How much older?"

"Oh, quite a lot." Simon leaned back in his chair and looked away, his eyes began to explore the photograph-laden wall beside him. "I'm..." he began again when his demeanor altered—a look so wild and so brief crossed his features that for a second or two it seemed his entire face was reshaping. Grief thinned his lips and paled him, the glow went from his eyes, every line on his countenance deepened. "Mamma," he whispered. "Mamma."

"What?" Sally stared. "What the hell...?"

"*There.*" Simon pointed to a photograph high above her head. "That's her picture."

Sally turned to look.

"*There.*" Simon's voice rose. He stood, knocking his chair away. The noise caused the barmaid to look up from her newspaper and frown; the couple in the far corner stared pointedly. "It's Mamma," he said excitedly. "I've seen that picture before."

"Hey, wait a minute."

"It is." Simon moved closer to the wall, and the shock began to disappear from his face. "It really is. What on earth can she be doing here?"

Sally peered at the photo. It showed a pretty, slight woman with raven hair escaping from beneath an open bonnet; she wore a check taffeta gown, below the hem of which the merest edge of a striped petticoat could be seen. She stood, leaning on a croquet mallet, looking beyond and to one side of the camera with an expression of gentle haughtiness. Beyond her, past the edge of the croquet lawn, was the corner of a stately home. The photograph must have been taken a hundred years ago; its sepia tones were faded; there were stains in one corner of the print. Sally could not take her eyes from it.

"You mean..." she suggested, "you mean...it looks like her."

"No, no, it *is* her."

"But..."

"*It's her.*" Simon turned on Sally. "Don't you believe me?"

"Sure," Sally replied, her mouth dry; slowly she sat down again. In that instant she wanted to see neither Simon nor the photograph. Hurriedly she swallowed a mouthful of Guinness.

"It's amazing." Simon glanced across the bareboard floor of The Half Moon. The barmaid was watching him carefully, the old man and his daughter stared at him with dislike. Simon's eyes flickered as a sickening realization flooded through him. He had revealed too much, had spoken when he should have remained silent, had not been nearly careful enough. It was not only from Sally he must conceal himself—they were all different; none of them was like him in any way at all. He could not afford to forget. Very deliberately, moving with extreme caution, he sat down opposite Sally again. "You must think me completely mad," he said with just the faintest tremor in his voice. "Please...I'm so impetuous."

"I..." Sally stared at him blankly. "I don't get you."

"Oh, we often played games at home and dressed up." Simon drank the rest of his whiskey. "All of us. Even Miss Harris joined in at times."

Sally watched without speaking.

"We had whole chests full of clothing that we'd use." Simon leaned away from the polished table. "Everyone would dress up and we'd have such fun." His eyes held Sally's. "You'd have loved it," he went on. "You really would have loved it."

"Yes..."

"And croquet." Simon leaned closer. "I'll wager you've never ever played croquet."

Sally shook her head. She felt miserable; there was no way she could touch him. She wished she were able to go to him, to pull him close to her and whisper that it was all right, that there was no need to explain. She understood his need and was unable to fulfill it; but she remained on her side of the table, transfixed, staring at him ineptly as she listened to his sad, over-bright explanation of his hallucination. At that moment there was no contact between them.

Simon put his head to one side; his eyes were strained. "May I offer you another?" he asked with light formality, pointing to the glasses between them.

Sally shook her head. "I'm a little tired," she whispered. "You mind if we go back to the apartment?"

"Of course not." Simon stood quickly, waiting for her to move. "I like it...there."

"Then let's go."

Outside, they walked slowly along the cobbled mews. They turned a corner, and when Sally saw the shapes of the trees of the square in the light from the street lamps, she felt a small surge of relief. She paused, Simon beside her, and glanced up at the dark, overcast sky. She saw the clouds break, and the moon, full-bodied and brilliant, sailed through the opening.

It seemed to be staring down at them both.

Sally heard Simon whimper. It was the faintest sound of fear and desperation, a keening for escape, the way an animal knowing it is cornered will whimper even before it is attacked. It chilled her to the bone.

Slowly, unable not to, yet afraid of what she might see, she turned and stared at Simon.

His head was thrown back, his gaze fully on the moon. His eyes were round; his cheeks seemed to have sunken so that the bones beneath the skin pushed through; his lips curled slightly upward; and his teeth were clear in the moonlight.

As Sally watched he lifted both hands, together and slightly apart, as if offering them to a captor. He raised them until they were level with his chest and stood for long seconds until the clouds caught the moon again and it disappeared back into darkness.

As it slid away, Simon's curled lips moved. "Bind me with silver," he whispered in a harsh, dry tone. "Bind me with the metal of the moon."

Sally felt her breath catch in her throat. She knew that if she attempted even to remain with him she would break, and her tears would spill. Quickly she went toward the door of the house in which she had her apartment. As she fumbled in her purse for keys she heard his footsteps behind her, and suddenly she was afraid. In spite of the affection that had been growing between them all afternoon, a chill went down her spine, forcing her to pause and consider.

She was certain now that she must seek help about his condition. There was an emptiness inside her she felt would remain hollow until she knew more about him, more of what she might be able to do to help him. Yet why she should feel his need so intensely, why she should be so prepared to assist, was beyond her understanding. She was only sure that for the first time in her life she had encountered someone who needed her desperately, whose insufficiency was such that she had no choice. Her heart went out to him; she would do whatever she could to aid him, to encourage him, to see him through his crisis.

She shivered briefly and inserted the key in the lock. Behind her she heard Simon arrive at the doorstep. Quickly she went inside and began to climb the stairs to her apartment, her mind dull and saddened, the fear within numbing to a dull ache.

It seemed that the house had never been so cold.

Albert Scot watched his mother busy herself in the kitchen, which smelled of bread and preserves. She was a small woman with short gray hair who never appeared to be still.

Albert, in all his life, could not recall her resting; sometimes he wondered if she even slept. Now she poured tea from a teapot that was older than he was, added milk and sugar to his cup, a segment of lemon to her own, cut a slice of fruitcake, and placed everything on a tray, which she carried over to the scrubbed kitchen table at which he sat. She placed the tray before him, immediately removed his cup and pushed it in his direction; the slice of fruitcake followed, and she picked up her tea and began sipping. Each movement was welded to the next.

"You're getting thin on top," she said, peering. "Have you thought of one of those transplants they advertise? It might work on you."

"Good God, no."

"You're young enough. Or almost. They say the younger you are, the more chance they have of taking."

Albert lifted his cup. Automatically he blew on the surface of the tea to cool it, realizing that only at home did he do this; he drank, and the warmth comforted. It had been a hard day.

"If you're going to get anyone, you've got to do the best with what you've got," Mrs. Scot continued, appraising her son and disapproving of what she saw. "Go bald and you'll have no chance at all."

"I'm not going bald."

"You are." Mrs. Scot was across the kitchen before

Albert saw her move. With a quick flick she parted his hair at the crown. "I'll get you a mirror if you like. It's going at the back here. You can see for yourself."

"It's all right." Albert patted his hair into place; he was dying for a cigarette. He cleared his throat and changed the subject. "You don't mind if I stay a few days?"

"Mind? Why should I mind? The room's yours. There's no one else staying here. In fact, if you were to stay instead of dashing off the way you usually do, I might get the chance to do something with you."

Albert closed his eyes.

"Get you onto a decent diet for a start. Sort your clothes out." Mrs. Scot was back on the other side of the kitchen, eyeing him again. "I don't know why you don't wear a uniform," she continued. "Make you look considerably better. Girls go for that sort of thing."

"We don't wear uniforms," Albert said patiently. "I've told you that before."

"More's the pity." Mrs. Scot finished her tea and began washing the cup and saucer. "*Anyway,*" she said emphatically, looking over her shoulder. "I'll bet no one insists you wear *dreadful* old suits and *terrible* roll-neck pullovers. Ye gods, why don't you spruce yourself up a bit? Look modern. Get into jeans or something."

"I'm comfortable...."

"*Comfortable.*" Mrs. Scot began drying the cup and saucer. "Life isn't a matter of being comfortable, Albert. Life's a matter of doing things. Making the most of yourself. Getting somewhere. I mean it, getting somewhere." She faced him. "What *are* you doing down here, by the way? You haven't given me one word of explanation."

"There's been a murder," Albert began uncomfortably. "Perhaps you heard of it?"

"Heard of it? No one's talked of anything else.

80

You'd begin to think there'd never been a murder in Tonbridge before. It's the press, mind you. They've made it into what it is. Sometimes I think they're worse than the television the way they glamorize violence." Mrs. Scot almost paused on her way to a cupboard. "Anyway, what's that got to do with you? You're London. You've nothing to do with Kent."

"I've been moved down here temporarily," Albert said slowly. "They asked for me especially."

Mrs. Scot did pause then; she stopped absolutely still in the middle of the kitchen, the cup in one hand, the saucer in the other. She stopped with the brisk-ness of a thrush listening for a worm: her head slightly to one side. The eye that Albert could see was bright and beady with curiosity.

"It's not complicated," Albert went on. "I can't think why they need outside assistance."

"You're working here?" The words came in a small, breathless rush. "In Tonbridge?"

"That's right. I..."

"Who brought it about? Bates?"

"The Chief Constable? Yes."

"My goodness." Mrs. Scot continued her way across the kitchen; she replaced the cup and saucer. "He always said he would. Has he said anything about your grandfather yet?"

"As a matter of fact, yes."

"What?" Again the bustling little woman stopped, absolutely still. "What'd he have to say?"

"He said something about an inquiry."

"He did, did he?"

"I'd never heard about it before."

"You weren't supposed to. Anyway..." Mrs. Scot picked up a cloth and began wiping the kitchen bench. "It's all over now. It was a very, *very* long time ago."

"Bates said that Grandad came out of it as clean as a whistle." Albert broke off a piece of fruitcake and put it into his mouth. "What was it all about?"

"Oh, something." Mrs. Scot brushed the idea aside

as she brushed away fruitcake crumbs. "Someone came down from London, ye gods, it was years ago. And your grandfather had to answer for things at this end, but it was nothing, just a formality, really."

"What did he have to answer for?" Albert ate more fruitcake. "Do you know?"

"Not really. You realize I wasn't even born when all this happened?" Mrs. Scot's sharp eye was on her son. "He married late, your grandfather. So did your father, for that matter. You know I'm twenty years younger than he was?"

"When did it happen?" Albert asked quietly. "The inquiry, I mean?"

Mrs. Scot wrung out the dishcloth and spread it to dry. "Over eighty years ago," she said as if she'd just worked it out. "Just after the turn of the century."

Albert's eyes closed thoughtfully. "Funny, isn't it, to think I'm connected with something that goes all that way back."

"You're not connected with it."

"He said something once, Grandad did," Albert went on slowly, "about Dad volunteering for Korea because he knew, because the old man had told him something. What'd he mean by that?"

"God knows. He was probably senile by then." Mrs. Scot began to clean the stove; she rubbed a cloth over its already polished surface, buffing the bright enamel. "He became a pest in his last years. My God, if I ever get that old I hope you'll have enough sense to do something about it."

Albert grunted. "Tell me," he went on. "Do you know what the inquiry was all about?"

"Not exactly. There was some talk of his working with a London inspector. Took his own life, as a matter of fact, but whether that had anything to do with your grandfather I really couldn't say."

"Who was the London inspector?"

"I don't think I ever heard the name."

"Never mind, I'll find out." Albert saw again his grandfather's half-closed eye; he felt an old warning move once more in the ageless kitchen. "Was there anyone else involved?" he asked.

"Anyone else?" Mrs. Scot's head came round. "What do you mean, anyone else?"

"At the inquiry, or in London?"

Mrs. Scot hesitated only a moment. "There was a German," she replied before she returned to clean the stove. "I think he had something to do with it."

Albert nodded. A piece fitted; a pattern was slowly taking shape, moving as it grew, forming as clouds form in late summer afternoon. He could feel the weight of the belt buckle in his hand; he saw the eagle it bore. His grandfather had been right about one thing: family blood was involved.

The realization was somehow comforting, Albert thought as he watched his mother's busy back. At last there seemed to be a reason for his return.

He realized also, quite abruptly, that he hadn't the slightest desire for a cigarette. "So," he said easily, "what've you been up to lately?"

Mrs. Scot's head turned briskly. "Me?...oh, the usual things. A bit of gardening, this and that."

"You never do any gardening." Albert's voice was gentle; he saw the uncollected leaves, the tangle of weeds outside the kitchen window. "You hate it."

"Are you being critical?" Mrs. Scot rubbed the stove a little harder. "Don't tell me you've come home to take your old mother to task."

Albert smiled. "It's usually the other way around, isn't it?"

Mrs. Scot put down the cloth, leaned against the shining enamel, and looked at her son. "I only want the best for you, Albert," she said quietly. "You know that."

Albert shrugged comfortably.

"You *do* know that? Ye gods, you must, in spite of what you tell your friends about me." The thin smile touched Mrs. Scot's lips again. "Don't think I don't know about that, my boy, but it's entirely beside the point. It's what *you* believe that matters." Her tone altered, became a degree more serious. "I do want the best for you, you know. I want to see you ... succeed."

For a moment Albert didn't reply; his mother's voice was sincere, the word *succeed* curiously selective. Then he said, "I am sure you do," and his own words were slightly muffled.

"Good." Mrs Scot turned away; she stared at the polished stove. "It's so very important that you do," she added almost to herself.

The Realization

Seven

~⌇~

RAY CLARK PUSHED chewing gum into the coin slot
of the public telephone with quiet anger.

He'd gone into twenty different pubs and asked
about his Lordship and he'd got nowhere. He'd drunk
half-pints of bitter until his stomach ached, and no
one had told him anything. Then, just after closing
time, he'd seen The Half Moon. He'd gone up the
three steps to the door and looked in. There was a
blond woman behind the bar, and she'd waved him
away. He'd called to her but she'd taken no further
notice. Hardly able to control his anger, he kicked
the door and walked away, furious. It was just the
place a ponce like his Lordship would go to. Ray
knew it, he could feel it, and there was nothing he
could do until tomorrow when they opened up again.

Mind you, the evening hadn't been a complete
dead loss. He'd talked about the Tonbridge murder
in just about every pub he'd visited. Wherever he'd
been he'd found someone who'd read about it or heard

about it from the telly. Scotland Yard was involved, he'd heard, and that was something that didn't happen every day of the week. There really was something big going on.

His bloody Lordship. The thought of how close he'd come made Ray furious again. He took a bunch of keys from his pocket and ran one of them down the paintwork of a little red sports car parked at the curb. As he watched the white line of the undercoat appear he felt better.

Ray put his hands into the pockets of his jacket and headed toward home. He'd make an early night of it; there wasn't anything else to do. In the morning he had to collect something for his uncle up near St. Albans, and by the time he got through the traffic and back down here again, the pub'd be closed for the afternoon, so he'd have to wait till evening. That might be better, anyway; there'd be more chance of catching his Lordship then.

Ray unlocked the door of the flat and went into its warm, stale interior. There was a light on in the living room and he could hear the sound of the telly; that'd be his mother watching rubbish.

"Is that you, Ray?" she called as he passed the living room door.

"Piss off," he replied and went to bed.

Sally Lawrence bent over the stove in her small kitchen and waited for the water to boil; coffee cups stood ready to be refilled. She shivered slightly although the kitchen was now warm. She felt ill at ease, uncertain. Simon had hardly said a word since they'd entered the apartment.

She'd made cheese on toast when they'd returned from The Half Moon, to give her something to occupy herself with while her head cleared and the nervousness went out of her fingers.

While she prepared the tiny meal, Simon sat in a straight-backed chair watching her. He said little and, at times, appeared to be on the edge of sleep; his eyelids drooped and his hands had lain unmoving on his lap.

Sally had not been able to take her eyes off his hands; they were so well formed, so elegant. But she could not avoid picturing them as they'd been lifted in the moonlight, held up toward the moon itself. She shivered again, in spite of the warmth of the stove and the two-bar heater at her feet.

When the hot cheese on toast had been set before him, Simon had eaten quietly, almost leadenly. Later he'd drunk a cup of coffee, and when Sally had offered another, he'd nodded and remained passive while she moved to the stove to reheat the water. He seemed like someone in a dream.

Sally could not imagine what had altered him so much. Perhaps the hallucination in The Half Moon had left him depressed; perhaps the sight of the photograph that reminded him of his mother had triggered something psychotic, the effects of which still lingered. Yet his performance beneath the fullness of the moon had been quite different, it was animated, weird, almost religious. Whatever conclusions she'd jumped to about drugs no longer seemed to apply. He needed help badly, and she realized sadly that there was no one but herself to give it to him. Without her he was completely alone.

Sudden pity made her move toward him. Without thinking of anything apart from comfort, she put her arms about him and drew him to her, fulfilling a longing that must have begun the moment she'd seen him, white-faced and trembling, the night before. She held him now, regardless of consequence, offering warmth and protection. She believed, as he laid his head against her, that she had nothing to fear from him at all.

"Simon," she whispered. "Simon, please tell me what's troubling you."

"I..." Simon began slowly. He pressed his head

89

farther into her warmth; his arms came up and held her. "I ... don't know. I really don't."

"Tell me. Talk to me. I can help."

"I'm ..." Simon breathed deeply. "I'm all right now." He closed his eyes and, in the dancing darkness, saw faces, dimly recognizable shapes; there was the whisper of ancient voices. No, he told himself fiercely, not her. She is innocent and must remain so. Above all, I must keep her whole. With an effort he spoke again, holding his voice steady. "Really, I am quite recovered."

Sally moved a hand over his head; she began to play with the copper-gold curls that grew in such abundance there. "Please," she whispered, "talk to me, tell me what's troubling you."

Simon rubbed against her like a cat. Her body was warm, and he could hear her voice through the woolens she wore; it was muffled, and with it began to return a sense of security. He held her and kept his silence—she must know nothing.

"My brother wouldn't talk, either," Sally went on. "He had problems. Maybe they were different problems, but if he'd talked about them sooner it would have helped."

Simon felt safer now. The voices were fading, the nightmarish shapes were going away, but it terrified him that for the first time since he'd been with her the horror had clearly returned. For a moment it had beckoned him; he'd felt the pull, the enormous moon tide, and with great effort he'd resisted it. She'd helped, this innocent, elfin girl, drawing him away from the fear, giving him something to cling to. He must keep her, protect her, not let her go. "Sally ..." he whispered.

"Please ... I'll help you."

"You are." Simon's hands locked her.

"But you must talk to me."

"It's nice." Simon's fingers explored the shape of

her. "I'm perfectly all right here with you. Don't send me away."

"No." Sally's voice was soft. "I won't send you away."

"Promise? I feel so safe with you."

"I promise."

"Thank you." Simon's arms were about her. "Thank you so much."

Sally felt, then, the first faint tinglings of sexual response, it was like a breath across her thighs, the lightest of touches over her stomach. It was sudden and delectable.

I wonder if it would help, she thought. If it would begin to break the barriers which remained between them. Perhaps, this way, he would tell her what she needed to know.

"Do you really feel safe with me?" she asked.

"Yes, yes, I do."

"My baby." Sally's voice was gentle. "You can trust me."

"Am I your baby?" Simon buried his head further into her softness; his hands seemed to encompass her more. "Really?"

"Of course."

"May I stay here with you?"

"Yes."

"Thank you." Simon sighed. "Holding you is so... nice."

Sally moved away. The water on the stove was boiling; she turned off the gas. "Come with me," she said, holding out her hand.

Simon stood uncertainly, he watched her switch off the kitchen light and lead him to her bed. There she stopped and put her arms around him and kissed him. For a moment his lips remained closed, and then her tongue came out to move them apart and he opened his mouth and pressed it into hers. He felt a fire begin, a fire he had not known before but which burned through him with a quick and vivid flame.

He found himself pulling her to him, trying to make her part of what he was.

"Wait," Sally said. She released her skirt, lifted her pullover over her head, and removed her underclothes. When he made no movement, she began to undress him. "Take them off," she whispered. "Get into bed with me."

Simon did as he was told. As she turned and peeled back the bedclothes he slipped between them. In bed he reached for her and pulled her closer. He found her mouth and opened his over it, and once again his excited tongue explored.

Sally ran her hands down his body, over the ribs and the muscle. She felt his stomach twitch as her fingers touched it; she put both hands around him and drew him toward her.

"Now, Simon." Sally's legs were apart. "Now. Do

Simon held her and pressed his lips into the throbbing of her neck.

"Now Simon." Sally's legs were apart. "Now. Do it to me now."

Again Simon's mouth went back to hers; his hands pulled her closer. He rubbed himself against her.

"My God," Sally whispered as she understood. "You're a virgin."

"What?"

"You're a virgin. You've never done this before."

Simon said nothing.

"Oh, my baby. My poor baby." The essence had altered, the passion remained, the need was as intense, but there was a newness now, a sensitivity that had not been a part of it before. "Here," Sally whispered, "let me show you."

"It is...strange," Simon said. "It is like nothing I have ever experienced."

"Shhh..." Sally moved beneath him. "Don't say anything."

Simon's mouth went back to hers as she positioned him. His tongue came out as she spread beneath him;

it forced itself into her mouth as she touched him and led him into her. He lifted his head and stared down at her in the half-dark as he pressed himself into her; the shock of the pleasure took his breath away.

"That's right," Sally said, and felt her orgasm begin, felt herself rush down to him, as if every nerve in her body was directed toward him as he moved in her. "Yes..." she cried. "That is...right."

Above her Simon responded to the incredible pleasure, to the darkness and the delight and the intoxication. Something new and strong and delicious grew within him; it contained a sensation of such intensity that he cried out as if in pain, a feeling of such joy that it filled him with a hideous dread. Every muscle in his thrusting body stiffened; his throat opened, and he gave rise to a deep and monstrous shout, a roar of deliverance, a bellow that was both a beginning and an end.

For a while neither of them moved. Simon lay as if asleep, covering her. Sally gazed, unblinking, past the shape of his curls to a pattern on the ceiling cast by the outside light. She felt buoyant, as if she were floating strangely free. Very slowly she lifted a hand and touched his hair. There were tears on her cheeks; they had sprung at the moment of her climax, and she could recall only one other time when this had happened. She hugged him softly, feeling such a depth of tenderness, she was afraid the tears might begin again.

"Oh, Simon," she whispered. "Dear, dear Simon."

"Mmmm?" Simon nuzzled against her, his cheek warm and soft. "What?"

"Nothing. Don't move."

"That was..." Simon murmured. "That was... marvelous. I've never felt anything like it before."

"Never?"

"No." He lifted his head and looked down at her. "Is it always like that?"

"Well...it *was* kind of special."

"Would it be like that again?"

"Who knows." Sally smiled; she could not keep her fingers away from his face. "It might be."

"Shall we try and see?"

Sally laughed lightly, in simple and pure joy, then she put one hand on either side of his face. "You're a tiger," she said happily.

"Wouldn't you like to?"

"I'd love to."

"Then..." Simon urged himself forward, and Sally felt him extend and fill her again until there was nothing else apart from the way he moved in her. "Is this right?" he asked.

"Yes." Sally felt herself opening in a new and different way: her legs came up as she tilted toward him; her hands went down across the muscles of his stomach until she was holding him as he moved in her. She lifted her head and kissed him so that they were totally joined; the way they locked was inseparable. "Oh, yes," she said, her climax beginning again. "My God, yes."

"Do...you...feel the same?"

"Yes."

"Is it...?"

"It is," Sally said as fire ran through her. "Don't stop."

Simon thrust as the scythe of pleasure cut through him again, threatening for the merest moment not to release him, then it rushed past in a sweep of glistening intensity. Once more his body stiffened, once again the deep shout of deliverance sprang from his throat as she flowed beneath him. There was nothing in her delicate, fine-boned body but tremblings and the beginnings of dreams.

This time they lay a long while, holding each other. They were thoughtless and still, and for a time the world allowed them to remain alone.

Then from within the building a voice called, and Simon lifted his head. Sally smiled.

"Should I move from you?" he whispered.

"No." Sally shook her head. "Don't go away."

"I am sleepy."

"Then go to sleep, Simon. Go to sleep and I'll hold you, but don't go away."

He smiled down with great tenderness. "Will you look after me?" he asked.

"I'll look after you."

"Thank you." Simon's voice was very faint. "And I will do whatever is possible to look after you."

Sally lay half beneath him, half beside him as he faded into sleep. She *would* look after him, if he would allow her to. She would do whatever she could.

If only there was someone I could talk to, she thought, as she, too, drifted into sleep. Someone like that priest in New York who had tried to help her brother. But there was no one like that here. Doctors wouldn't help. If she were to tell them what had happened in just one day, they'd more than likely put him away or get in touch with his parents, who'd take him away. That was the last thing she wanted now that she was close to him; now that they were lovers.

Sally's mind clouded as sleep overtook her. There was no one she could think of.

Sally woke suddenly. A name and a face had come to her with such simplicity that she smiled openly into the darkness.

Cyril Fenick, of course.

God knows what had brought him to mind, but he was right, he was so absolutely right that she wondered why she hadn't thought of him before. Cyril Fenick, the fortune-teller she'd consulted when she'd first come to London. Cyril Fenick, who was more than a fortune-teller, so very much more: he was a man who understood.

Sally remembered the basement flat he had near the Sloane Square tube station and his large, slow-moving figure as he'd opened the door and led the way into his study. The walls were lined with maps and charts that seemed to be connected not only with the signs of the zodiac but appeared to contain elements even more mysterious. There were symbols and geometric patterns, writing and scripted messages, elements that belonged to a separate dimension of his pursuits. She'd understood, then, that he was more than an ordinary fortune-teller. He reminded her more of a painting she had seen somewhere of an astrologer in his den of charts and books, globes, and comfortable, purring cats. He had seven cats, all black, who sat watching him.

He took her hand and looked at it and felt the bumps on her head and told her to walk as best she could among the overstuffed chairs and the piles of books that littered the floor. When he spoke, his voice was solemn, and yet there was a touch of whimsy in his eyes.

He suggested that she'd suffered a tragedy, and she told him about her brother. Her life would be crossed by such tragedies, he'd said; he knew it from the way she walked: her hands were always held before her as if she were attempting to ward off disaster. But there was happiness, he'd added with the smallest smile; a child would enter her life and change it.

Sally had listened, fascinated, not only because he seemed to understand but also because there was a depth to him, an insight she'd not encountered before. Other fortune-tellers she'd seen had been brief and busy and superficial, but Cyril Fenick was different. He seemed to care.

He'd told her to come back whenever she felt the need to talk to someone, whatever it was that worried her, however unimportant or trivial it might seem to be. As she'd left the small, overcrowded flat, he'd taken her hand and looked deeply into her eyes and told her that she *would* return. He knew it, he'd said, and he was never wrong about such things.

Now, the warmth of Simon all about her, Sally smiled at the image of the wise old man and his family of cats. She would call on him, tomorrow after work, and she'd talk to him about this strange young man who had come into her life.

Eight

DETECTIVE SERGEANT ALBERT SCOT shook wet snow from the collar of his raincoat and examined the trench in which the bulldozer driver had died. He wore a pair of rubber gum boots, and cold came through them, numbing his toes; it came through his raincoat and his jacket and his roll-necked pullover, seeking his bones.

It was a miserable morning, Albert thought. It was a miserable place to die.

Beside him the Chief Constable breathed deeply and rubbed his gloved hands together briskly; his breath came out in steamy plumes. His skin had reddened in the weather; his bright blue eyes watered but his voice was cheerful when he said, "Tells you nothing, does it? Everything washed away," and pointed to the hole in the mud that had contained the carved box with its silver clasp and the mystery that had not quite touched them yet.

"I wasn't expecting anything," Albert replied. "I just wanted to see the site."

"Yes, yes, I understand."

"Who found him?"

"Oh, the watchman, when he made his morning rounds."

"No one missed him?"

The Chief Constable shook his head. "Lived alone. Wife went off with someone else about six months ago." He tapped his forehead with a gloved finger. "Been a little odd since then."

Albert stared at the hole in the mud where the box had lain for over eighty years, the German's belt buckle and his bones beside it.

"Seen enough, have you?" The Chief Constable shrugged at the cold. "Care to discuss things over a drink?"

Albert nodded.

The Chief Constable led the way back to his Range Rover. They drove out of the building site, away from the mud and the stacks of concrete blocks, the twigs of reinforcing steel and the cement-colored shuttering. Already work had begun on the wall the driver had been digging the foundations for; no time had been lost. Soon there would be no trace left in Tonbridge of what the driver had uncovered—apart from the remains that lay on the bench in the police storage room.

The Chief Constable drove back to the town, past the wet yellow-sandstone of the Norman castle, into a narrow street with stone-faced buildings glistening in the sleety rain, and parked beside a black wrought-iron railing on which there was a discreet sign that read: CONSERVATIVE ASSOCIATION.

"Hope you've no objection," he said, clearing his throat. "But it's quiet here. We can chat."

Albert smiled. "I've never thought politics had much to do with police work," he replied.

"That remains to be seen," the elderly policeman commented cryptically.

They went from the sleet and the pinching cold into a warm, carpeted room, its walls lined with photographs of former Conservative prime ministers; over the fireplace, commanding the entire room, was an oil painting of Margaret Thatcher. The Chief Constable took off his coat and gloves and tossed them onto a chair in the corner; Albert did the same.

"Used for committee meetings," the Chief Constable explained. "No one'll disturb us here."

Albert went to the fire, which crackled in the grate, and stood with his hands toward it; he thought of Chris Wilkinson and smiled to himself.

The Chief Constable pushed a bell, and a waiter appeared. "What'll it be?" he asked Albert. "I think malt on a day like this, don't you?"

Albert nodded, his eyes on the flames.

"A bottle of Glen Grant and two glasses," the Chief Constable told the waiter.

"Water, sir?"

"Oh, yes, I suppose so."

The waiter disappeared. Both policeman stared into the fire as it tossed and spun gleefully until the waiter returned with a tray containing the whiskey, two cut-glass tumblers, and a matching jug; he placed the tray on a marble-topped fireside table. "Will that be all, sir?" he inquired politely.

The Chief Constable nodded. "You have the chit?" He held out a hand.

The waiter produced a slip of paper, which the Chief Constable signed with a flourish, smiled tightly, and handed it back; then he picked up the already opened bottle, poured himself a generous measure, and turned toward Albert, his eyebrows raised.

"Yes, please," Albert replied. "With a little water."

The Chief Constable grunted, mixed the drink, and handed it over. "Cheers," he said, and drank half his own.

"Cheers," Albert replied, and sipped the warm, softly invading spirits; at the moment he couldn't think of anything he'd rather be doing. "Are there rats down at the building site?" he asked easily.

"Rats?"

"Yes, sir. Rats."

"I suppose so." The Chief Constable was clearly confused. "Why do you ask?"

"Constable Hooper thought they might be responsible for the state of the dead man's throat. He thinks there was a fight and the rats did the rest." Albert sipped a little more whiskey. "The driver's made a few enemies, I hear."

"Well..." The Chief Constable shrugged the thought away. "It's possible."

"But you don't think it's likely."

"Frankly no, but the important thing is what you think, Detective Sergeant. You're the expert."

"What about Wilson, sir? The doctor who did the medical report?"

"They've been talking about him?" The Chief Constable's eyes lost a little of their innocence. "Ah, I see from your face that they have. Well, let me tell you something. For some time things have been a bit slipshod around here, not up to scratch, if you understand my meaning. That's one of the reasons I wanted you down. To show them how a real policeman works, put some steam into them."

"How much would you rely on the report, sir? Wilson's, I mean."

"Oh, it's sound enough. Don't worry about that. Routine work. He's quite reliable."

"And if it's not routine?"

The Chief Constable blinked. "What exactly do you mean?"

"What's he likely to miss, sir?"

The Chief Constable took a mouthful of malt whiskey and held it, feeling the gentle spirit move about his tongue. Detective Sergeant Scot was proving to be quite difficult. He seldom answered a question; the ones he asked were, to say the least, tricky, and he'd yet to deliver an opinion. Not even on the whiskey. "You enjoying this?" The Chief Constable held up his glass.

"Very much, sir." Albert smiled. "What I mean is, his report didn't mention the hairs."

"What hairs?"

"The ones on the driver."

"Oh." The Chief Constable turned his back on the fire. "You've sent them up to London?"

Albert nodded.

"He had a dog, you know?"

Albert sipped a little whiskey.

"Well, we'll just have to see what London has to say." The Chief Constable looked at his glass. It was empty. He walked to the marble-topped table and poured himself more malt, then turned and stared at Albert's back, at the thick shoulders, at the head bent toward the fire. "Before we discuss this any further, Scot," he said quite slowly, "there is something that I think you should know."

"Really, sir?" Albert turned to the elderly policeman. "What's that?"

The Chief Constable coughed, then lowered himself into a stuffed leather chair. Albert paused, then sat in another; he pushed his rubber gum boots out toward the fire and watched steam rise from them in tiny wisps. "You'll have seen a belt buckle?" the Chief Constable began. "Found on the building site?"

Albert nodded.

"German. I supposed you noticed that."

"Yes, sir."

"Well, it was over the death of a German that your grandfather's inquiry was held, Scot. I think that's something you should know."

Albert barely moved. "Who was he, sir?"

"An inspector from Munich who came down on some business or other. Your grandfather was his contact. He was never heard of again, the inspector that is. Result was the inquiry."

"Was it the same German, sir?"

"What? Oh, he of the inquiry and the belt buckle? It's possible, don't you think?"

"Is that why you thought it was an old murder site?"

"Quite frankly, yes."

"Do you think my grandfather knew anything about it?"

"I'm sure he didn't. He would have said so if that'd been the case. He was that sort of man."

"But, he was involved?"

"Innocently, I'm sure."

"That may have been enough," Albert said quietly, then added, "What about the London inspector, sir? The one who killed himself?"

The Chief Constable looked away. "What do you know of him?" he asked.

"Nothing much. My mother mentioned him last night."

"Kearsley. His name was Kearsley. It was he who first contacted your grandfather. Before the German came down." The Chief Constable swirled his whiskey and stared at it solemnly. "No one knows why he shot himself," he added. "There was no note. No reason was ever discovered."

"Why was the German in Tonbridge? What was an inspector from Munich doing here?"

"No one is exactly sure of that. The only person who might have known was Kearsley and, well, he didn't tell anyone anything."

"Was it assumed the German had died?"

"Yes, seemed logical, I suppose. He came down here, got in touch with your grandfather, wanted to see some old maps, ordered a carriage, and went off the following morning never to be seen or heard of again." The Chief Constable emptied his glass. "After a while his superiors wanted to know what had happened, and no one could supply a satisfactory answer. In the end an inquiry was held and it was assumed he'd died."

"No one in Munich knew what he was after?"

"Not really. He worked alone. There'd been a series of killings on the Continent, and it was assumed he'd come here to check on something." The Chief Constable poured himself a further measure of malt. He looked at Albert, who leaned forward to have his glass refilled. "It was when the Germans found themselves up against a stone wall that they asked us to see what we could do."

"You..." Albert hesitated fractionally. "You seem to know a great deal about all this, sir."

The Chief Constable said nothing.

"Rather more, if you'll forgive me, than I'd have suspected."

"Well, as I've told you, I met the old chap, your grandfather. He impressed me greatly. I fished out the inquiry verdict and read it. Out of curiosity, you understand. Then over the years I've picked up a bit more here and there. It's become a sort of hobby of mine, if you know what I mean."

"Tell me, sir," Albert asked very deliberately. "What sort of killings on the Continent was the German inspector investigating?"

The Chief Constable's clear blue eyes fixed themselves on Albert. "They were particularly nasty, Scot. Three people died of neck wounds. It seems their throats had been torn out."

Albert felt the ghost come into the comfortable room. Very slowly he lifted his glass and sipped from it; the whiskey tasted flat and cold. He noticed that his hand was trembling.

Simon Blackstone sat in Sally Lawrence's flat above the square near Victoria Station for as long as he was able. He knew he must wait, but he was uncertain how long it would be before he could go back to The Half Moon to examine the photograph of his mother. From a chair by the window overlooking the skeletal trees, their black, bare branches framing the small gray stone church at the far end of the square, he watched cars go past in the street below, people hurrying through the cold, wet London air with mounting impatience.

It had been raining when Sally woke him. She wore her cape, a long hand-knitted scarf about her throat, a woolen hat pulled down over her dark hair. She must go to work, she'd told him; there was food in the kitchen and she'd not be late.

"Work?" Simon blinked, obviously puzzled.

"Yes. Simon, work."

"What...?"

"I'm waitressing at a hamburger joint in the Fulham Road." Sally laughed lightly. "Not exactly your quaint old London, but it helps to pay the rent." She looked down at him from beside the bed; her expression was soft and longing. "I could stay, but I really should go," she said very gently. "I wasn't there yesterday, remember." She bent and kissed him with great tenderness, her lips as soft as down. Simon reached for her immediately; the warmth and the need and the memory of the night before came back to him in a rush. "No..." she murmured. "I must go. I've made up my mind."

"Couldn't we...?"

"No..." Sally whispered, knowing she must leave at once; to linger for any time at all would keep her from the appointment with Cyril Fenick she knew she had to make. "Not now."

"It wouldn't take very long."

"If I got back in there beside you I'd never get out." With an effort, Sally moved away from the bed; she pulled on a pair of gloves, and her manner became more businesslike. "I've left a spare set of keys on the kitchen table," she told him. "And there's a razor I put out for you in the bathroom."

"A razor?"

Sally nodded, fixing the woolen hat more firmly on her head. "About time you shaved." She smiled. "I noticed last night. It's soft, but it needs cutting, if you know what I mean."

"Of course." Simon put a hand to his cheek. "When will you return?" he asked.

"Oh, about six." Sally blew him a kiss from where she stood, and her eyes were suddenly misty; she felt as if she were melting inside. "I'll get back as soon as I can," she added quickly, then turned and left, going abruptly, before the temptation to join him overcame her. "I won't be late," she whispered as she closed the door behind her. She ran down the stairs, wondering at her emotions; they seemed to be extreme.

Simon had remained in bed a little longer; after a while he went into the tiny bathroom and discovered the small, plastic razor Sally had spoken of. He held it uncertainly as he stood before a mirror, an image of his father in mind. The tall man's face was covered with thick, creamy lather; a shaving brush stood in a heavy, steamy mug; with a straight razor in one hand, a leather strap in the other, his father stropped the blade to a fine edge. The image was so vivid, Simon dropped the plastic toy he held into the washbasin. He picked it up gingerly and used it, then went into the kitchen and ate a bowl of cereal Sally had left for him.

After that he sat in the chair by the window and stared across the square, willing time to pass so that he could return to The Half Moon.

He was impatient to view his mother's picture again, hoping that it would tell him more about himself, strip away a little of his blind and groping ignorance. It was the only real link he had with the past.

The words he recalled from the crone's lips were not enough: they failed to explain his presence here and now; they told him nothing of his essential being. They predicted nothing of the great changes he sensed were about to occur.

For he was sure he would not remain as he now was: an inept creature, a half-person, torn between the temporal innocence of a guileless boy and a force more sinister, a presence all-knowing, defiant, and utterly damned. He knew the seeds of this greater power lay within him. He had felt it as he'd run through deserted streets the night he'd come to London. He was becoming more and more conscious of the temptations it offered, the strength it would bring, even as he fought against it with whatever determination he possessed.

Simon put his head in his hands and struggled anew with that which had neither shape nor dimension. He pressed his fingers into his forehead until they threatened to snap, and trembled as he'd trembled when he'd hung against the brick wall with Sally's eyes upon him.

Finally he could contain himself no longer. He hurriedly pulled on his padded jacket, stuffed the spare set of keys into a pocket, and went downstairs into the bitter, damp, diesel-smelling air.

The cold and the noise of the traffic halted him for a moment, and he paused uncertainly on the footpath, not sure of which way to go. A middle-aged woman, her head wrapped in a sheet of clear plastic, bumped into him. Simon stepped aside apologetically, and the woman went off muttering.

The street seemed foreign to Simon. It was as if he had never been in it before. For a frightening second he was tempted to return to the safety of the rooms above and wait for Sally. He half-turned toward the security of the apartment but stopped. He *must* go on to The Half Moon. Gritting his teeth, Simon set off in the direction he believed the public house to be.

He went into a street lined on both sides with

small shops; he passed people with pinched faces, bent against the freezing rain. He turned a corner and thought he saw the mews he was looking for. With his head down he went quickly to where the mews cut away from the shop-lined road, and then realized that it was not the one he was seeking. There were no narrow, locked together houses, there was no signboard with its sickle of yellow moon against a blue-black sky. Simon stared down the alley in disbelief: there was a garage on the corner where the inn should have been.

Breathing deeply he ran back to the square. In panic he looked about him, then started off again. This time he took the opposite direction and suddenly came to a section of the road that seemed familiar. Then, almost in the same instant, his eyes caught a glimpse of the mews he was searching for. He let out a small sob of relief and quickened his pace.

Once in the mews, he rushed down past the narrow houses until he saw the signboard. He ran up the three stone steps of The Half Moon, grasped the shiny brass door handle, and pushed.

Nothing happened. The door remained closed. He had arrived too early.

Nine

❧

MOLLY WHITE LOOKED UP from the paper she was reading to see Simon Blackstone standing bewildered outside The Half Moon. My God, what's happening round here? she wondered. Last night it was a skinhead kicking the door after closing time; now we've got a fairy bleeding to death in the rain. She flicked the paper angrily and reached for a cigarette. There's another twenty minutes to go before opening, dear, she said to herself, go and wait in a public lavatory.

Her eyes went back to the paper, but the face outside the door wouldn't go away. He won't have seen me, Molly thought. Not with the lights off. She looked up carefully again. He *was* very handsome. Much better-looking than the male model she'd first thought him to be, the one who lived round the corner, drank port and lemonade, and always wanted a knife and fork for his scampi.

She drew in a lungful of smoke. Don't be a bitch,

Molly, she told herself, go and see what the poor bleeder wants, but don't let Fred catch you. If he was to see you letting in a good-looking boy before opening he'd black your other eye.

Molly White smiled, slid off her chair, and went to the front door. Simon's wild look caught her. He's a nutter, she thought, but I'll see what he wants. I'll just poke my head out and tell him to go away.

Through clear spaces in the frosted glass Simon watched the blond woman approach; her image was misty in the darkened interior.

"What you want, love?" Molly asked when she'd unbolted the door. "Don't you know it's before time?"

"I..." Simon breathed deeply; he must learn to be patient. "I do apologize, but may I come in for a moment?"

I do apologize, Molly thought. Manners he has, and style. "It's too early for a drink, you know that, don't you?" she said.

"I wasn't seeking a drink." Simon replied politely. "Really, I merely wanted to look at the photographs."

"You was here last night." Molly recognized him. "You and a girl?"

"Yes, that's right." Simon managed to smile. "We came in for a drink."

"I remember now. Scared old Alf half-silly, you did." Molly put her hands on her hips. "Put on a turn or something, didn't you, dear?"

"It was the photographs." Simon willed himself to wait; he was too close to be sent away now. "We were very interested and, well, I suppose we got rather excited to see so many."

"In the business yourself then?"

"As a matter of fact I am." Simon's smile grew, his eyes crinkled at the corners. "That's exactly why I came early, to examine them while it was quiet. That is, if you don't mind."

"No, well..." Molly White glanced at her watch; Fred should sleep for another hour at least, and it couldn't do anybody any harm to let this pretty feller in for a look. She pursed her lips mischievously. Depended what he wanted to look at, mind you, not that she'd put up much of a struggle. "Come in." She stepped away from the door. "Not much point in standing out in the rain, is there?" He definitely wasn't a fairy.

"Thank you, you are most kind." Simon entered The Half Moon; it smelt vaguely of cigarette smoke and stale beer. His eyes went past the zinc-topped bar with its ceramic pump handles to the wall of photographs; they were an indistinct maze in the semidarkness. "Do you mind if I look more closely?"

"'Course not, love. I'll put on a light."

"That is very kind of you." Simon went to the wall. "You do have a lot of them, don't you?"

And I'll bet you do, too, dear, Molly thought as she adjusted her dress and followed.

"Where did they come from?" Simon asked.

"Ah, you've got me there, love. They were here when we came. Only been in the place a couple of months, Fred and me." She shook her head. "He wants me to rip this lot out, Fred does. Put in Formica and some of them space games. That's where the money is, he says, but I rather like these old pictures."

"Then you would not know who the people were?" Simon asked, his eyes going to the photograph of his mother on the croquet lawn. The last time he'd seen it, it stood in a silver frame on her dressing table between tortoiseshell hand mirrors on a case of polished mahogany. She'd been proud of it; it showed her figure without revealing it, made her look quite handsome, she said. "You wouldn't know their names?"

"Good God, no." Molly laughed. A hand went to her dyed blond hair. "I might be getting on a bit, love; but I don't go back that far."

"Who would? Who would know?"

"Haven't the faintest." Molly looked at the handsome features, at the light in the beautiful eyes. Perhaps there was something funny about him after all. "They've all been dead and buried several times over by now. Why? What difference does it make who they were?"

"Well, none, I suppose."

"What's your interest then?"

"Well, I'm... I'm a collector and..." Simon kept his voice even; he must reveal neither his excitement nor his fear; he must learn what he could and then he must leave. "And one wonders, I suppose, who the people were and what they did. It really does capture one's imagination."

AC-DC, Molly thought, but I'll take what's going. "Could I just browse amongst them a little?"

"Go ahead." Molly went back to the bar. "I was going to have a cup of tea before we opened. Like one?"

"That would be most kind."

"It's only tea bags."

"Thank you." Simon's eyes were on the wall. "I'd love a cup of tea."

Molly White whistled as she waited for the plug-in kettle to boil; she watched him study the photos. One in particular seemed to have taken his fancy. He moved a chair closer, stood on it, and stared with curious fascination. Molly screwed up her eyes to see more clearly which it was. After a moment she recognized it as the one of the woman with her bum stuck out as she leaned on a cricket stick. No, it wasn't cricket, it was that game where they hit balls through hoops with a bat. I'd play it with you anytime, love, she thought as she watched Simon lean into the wall; we could run up a decent score, you and me, get a ball or two in the right place. She smiled as the kettle boiled; she made tea and took a cup over to Simon as he climbed down from the chair.

"You seem to like that one, dear." Molly handed

him his cup. "Anything special about it? I mean, she's quite nice looking isn't she?"

"She's beautiful."

"Well, perhaps that's going a bit far." Molly smoothed her dress over her hips. "But, it's what turns you on, isn't it, love?"

"Yes, of course." Simon saw the warmth in Molly's eyes. "Do you have any more photographs of that . . . that particular person?"

"God knows." Molly went back to the bar and lit a new cigarette. "Haven't had time to look at them all myself, if you want to know the truth. But . . ." Her face altered. "Come to think of it, there *is* another one of her. I remember the gear, that striped shimmy. Now I wonder where it was I saw it."

"Please, do try to find it."

"You're really stuck on her, aren't you?"

"It is . . ." Simon thought desperately. "It's that, as a collector, I'd rather like to see a selection that was related, if you know what I mean."

"You thinking of making an offer, then?"

"Well, yes, I would be quite prepared to do so."

"You'd have to talk to Fred about that. He's the one who wants to sell."

"Perhaps if I could see the photograph . . . ?"

"Yes, well . . ." Molly drew in smoke. We could have some fun with this, she thought, if we had the time. "Now, where was it?" Her eyes went over the image-laden walls, past groups and landscapes, buildings, and flights of sepia-colored birds. "Was it over here somewhere?"

"Where?" Simon was beside her.

"Let me think." Quite casually Molly took him by the arm. Strong, he is, she thought. "Down in this corner, if I remember rightly."

"I do hope we can find it."

"Oh, I think we will, love," Molly said with a smile. "It's got to be here somewhere."

"Where?"

"Over there, perhaps."

"I see it." Simon's voice became a whisper; he moved away quickly, but even as he went, Molly felt a tremor go through his arm. He crouched, staring at a photograph. "It is ... *she*," he whispered. "The same ... person."

Simon was staring at a group walking on the gravel driveway of a country house; brickwork was softly lit by late, slanting light; shadows lay long across the lawns. The group consisted of the woman wearing her checked taffeta gown, a swirl of striped petticoat caught in the movement of her foot. By her side walked a tall man wearing tweed plus-fours and a broad-peaked cloth cap. They strode toward the camera, passing beneath the spread of an oak so that sunlight scattered above. But what captured Simon's attention most was the image of a small boy who walked between them wearing a Victorian sailor suit. He could have been no older than six or seven, and yet he had the presence of someone much older. Light caught his hair in a halo, a spindle of living luminosity, and his features were lost in a blur of movement. At the instant the photograph had been taken, the child's head had turned away; there was no detail visible, merely the spinning of light and a glow where the face should have been. The effect was magical, the trick of an instant. Simon stared at it and could barely control his trembling. He heard his teacup rattle on its saucer, and with great effort he placed it carefully on a table as he stood upright and stepped away from the time-laden wall; his face was ghostly pale.

"That what you was looking for, love?" Molly asked, watching him carefully.

"Yes." The word was a whisper. "It is." Simon could not take his eyes from the photograph—it was magnetic. It told him more than he wanted to know. As he stared into its distant landscape he heard the voices begin their whispering and saw the images begin to assemble. They all came out at him suddenly, their torn and bloodied throats agape; they spun about him urging, calling for the force that was their master. It was as if the faceless child in the almost century-old photograph had turned a hidden key releasing these eerie powers with their hideous demands.

No, Simon told himself, not here, not immediately.

He needed time, the security of Sally's rooms above the square, a space in which to reassemble himself. There was too much pressure—and too many demands—for him to even begin to confront them here, in this place. He knew now why he had been attracted here, why he had been called. This was where they had lodged, some of them, some of the forces that seduced and threatened, while he had remained ... asleep. All the while he had lain dormant they had waited for him in the blacks and grays of the assembled images.

With great effort, keeping his voice as even as he could, he turned and spoke to the woman beside him. "It is exactly what I have been looking for," he said in a voice that was not his own. "Exactly."

"Really?" Molly watched him carefully. "You must be a very keen collector, the effect it's having on you."

"I..." Simon folded his arms about himself. "I... do find it remarkable."

"You...ah, you often get excited by things like that?" Molly asked. "Kinky gear, that sort of thing?"

Simon turned and stared at her.

"Dressing up? Playing games?"

"Oh..." Simon forced a stiff smile; he felt blood come back to his face. He must leave but he must be able to return. "It's merely that..." he said unsteadily, "I find there is something quite thrilling about old photographs."

"I'm sure there is, love." Molly moved closer. She felt him quivering from where she stood; he was like a young animal surprised in the dark. Well, now, she told herself, he's a strange one. If we could only get him on the right track we'd have a lovely time. "There's lots of things to get thrilled about, if you take my meaning."

"Oh, yes." Simon's eyes darted to the group striding through the late sunlight and the sinister magic it contained, then back again to the woman and her appetite. "I do understand."

"Do you, dear?" Molly put out a hand.

"Well...of course."

"Perhaps we could..." Molly began, when there was the sound of a door closing above followed by a long body-wrenching fit of coughing. "Blast." Molly took her hand away. "It's bloody Fred. Early."

"I beg your pardon?"

"Me hubby, dear. He's up. Coughing himself to life. Don't tell me you can't hear it."

"Yes, yes, I can." Simon breathed deeply, relief flooding through him. "Should I speak to him about purchasing the photographs?"

"I wouldn't do that now." Molly could have spat tacks, things were just getting interesting. "Come back later when he's got himself together."

"Very well, then."

"This evening, maybe?"

"No." The reply was instinctive. This evening was too soon. He must concentrate, try to assemble the assorted fragments that cluttered his brain, try to piece them together. "I mean," he added, recovering, "I should like to consult my friend. Could we make it tomorrow?"

"The dark one, your friend? Looks like a gypsy?"

"That's her."

"'Course, if you go for that sort of thing."

"She's very nice, really she is."

"Oh, I'm sure, dear. They all are." Molly's eyes went upward; she could hear Fred beginning to descend. "Well, let's leave it until tomorrow, love." She moved closer for a moment. "Mind you, if you want to come back and have another quiet look at the pictures on your own, don't hesitate. I mean, like this time tomorrow morning." A clever gleam came into her eye. "I might even be able to find more of that lady with the shimmy you like so much."

"Do you think so?"

"Now, I'm making no promises." Molly smiled; he was very sweet and awfully strong for his age. "But I'll have a look, don't worry." She crossed to the door and opened it. "Off you go now. See you tomorrow."

"I must thank you so much for all your help."

"Anytime, dear." Molly smiled. "That's what I'm here for really. To help young lads like you."

"Thank you again."

Simon hurried out into the rain. Hunching his shoulders, he walked quickly up the mews. Molly watched for a moment, then slowly closed the door; she turned to find a thin unshaven man looking at her through red-rimmed eyes. "Who was that?" he asked sourly.

"A feller." Molly smiled. "Thinks he might like to buy some of the pictures."

"I know him?"

Molly shrugged. "He's been in a couple of times," she replied indifferently.

Fred's eyes flicked away; he reached for a cigarette, lit it, and immediately began to cough again. He put one hand on his chest and the other on the bar and coughed until he was red in the face, then thickly spat into the sink below and shuddered.

"Oh, Fred," Molly said quietly. "You really are the answer to a maiden's prayer."

Albert Scot's fingers spread clothing on the bench in the storeroom at the back of the Tonbridge Police Station. He laid pieces out in order, attempting to fit them together.

"I've already done that, sir." Constable Hooper

stood beside him. "It was one of those sailor suits they used to wear."

"Why didn't you tell me more about it?" Albert placed the split remains of an arm alongside the tunic.

Hooper shrugged. "Didn't think of it... Albert," he replied.

"What else is there?"

"That's all. Just the one set of clothes. That's intact, if you understand me. The rest is rubbish."

"That belonged to the German?"

"I suppose so. It was with the belt buckle, if that's what you mean."

"That's what I mean." Albert assembled the tiny jacket. "This must have been inside the box. It's been protected the same way as the lining."

"That's what I thought...."

Albert straightened and looked at the hollow-chested policeman with the hooked nose. "What else did you think, Tony?" he asked quietly.

"Well... speaking of clothes..." Hooper dug into a pocket of his tunic and took out a slip of paper. "We've had a report about some that was stolen. Jeans, pullover, and an anorak," he read aloud. "With shoes. Taken the night the driver was killed, not that I suppose there's any connection."

"Where was it taken from?"

"Farmhouse. On the London road just out of town."

"No idea who took it?"

Hooper's lean features went back in a grin. "None at all, sir. The feller who made the complaint could've lost it the condition he was in. Didn't make it to bed. Got to a sofa in the front room and went out like a light." The grin grew. "Had a bit of trouble with his back and took too much lotion on the way home. Fact is, he was too hungover yesterday to even report it."

"How's his back?"

"Oh that?" Hooper wiped his lips with long fingers. "Worse than ever, I should think."

"What size is he?"

"About your size... Albert. Only not so..."

"Fat?"

"Well, he's at it all day on a farm, that is, when his back doesn't play him up."

"We've got the colors of the clothes, things like that?"

"It won't help us much. Jeans are all the same. The anorak was blue, the pullover navy. We didn't get much on the shoes."

Albert nodded thoughtfully, he looked at the ragged remains of the sailor suit laid out on the white Formica bench. Eighty years ago it would have been fashionable, almost commonplace; children everywhere would have been seen wearing them in the High Street in Tonbridge or as they were taken for walks along the winding river. He wondered if the missing German inspector had ever set eyes on this particular garment, and who the child was who had worn it.

"What do you make of it, Albert?" Constable Hooper asked. "Who'd have treated it like that?"

Albert shook his head.

"It's gone in the seams." Hooper leaned forward and touched the ripped jacket. "Torn apart, it's been."

"Perhaps they were looking for something."

Hooper raised his eyebrows and said nothing.

"I don't know either." Albert smiled slightly. "Any one mind if I leave it out here for a bit?"

"Shouldn't think so." Hooper's eyes went round the storeroom. "Lost bicycles is what we have in here mostly. Stolen goods, things like that."

Albert reached for the raincoat he'd hung on a hook by the door; automatically his hand went to the shape of the cigarette packet in one of the pockets. He'd not felt like smoking all day. He slipped the coat on and was reaching for the door handle when the door opened and a uniformed constable stepped into the room, half-saluted Albert, and handed Hooper a message. "Call from London for you, Tony," the constable said. "Lab at Scotland Yard."

"Thanks, Jim." Hooper read the message once and frowned; he read it again and looked up at the constable who'd brought it. "You can leave this to me," he said in a quiet voice. When they were alone, Hooper's eyes turned to Albert. "They can't identify them," he said in the same empty tone.

"The hairs?"

"That's right. They got no idea what they are."

"They've tried everything?"

"Everything that's got hair on in this country." Hooper read the message for the third time. "They'll try again, but they're not hopeful. They've got no idea at all what sort of animal it came from."

Albert Scot pulled his raincoat about him more firmly. Once again he was aware of a ghostly chill coming into the room. He turned and looked at Constable Hooper and knew that the lean policeman felt it also.

Ten

SALLY LAWRENCE arrived at Cyril Fenick's basement flat as darkness settled over the city; the air had become colder, and rain had turned to wet snow, which fell and melted on the running pavement. She was grateful for the warm, cat-smelling atmosphere of the closed apartment and to see the slow-moving, heavy old man bow slightly and smile as he closed the door behind her.

"I thought it was you, my dear," he said in his rumbling voice, "but I couldn't be sure. It's not often they come back, you know. Something I find strange, myself."

"I told your secretary..." Sally hesitated, nervous now that she was here; she would find it difficult to begin. "I said I'd been before."

"Oh, that Eric...." Cyril Fenick dismissed him with a wave of his hand. "He never tells me anything." Ushering her into the crowded study, he pointed to an overstuffed chair among piles of books.

"Take a seat, my dear. What can I do for you this time?"

Sally sat on the edge of the chair and watched Cyril lower himself into another so close that their knees almost touched. "You don't think I want my fortune told again?" she said as lightly as she could.

Cyril shook his head. "They never do, they never do. I suspect they think it might change, and then they wouldn't know what to believe." He smiled a gentle smile. "But, I'll tell yours again if you like."

"No." Sally realized he was making it as easy as he could. "It's not about me this time. It's about a friend."

"I see." Cyril reached down into the semidarkness at his feet and scooped a large, black cat onto his lap. "This is Sootums," he said. "I'm afraid I'm not very imaginative with names."

"You had lots last time."

"They're all still about somewhere." Cyril stroked the black cat's fur. "Tell me about your friend," he said comfortably.

"Well"—Sally found herself unbending—"last time I was here I told you about my brother."

Cyril nodded; the cat had begun to purr.

"You remember?"

"My dear, I never forget anything." Cyril's voice rumbled even lower. "That's one of my shortcomings, and with someone like you, who told me so much ... I recall it all."

"Then you'll understand what I mean when I say I've met someone here in London who has ... who has what I think is a similar problem, and I'm not sure what to do about it."

"You don't have much faith in doctors, do you?"

"I don't think they'd understand."

"And, you love ... this friend of yours?"

"I ... ?" For a moment the question took Sally's breath away. It was so abrupt, so accurate, and yet she'd not even asked it of herself. There had been tenderness and passion, but she'd not really thought of love, although she realized as soon as Cyril Fenick spoke the word that love was exactly what she felt for Simon. The soft melting inside when she looked at him, the way she'd thought of him all day, could not mean anything else. She smiled, almost with relief. "I ... I suppose I do love him," she admitted at last. "It's just that ... that it's been so quick."

Cyril smiled. "Velocity has very little to do with love," he said. "But, take your time and tell me more about the problem this friend of yours is suffering from."

Sally settled further into the chair. She found that the admission of love had relaxed her; whatever else she had to say would be easier now. "The trouble is," she went on, "I can't get him to talk to me. I've tried, but he won't even admit he's got a problem."

"What's his name, my dear?"

"Simon."

"And how long have you known, Simon?"

"I met him ..." Sally paused, finding it difficult to believe there really had been so little time. "My God, it was only the day before yesterday."

"But, in that short time a great deal has happened?"

Sally nodded, and her gaze moved away. She found herself looking at the charts she'd recalled, with symbols she didn't understand, that lined the walls. She knew that Cyril Fenick was forcing her to face herself. As he sat with the purring cat on his lap, his intelligent eyes fixed on her, he was making her answer questions she'd so far avoided. "Yes," she whispered finally. "Lots of things have happened."

"What, my dear?"

"Things ... things that are kind of ... weird."

"Things you can't explain?"

"I can't explain any of it." Sally sat forward in the chair. Words came in a rush now; they bubbled on her lips. She began to tell Cyril Fenick everything.

"I came to you because I thought you'd understand. You're the only person I know in London who might understand. Last time you told me you knew what it was like to love someone and to want to help them and...and not be able to, because they wouldn't let you, because you couldn't get to them. Well, that's what it's like with Simon. I can't do anything for him because he won't let me. I mean, I'm close to him and...and everything, but he won't talk to me about what's worrying him. He won't say a word."

"And you've tried."

"Yes, I've tried and tried. I've..." Sally began, then paused. "There's something else," she began again, "something...strange." Her voice fell to a whisper. She could feel the concentration in Cyril Fenick's eyes. "I don't know what's got into him."

"Got into him?" The question was rapid. "What do you mean?"

"The way he acts." Sally watched the fat old man; he was suddenly very still. "He's strange."

"When did you first notice this strangeness?" Cyril's voice deepened; each word appeared to be spoken singly as if no other existed. "Was it from the very beginning?"

"Yes...it was."

"Where did you meet this...Simon?"

"I didn't meet him, I found him." Sally closed her eyes. "I know it sounds silly, but I was coming home the night before last and I found him in an alley near to where I live. He was frightened, and I stopped to see if I could help him and, well, I took him home."

"Then what happened?"

"Nothing. Well, I mean, nothing like that. We had coffee and he told me he'd just come to London, said he hadn't been here before and he had nowhere to stay, and so I told him he could stay with me and he did. He slept on the divan. There was nothing... at first."

"But there has been?"

Sally nodded. "I know what you're thinking," she said in a small voice. "But, well it seemed right. It was right. I didn't go to work yesterday, and we just played around in the park and bought chestnuts, you know the sort of thing. It was fun, we had such a good time, and he, he was happy, you know, so... relaxed." Sally paused. "We're right for each other; that's why I want to help him so much. That's why I came to you."

"What has frightened you, my dear?"

"Frightened me?"

"There is fear in every gesture you make," Cyril said softly. "I noticed it the moment you came through the door."

"Does it..." Sally swallowed. "Does it show that much?"

Cyril nodded. "Try to tell me what has caused it," he urged, his hands kneading the big black cat.

"Don't you... don't *you* know?"

The fat man's expression did not alter. "Me?" he asked, his voice a distant rumble.

"Yes, when I thought of you I... hoped you would." Sally let her breath out in a long, sobbing sigh. "Last time I was here you asked me if I believed in fate or destiny, things like that. You wanted to know if a person's life was... foreshadowed by anything or if I thought it was. Well, I do now. And it scares me." She stared down at her tightening hands. "I think that Simon and... what's going to happen to us was decided a long time ago. And I find it very, very frightening."

Cyril Fenick listened intently; he said nothing as she told him all that had occurred. The little words and the delicate memories drifted between them. Only once did he move, and that was when Sally spoke of the look on Simon's face and the way his hands were lifted when he said, "Bind me with silver. The metal of the moon." Then Cyril's breath sucked in sharply, and he lifted his head back, away from the sound.

When Sally had finished, there was silence in the crowded study. She lay back in her chair; the effort of telling had both drained and renewed her. But it was a long time before the fat man said anything. He appeared remote; his eyes were on her, but they gave the impression of looking through her, and when he spoke, his voice was distant.

"You must give him what he wishes," he said in a cold and different tone. "He must be denied nothing."

"I...ah..." For a second or two Sally did not understand. "I've given him..."

"If it is silver he asks, give him silver." Cyril closed his eyes. "He will not harm you. Of that I am certain."

"*Harm me?*" Sally sat forward sharply. "I don't get you. Why should he harm me? I mean, I'm scared of what's happening to us, to both of us, but it never crossed my mind he'd...harm me."

"He won't."

"What do you mean?"

"I mean that there is great danger in everything about him." Cyril's eyes snapped open. "You were wise to come to me. I am one of the few people in London who can help you but not now. I must consult my library, make calculations. Then I will be able to confirm everything. In the meantime give him what he asks."

"But..." Sally scrambled out of her chair and stood over the bulk of the man who seemed to have turned into a sorcerer. The mood in the study had altered. There was more being said than she could possibly understand. "What...what are you trying to do? You talk about him as if he was some sort of...monster."

"He is."

"*What?*"

"Believe me, he is."

"No...please..." Tears were suddenly in Sally's eyes; she heard a ringing in her ears. She looked about her wildly. "What are you trying to do?"

Cyril Fenick stared up at her. "In your heart you know I am speaking the truth." His eyes seemed to pierce. "That is why you came to me. Like me, you are a believer."

"Stop...." The word was dry in Sally's throat; it lay like a leaf on her lips. "I came because I thought you'd understand."

"I do. I understand everything. There is more to my life than the mere telling of fortunes. There are mysteries I have studied, experiences I have had that are given to few. I understand what you are talking about...and therefore I must warn you."

"Warn me?" Sally sank to the side of her chair. She was terribly aware of the growing truth of what she was being told. "No..." she whispered, denying it, "there is nothing to warn me of."

"There is," Cyril continued relentlessly. He watched her face move with pain as each utterance struck. "There is much to warn you of. But, remember, he will not harm *you*."

"Please...don't say that again." Sally wished she could hide from Cyril Fenick's dreadful words and the cold, positive way in which they were spoken. She wanted to be with Simon, to hold him close to her, to shut out what was being said to her completely. "Oh, my God," she whimpered. "What is happening?"

"What is happening *was* decided a long time ago," Cyril went on steadily. "He is not to blame, nor are you or anyone else who has anything to do with it. It began before any of us was born."

"No." Sally saw again the slight, haughty woman in checked taffeta; she seemed suddenly alive. "That *couldn't* have been his...mother in the photo I told you about."

"There is no doubt." Cyril's tone altered slightly. "Tell me, is he out of touch with everyday matters?"

"Yes," Sally whispered, "he is. He thought five pounds was an awful lot of money."

"He had none of his own?"

"Nothing. Oh, my God." Sally sat unsteadily on the arm of the chair. She looked at the walls with their symbols and their charts; they seemed to have new meaning. "What can I do?"

"For yourself, nothing. As far as Simon is concerned I will have to think. Tomorrow? Do you think you could come back tomorrow?"

Sally stood abruptly, moving away from the fat teller of fortunes, her hands held up defensively, some of the horror, some of her despair turned against him. "How do you know so much about all this?" she asked harshly. "What's it got to do with you?"

Cyril Fenick did not reply.

"You sit there like some sort of guru, passing goddamn judgments, telling me that Simon's a monster. What do you think you're trying to do?"

Cyril Fenick remained impassive.

"You... You're trying to frighten me." Tears ran freely down Sally's cheeks, a web of saliva formed at her lips, and her words were choked. "You're trying to scare me... you and your... cats and your... pictures." Her hands went up to her face. She backed into a corner of the study as far away from Cyril as she could possibly be. "You're trying to make it worse."

"I'm trying to make you understand." Cyril's voice was extremely gentle. It had eased, the monkish quality gone. He now appeared merely to be a kindly old man stroking a cat. "You must understand, because we have a lot to face together."

"We?" Sally's voice was small. "What do you mean, we?"

"You and I, my dear. You have brought this matter to me; now I am part of it." He sighed very softly.

"Perhaps that was also written, perhaps that too is inescapable, but whatever the case, I am now involved."

"How do you know so much?"

Cyril smiled softly. "I am a believer. Some of us are, some of us could never be, and, of those who believe, there are a small number who ... *know*. Who have had their beliefs made manifest, who have seen what the forces of darkness and death are capable of." He looked at her simply, and his old eyes were sincere. "I am one such, my dear. I have ... *seen*."

"What have you seen?"

"That is not important at the moment. I would need too much time to explain everything, but it is enough that you understand that I know, and it is enough that you believe I can help you."

"What ... what can you do?"

Cyril looked at the frightened figure of the girl in the opposite corner of the study. He saw the despair, the need, and regretted the harshness of his reaction, but it had been necessary. She must comprehend clearly the danger she was in. She must be told of the strange power that surrounded her. She would need to believe in her heart that this was not another fortune-telling session, that it had nothing to do with the trivia of everyday life. And she must take that knowledge with her when she returned to whatever it was that awaited her. She must be strong, as I also must be strong, Cyril thought, for I am now almost as involved as she. An imperceptible shiver ran through his bulky frame. I will be the bearer of bad tidings and, as such, I may also be destroyed. His eyes went down to the cat, and he pressed it for a moment in comfort and in strength.

"Tell me." Sally's voice came across the study. "What can you do?"

"I can tell you how to save him," Cyril answered simply. "And how to save yourself." He paused and stared at her fully. "In the meantime, my dear, give him what he asks for."

Sally moved her lips. "Silver?" she whispered.

Cyril nodded. Very slowly he stood and, with the cat under one arm, opened a drawer of his littered desk. He reached into it and took out an object that glittered between his pudgy fingers. "Here," he said softly, walking toward Sally. "Give him this."

Eleven

RAY CLARK DROVE slowly through the London rush hour. Wet, sleeting snow cut visibility down to nothing; everything was reduced to a crawl. Anger bubbled inside him like acid. He'd had a swine of a day. He'd been late getting to St. Albans, and they'd held him up there all afternoon. Now he was stuck in bloody traffic and, unless things went his way, he wouldn't make it to that poncey pub in the mews before it filled up with all those gits, their posh accents and their pints of bitter standing around talking about their wanky sports cars.

He had to get in early, had to talk to that bitch behind the bar, make friends with her, turn on a little of the old charm after the way he behaved last night. Well, he could do it if he had to, especially with them fat, hungry ones; they seemed to like a little rough stuff now and then. But he needed a break badly.

Using all his skill he edged through the packed

vehicles, hoping that the police didn't spot him and ruin his plans completely. Gradually he made ground.

After Hyde Park Corner the traffic moved a little more rapidly, and Ray's bitter mood eased. By the time he got to Victoria Station he was close enough to where he wanted to be; he looked at his digital watch and nodded. He'd make it in time to have his chat. It seemed, at long last, that things were going his way.

When Molly White saw Ray come into the bar of The Half Moon, she recognized him immediately. The little bugger, she thought, what's he doing back here? Her first instinct was to call Fred, who was down in the cellar changing a keg. But the cheeky little sod was smiling, and she decided to give him a chance. She looked across at old Alf and his daughter; they were at their usual table with their usual drinks; apart from that, the bar was empty. She turned and stared at Ray Clark coldly.

"Evening, miss," Ray said as he sat on a stool and pointed to the ceramic-handled beer pumps. "Is that real ale you've got there?"

"As real as you're likely to find, sunshine."

"Yes, well..." Ray smiled. This was going to be harder than he thought. "I'll have a half, if you don't mind."

"I don't mind at all." Molly reached for a mug, put it under a handle, and drew a half of ale. "Just don't go kicking the place to bits," she said as she put down the drink and took the money. "We like it the way it is."

"Oh, yeah, you remember me then?"

"Never forget a face, sunshine." Molly leaned away and lit a cigarette. "Especially yours."

"I, ah, I came back to apologize for that," Ray said, forcing a smile. "I must've forgot meself or something."

"What'd you get upset for, anyway?" Molly studied him carefully. He wasn't a bad kid, she thought; and

132

wiry. I'll bet he's got a tough little body. "We got our hours to keep, you know that."

"I was looking out for a friend of mine." Ray sipped ale and nodded appreciatively. "And, just when I thought I'd found him, I mean, somewhere where he might've been, I was too late."

"Who's your friend?"

"The thing is, I run a delivery service down Tonbridge way." Ray put his elbows on the bar, his chin on his hands, and looked up at Molly appealingly. "And there's this feller I give a lift to the other night. Really nice he was, I think he's a rock star meself, and he lives round this way. Well, you know how it is, we said we'd have a drink together, and he told me about this pub and, like I said, when I got here, you was closed and I lost my bottle a bit." He made a gesture of reaching for his wallet. "I'll pay for any damage I did."

"That's all right." Molly's eyes were interested. "What's his name, this friend of yours?"

"Ah, you've got me there. He did tell me, early on, but it went right out of my head. His Lordship, I call him. He's like that, if you know what I mean."

"What's he look like?"

"A good-looking feller," Ray said sincerely. "Got a good head, if you know what I mean. Red hair. Looks like one of them you might see in the adverts on the telly. You know, a real handsome geezer." He watched Molly with his shrewd little eyes. "You'd notice him, you would. A good-looking woman like yourself would've noticed him right off."

"You think so, do you?"

"I'm sure of it, miss."

Molly held the cigarette in front of her and watched smoke curl upward. "He interested in photos?" she asked casually.

"Could be," Ray answered promptly. "His Lordship'd be interested in things like that."

"Got a girl? Looks a bit like a gippo?"

"He didn't say anything about her to me."

"How tall would you say he was?" Molly was enjoying herself. He could be quite nice, this wiry little feller, when he tried. "A big feller, did you say?"

"Well, no. Not that big." She knows, the old tart, Ray thought, and she'll tell me in a minute. "About average. Why? You seen him, have you?"

"Could've done."

"He come in here often, then?"

"*If...*" Molly said emphatically, "if, it's the feller I think it is, he won't be back again tonight."

"Oh." Ray exaggerated his disappointment. "I was sort of looking forward to having a few with him." He smiled ruefully. "It's not often you run into a geezer like that, with that sort of class. What's human with it."

"Well, I'm not saying I'm sure, mind you." Molly turned away as Alf's daughter came up carrying an empty pint pot and a large sherry glass. "Same again, Myrtle?" Molly asked with a smile.

Myrtle shook her head. "Better make Dad's a half," she said with a sidelong glance at Ray. "He's having trouble holding the big ones tonight."

"Yeah, well, it gets to that." Molly began to fill a half-pint. "Schooner for you?" she said, indicating the sherry.

Myrtle nodded, then sniffed. "Clientele's changing," she muttered, her eyes going toward Ray. "Last night you had those hippies. Now this..."

"Gives the place a bit of character, Myrtle. Look at it that way, love." Molly took the sherry glass and filled it. "I'll bring these over," she said. "You go back to the dad."

Myrtle's face brightened. "Thank you, Molly. That's very kind."

"Allow me, miss." Ray moved off his stool and picked up the full glasses. With a slight flourish he carried them to the corner table. "There you are, squire," he said, placing the half in front of Alf. "And for you, ma'am," he added, handing the sherry to Myrtle. "My pleasure, I can tell you."

Molly watched the performance and giggled. He's a card, this little toughie, she thought; I'll bet he knows a trick or two. "Listen," she said when Ray came back. "I think I do know the feller you're talking about. He was in here earlier, I think he's keen on buying some of these old pictures. Said he'd be back tomorrow, so why don't you call back then?"

"Got to go to Tonbridge in the morning."

"Make it the evening then."

"Think he'll be here?"

Molly smiled. "If he comes in early I'll tell him a friend's waiting."

"I wouldn't do that," Ray said quickly. He didn't want his Lordship warned off. "I mean, I was going to make it a surprise, if you know what I mean."

"All right, love, but if he does come in early I'll get him back. Like I say, he's interested in them pictures."

"Well, that's great." Ray smiled at Molly warmly and saw the responding twinkle in her eye. He felt immensely pleased with himself. "Can I offer you a drink, miss?" he asked. "To sort of thank you for your trouble."

Molly stubbed out her cigarette. "Well, just this once," she said, and poured herself a nip of gin. As they lifted their glasses to toast each other there was a sudden heart-wrenching burst of coughing from the doorway behind the bar, and Fred stepped gingerly into the room; he put one hand on the door frame and held the other to his face, which was going gradually blue. "Hello, Fred," Molly said quietly. "Come up smiling again, I see."

Ray laughed as he finished his drink.

Sally Lawrence listened to the clacking of the tube train that carried her underground from Sloane Square to Victoria Station. She tried not to think of arriving, as she tried to put from mind where she had been and what she had been told. She stood in the half-empty carriage, ignoring the vacant seats about her, and stared out into the passing darkness, wishing that she were back in her apartment already, that the meeting with Simon was over.

In spite of her efforts to keep them away, Cyril Fenick's words forced themselves into her consciousness. Sally bit her lip, felt the warmth of tears in her eyes. She wondered, with a bleakness that filled her with despair, what else she would need to know. She might learn that to love him was not enough.

Sally closed her eyes and leaned her head against the carriage wall.

Oh, my God, she whispered. What is this turning into? I wanted to help him, that's all. I stopped and talked to him because I thought he needed it, not to fall in love with him.

And the love? So sudden...and so strong. She'd been in love before, but it had never been like this, as intense, as unselfish. She couldn't think why. Perhaps he fulfilled something in herself that had remained untouched until this moment. Whatever the reason, it was something from which she would never escape.

Sally felt the train begin to slow as it came into Victoria. One or two other passengers got up from their seats and began to move toward the door by which she stood. She shivered and wiped her eyes. It was time to return to her tiny flat. It was time to face Simon.

Simon Blackstone lay on the bed he'd shared with Sally Lawrence and tried to keep the images at bay. All afternoon, ever since he'd revisited The Half Moon, they'd come crawling out of the woodwork, whispering, informing, unraveling the fibers of his memory, telling him what he was.

They'd been brought to life by a photograph he

could not ever remember having seen before—the group of three striding down a gravel driveway. The faceless child in the sailor suit, the ghostly imprint of something that might not even have been, carried with it a force so dreadful that he knew he could not deny any part of what he had been made to know.

He was no longer a Moonchild, not now—no longer a simple being whose empty soul had become possessed, a seemingly dead infant who'd had to be carried halfway across Europe, to the town he had been born in, to be buried there.

Conceived, born, interred above and below the same piece of earth.

That is what had been said over eighty years ago, but no one had known then of the changes all those years in the ground would bring, how the evil would develop and mature. No one had known how fertile the earth would be.

For he was a Changeling now.

The accident that had released him, set him free again, had initiated the sweep of another cycle. Possessed by the same demon, grown stronger now, more vital, he was destined to wreck and devour and kill.

He was moving much more swiftly now, becoming rapidly closer and closer to the beast within. Each time its power was released the alteration would be more dramatic. Already he had changed once, from a child to a man, as he'd lain beside the dead bulldozer driver who'd uncaged him. And he'd change again and again, until the beast assumed the final shape.

Now he lay in Sally's bed trying to hide from the knowledge of himself. Only the thought of the dark and lively girl, whose eyes held such sympathy and whose body had awakened such pleasure sustained him, kept the insistent voices and their vile demands at bay. When she came back her goodness would give him new strength—if only for a little while.

But she didn't return. Pale light outside the window turned to gray, then to final blackness. A faint glow came up from the street; muffled sounds of homeward traffic droned in the background, but there was no sign of the girl. And, as clearly as he was able, he tried to think of a way of excluding her from all that was destined to occur.

He could leave, before it was too late. He could crawl from the bed and leave the flat and try to forget her; that way she might not become contaminated.

If she was not so already.

The thought went through Simon like fire, destroying his ability to concentrate. He put his hands to his head and pressed as if in pain, trying to hold himself apart from the presences that chanted all about him.

The sudden galloping of steel-shod hooves, voices whispering in an icy dawn, the sound of a steam locomotive, the pinching smell of black smoke in the searing air. They shouldered all thought of Sally aside, murmuring, shouting, grinding closer. They waited for the moment when his strength or his will failed sufficiently for them to sweep down and carry him off into the darkness they lived in, for the violence they demanded.

It would happen soon. It lacked only the moon in its fullness to light their way. He was without protection now, and felt his resistance draining.

Finally a sort of sleep overcame him. He curled, knees under the chin, elbows at his sides, in the position of an unborn child; the singing, chanting, syllabic shapes began to draw closer and closer. The last vestiges of his resistance died, and he allowed them entry.

The one-eyed coachman was the first.

The tall, gaunt figure, with its blind left eye, emerged from the gloom to stand at the foot of the bed. Simon saw it clearly, although his face remained buried in the blankets; he saw the half-stoop, the ravaged countenance, the lips pulled back into a welcoming smile.

"Poor little one," the coachman said in his mountain voice.

Simon pressed his hands to his ears.

"Poor little one," the coachman repeated.

Simon kept his eyes from the throat of the vision. It was there, he knew, that the full horror lay. It was to that point the arm had gone, and the horned nails had torn, until the gaunt, one-eyed shape had been hurled into the limbo in which it now lay.

Simon whimpered and pressed the blankets about him, but the mountain voice and its gentle comment were not to be denied. Simon dug his fingers into his eyes so that they would not drift to the bloodied throat and the thin whisperings of death it held.

"No," Simon shouted. "Leave me alone."

"Simon."

"Get away...get back."

"Simon." It was Sally's voice, filled with anxiety. The hand on his shoulder was hers. "Simon, wake up. It's me."

"What?" Simon saw nothing.

"Simon, please, what's the matter?"

Simon lifted his head from the covers and looked up into the concerned eyes of Sally Lawrence. He saw the shape he had come to trust, heard the only voice that might possibly save him, and his fears burst from him in a great and needful cry as he reached out and pulled her down onto the bed alongside him.

"It's all right," Sally whispered. "It's okay now. I'm back, I'm here."

"I was...I was..."

"What?"

"A nightmare. It was awful."

"What about?"

Simon shook his head and buried it in her warmth.

He must tell her nothing. Above all, he must tell her nothing.

"Tell me. Talk to me."

"I cannot...it was too hideous." Simon shivered and looked at her with such need, with such a demand for compassion, that Sally's own arms tightened about him and held him dearly. "I am better now," he whispered. "You are with me again, and I am recovered."

"Oh, Simon, my dear Simon...my God."

"Don't go from me."

"No, no, I'll stay." Sally pressed him closer, putting aside the questions that had troubled her since Cyril Fenick had uttered his mysterious words. Now, when he seemed so lost, so needful, so afraid, what he required was her comfort; she closed her eyes and held him tightly. Together they would face what lay before them; she would give him whatever it was he needed. She remembered the silver. "I have something for you," she said, attempting to reach for her bag. "I've brought you a present."

"Don't leave me."

"I have to, for a moment."

"What is it?"

"You'll see." Slowly Sally released herself from Simon's clinging arms; she felt about the end of the bed where her purse had fallen and, when she found it, drew it toward her, keeping her eyes all the time on Simon and the mixture of fear and relief that moved over his face. "I hope you like it."

"What is it?"

"Something you asked for."

"What?" Simon sat upright in the bed. He watched her open the purse and take from it a small item wrapped in white tissue. "Here," she said, "it's yours."

Simon took it, felt the shape of the gift through the thin paper. Abruptly he tore the wrapping away and stared down at the heavy, silver-chain bracelet that lay in his fingers. Each link was made in the shape of a heart, and from a central link, larger and heavier than the others, a silver cross dangled. In the half-light from the outside street lamps, the thick metal glowed softly in Simon Blackstone's hand.

"Let me put it on for you," Sally said. She reached forward and attached it to his left wrist. "I hope you like it. Please"—there was the faintest catch in her voice—"please say you like it."

"I do," Simon said simply. There was courage in his words, there was new life in his face. He stared at the chain and felt his breathing ease. The shapes no longer existed, the whisperings had ceased. His eyes came up to Sally's in a mixture of gratitude and dread. "Thank you," he said again, his voice desolate and joyful. "I will keep it with me always."

Sally was unable to speak.

She watched Simon's expressions, and she understood. She heard the twin notes of hope and despair and felt as if her heart had frozen within her. She put her arms about him and drew him back down into the bed and held him as the tension went from his body and the pain disappeared from his face.

As she held him she felt new tears on her cheeks; she stared up into the semidarkness and watched the faintest of patterns drift over the ceiling, and she tried desperately not to cry, not to allow the sound of her own sorrow to escape her lips and be heard.

He belonged to her now, of that she was certain. Whatever he was or might become, he was now hers, something lost she had saved, something she could not now abandon.

Twelve

ALBERT SCOT SAT in his mother's kitchen and watched her clear away the remains of their evening meal of carrot-and-tomato salad, whole-wheat bread, and low-fat cheese. He'd consumed as much as he could and was still hungry.

"A few days down here and you'll soon get into shape," Mrs. Scot said as she ran hot water into the sink and began washing dishes. "Might be able to make some change for the better with what you wear," she added, glancing over her shoulder. "Your shoes, for example, look like loaves of bread."

Albert looked down at his ungainly footwear. "They're comfortable," he murmured, knowing it was the wrong thing to say.

"I've tried to tell you, comfort's got nothing to do with it." Mrs. Scot picked up a towel and began drying dishes. "I hear you had lunch with Bates," she said presently. "At that club of his."

"Conservative Association."

"That'd go with your shoes." The briefest smile flickered across Mrs. Scot's features. "What'd they give you to eat? Steak and kidney pie? Cabinet pudding? Stodgy stuff like that?"

"I had grilled trout." Albert cleared his throat. "Is there any coffee?" he asked uncertainly.

"Tea. *Camomile* tea. Very good for you. It'll make you sleep."

Albert closed his eyes. "Do you have any of the fruitcake left?"

"Not at this time of night." Mrs. Scot put the kettle on. "Anyway," she added, "that was a special treat because I was so glad to see you after all this time." She reached for a canister on a shelf above her head. "By the way, have you discovered who committed the crime you were brought down to solve?"

"Yes."

"Oh, who was it?"

"A boy in a sailor suit," Albert replied, and watched his mother carefully. She stopped in midmovement, then whirled to stare at him intently; her bright little eyes were as sharp as flints. "What? Who did you say it was?"

"Oh...I was only joking. I really don't have any idea who did it."

"But why did you say that, Albert?" The birdlike head was listening; the thin, well-groomed body was almost still. "Where *did* you get the idea that a boy in a sailor suit had anything to do with it at all?"

"They found a sailor suit on the site where the driver died."

"Did they now? That's interesting." Mrs. Scot resumed her movements; she took down the canister of camomile tea, spooned some into a teapot, and stared at the kettle, willing it to boil. "What else have they found?"

Albert looked at his fingernails; they were beginning to grow again. It must be a couple of days since he'd bitten them. He wondered idly what was happening: he'd altered since he'd been attached to the Tonbridge Force.

"Well, go on, tell me." With some satisfaction Mrs. Scot picked up the boiling kettle, turned off the gas, poured water into the teapot. "I'd like to hear about your work."

Albert smiled softly; there was no stopping her when she was like this. Get a mouse out of its hole if she wanted to, he thought, and the mouse'd be grateful.

"Come on, tell me." Mrs. Scot placed a cup of herby-smelling tea before him. "I'll give you a *small* piece of fruitcake if you do."

"Make it a big piece."

"Medium."

"Well," Albert began, "I know who that German was who came down here and where he ended up. I know who the London inspector was who contacted Grandad. I seem to be getting on quite well with what happened round about the turn of the century, though not too cleverly with what went on two days ago."

As Mrs. Scot listened she reached into a cupboard, took out a cake tin with a picture of George V on it, cut a semi-thick slice of fruitcake, and placed it on a willow-pattern plate. "Tell me more about the sailor suit," she said, licking a crumb from her finger.

"There was an old box on the building site." Albert's eyes were on the slice of cake; he picked out a raisin and ate it thoughtfully. "Inside was a little boy's sailor suit. Ripped to pieces."

"That the box the papers said was full of silver?"

"It had a silver lock, that's all."

"Nevertheless, that'd be it."

"The bulldozer driver dug it up before he died. There could have been someone with him we don't know about. Perhaps they thought the chest was full of silver and fought over it, but we've no idea really."

"One of the papers said he was killed by wild dogs."

Albert glanced at his mother. She was on the far side of the kitchen sipping camomile tea, her bright little eyes fixed on him.

"Well, they *did,* you know," Mrs. Scot said defensively. "One of the less respectable ones, of course."

"You seem to have read them all."

"Oh..." There was the slightest flicker of the attentive head, the vaguest smile. "It's not every day you get a really grisly murder so close to home."

"I've sent some hairs up to the lab in London." Albert broke off a piece of fruitcake; his fingers were steady. "They've not been identified yet."

"Why not?"

"It takes time."

"What else?"

Albert looked at his mother. "I'd have said that wasn't bad for a couple of days. Did you know the dead driver by any chance?"

Mrs. Scot blew on her tea. "Never even heard of him," she replied. "What'd Bates have to say?"

"About what?"

"About *anything.* Ye gods, Albert, this is your mother you're talking to. Don't be so damned uninformative."

Albert smiled. "It was Bates who told me about Kearsley," he said. "He was the London inspector who committed suicide. It was Bates who told me who the German was; in fact, he said it was because the German was missing that they held Grandad's inquiry. He's been a lot of help."

"He say anything about the report?"

"What report?"

"The one the German sent." Mrs. Scot turned from her son and tipped the dregs of her tea into the sink. "Mind you," she went on, "there was only talk of it. Rumors, things like that. Perhaps Bates never heard them. Perhaps he'd forgotten."

"He wouldn't forget. He told me this whole business is a hobby of his."

"A hobby?" Mrs. Scot glanced over her shoulder. "Ye gods, what a thing to say."

"Tell me about the report."

"Well, as I say, there was never anything definitely *known* about it. There was talk and, well, you know how people are."

"Did he give it to Grandad?"

"What?"

"You heard."

Mrs. Scot smiled then, a small, tired smile that contained something of relief. "You're quick, Albert," she said softly. "You mightn't be anything to look at, but there's nothing wrong with your mind. He always said that, your grandfather did. He said you'd get there on your own."

"What happened to it?"

"Oh, your grandfather sent it up to London as he was asked to." Mrs. Scot folded her arms about her narrow bosom. "It went to Inspector Kearsley, the one who . . . killed himself."

"But Grandad read it first?"

"Yes, Albert." Her eyes were slightly melancholy as she gazed at her son.

"What did it say?"

Mrs. Scot's hands came out. "Of *that* I have no idea," she said positively. "None whatsoever." Her voice became quieter. "But it affected him, it affected him deeply. He was never quite the same after that. He felt as if he'd been . . . touched. That's the word he used, Albert, touched. On the few occasions he talked about it he said nothing of what it contained, but he said it had touched him and his family. He thought it would go through us all."

"Has it?"

"I don't know. Your father wouldn't join the force here. He went into the army instead, and look what happened to him." She closed her eyes. "I always thought it was unfair of him, you know. I always thought he was just passing it on to you."

"What is it," Albert asked carefully, "this thing we have to face?"

"I don't know. Truly I don't."

"But Dad did."

"Yes," Mrs. Scot replied quietly. "Your grandfather spoke to him."

"And he said nothing to you?"

Mrs. Scot shook her head.

"Well..." Albert sighed. He reached for the remaining piece of fruitcake and paused; his hand went back to the table, leaving the cake untouched. "At least it's not all nonsense, is it?"

"What is?"

Albert smiled. "I can't put it into words without sounding spooky, but before I left the Yard, the old man's remark came back to me. The one he made that day in the kitchen here when he spoke about family blood being involved. It makes sense to me now."

"He left something for you."

Albert glanced quickly at his mother; she was as still as stone. "What is it?"

"He said you'd know what it was for."

Without another word Mrs. Scot left the kitchen. Albert heard her footsteps ascend the stairs to her bedroom, heard a heavy piece of furniture move, then there was silence. After a while his mother came back into the kitchen carrying a small object wrapped in soft black cloth and laid it on the table before him. Then she went back and leaned against the sink, watching him with her sharp, clear eyes.

Albert reached for the object, and as his fingers touched the cloth he knew what it was. He felt the shape of the barrel; his palm sensed the heft of the grip even before the cloth was removed. He unwrapped it, picked it up, and slowly turned it over in his hands. It was a Victorian pistol with a single chamber. It had a curved, polished walnut stock, and the barrel was octagonal-shaped, chased in a pheasant-wing design. The small, neat hammer and the curved trigger balanced the exquisite workmanship. With the pistol was a single cartridge; its bullet appeared to be solid silver.

Albert stared down at the pistol in his hand; it seemed to fit perfectly. He picked up the cartridge, testing its weight; it was heavy and it shone. Albert felt the hair at the back of his neck prickle slightly.

Albert looked at his mother; the neat, well-dressed little woman had not moved on the far side of the kitchen. She stared back at him; in her eyes there was pain and pity.

"He said you'd know what to do with it," she said.

When Sally woke the following morning, Simon was not asleep. He lay beside her in the shared bed, his eyes on the bracelet she had given him the night before. As Sally watched he fondled the heavy, heart-shaped links. His fingers touched and turned the dangling cross, his attention absorbed. His face was smooth and his eyes were clear; there was no sign of the confusion that had marked his features the night before. He turned and smiled at Sally with a full and enchanting radiance, touched her hair, drew her close and held her.

"You okay this morning?" she asked hesitantly.

Simon nodded against her.

"No...no more nightmares?"

"None," Simon said softly. "Did you also sleep well?"

"Yes," Sally admitted. "I must have."

They'd not left the bed since her return but had lain close and comforting, sharing warmth and presence without passion. They'd drifted into sleep holding each other, and from there exhaustion had taken them through the night. It seemed to them both that a new day might bring new promise, and this was enough to enable them to continue.

After a while Sally moved. "I must go," she said. She wore yesterday's clothes and felt a need to wash and change and begin again. "I must go to work."

"Must you?"

"Yes." Sally thought of Cyril Fenick and her promised return. She held Simon close a moment longer. "Will you be all right?" she asked, watching him intently. "Will you?"

"I will." Simon touched the bracelet. "I am protected now."

"Are you sure?"

"Yes." Simon sat up in the bed. "I cannot begin to tell you..." he began uncertainly, and Sally's fingers came up and covered his lips. "Shh," she whispered, "don't say anything. Not now."

There was nothing he could say that would make any difference now. She had seen him in passion, she had witnessed his pain; and she loved him still. All night long her hands had moved out toward him; she found herself holding him whenever she awoke. It seemed not to matter what he was. She knew only that she would care for him—that was part of what she had accepted.

"Say nothing," she repeated. "I understand."

"Do you?"

"Yes."

"How...how did you...know?" He stared at the silver. "What I...wanted?"

"You told me," Sally replied, not taking her eyes from him. "The other night in the mews, you told me."

Simon could make no reply.

"I will help you," Sally said. Simon turned to her, his face drained. He would have spoken, but Sally prevented it; once more her fingers covered his lips.

"Say nothing," she whispered again, and slipped from the bed.

Later, as they sat at the small table in the kitchen, sipping hot, milky coffee, seeing an aspect of hope mirrored one in the other, Simon asked, "Will you be late tonight?" His voice was steadier now; he touched the bracelet constantly.

Sally shook her head. She would leave work early and make her visit to Cyril Fenick and be back in the apartment as soon as she could.

"Do you promise?"

"I promise."

"Then I'll wait for you in the public house in the mews. There's something ... something there I think you should see."

Sally's eyes were cautious; a new door was being opened. "What is it?"

"Another photograph," Simon replied. He must have her with him all the time now; there was no other way he could imagine being able to continue. Alone, even with the bracelet, he was incapable of surviving. With her he might just discover an avenue that could lead them both past the darkness that stretched ahead. She knew enough to have given him the protective silver when he needed it most. He would defend her as best he could. He would tell her nothing more than she already knew, but he could no longer keep her apart, not now. "There's another photograph," he went on. "I think you ... should see it."

"Why?"

"It will help me ... if you do."

Sally lowered her eyes; sadness shook her. "You've been back there," she said quietly. "Yesterday you went back."

"Yes," Simon replied, equally softly. "Yesterday morning. That's when I found this other ... photograph." His fingers closed over his braceleted wrist. "I'm sorry, didn't I tell you?"

Sally shook her head. She might have realized that something like that would have caused his nightmares. My God, she wondered, what was it that tormented him? She had no choice but to accompany him back to The Half Moon, to see for herself what it was he'd discovered.

"I'll be there," she said, looking at him, seeing something in his eyes she didn't understand: a mixture of pain and gratitude and, she couldn't be sure, but it appeared to be relief. "It'll open about six this evening," she continued. "I'll be waiting."

"Thank you. It's important."

Quickly Sally glanced at her watch. "I've got to go," she told him. "If I don't go now I'll be late. Here"— she wrote a telephone number on a piece of paper and pushed it across the table to him—"call me if you need anything, anything at all, understand?"

"Thank you." Simon moved from the table and stood close to her; his hand was on the bracelet. "But I shall be all right, I know it."

"I...I guess you will." Sally put her head on Simon's chest. She reached up and touched the copper-gold of his hair and felt as if something inside her was about to break. "Take care," she whispered. "If you need anything just call me. There's a phone at the bottom of the stairs."

"Don't worry, please don't worry. Go now." He touched the curve of her cheek and felt the warmth of her lips as they turned into his hand. "I shall await you at the public house. At six this evening I'll be there."

Sally turned and left quickly; she paused once, her hand on the door, and looked over her shoulder to see Simon watching her. He smiled. "Good-bye," he said softly, then she was gone.

Simon stared at the door for a long time after it closed behind her. They had come now to a turning point: there was danger all about them; it was close and moving closer. Soon the forces of evil would demand their confrontation, and regardless of the protection he carried or how much power the girl's good and innocent heart possessed, he was afraid of the outcome.

Thirteen

෴

BY MIDAFTERNOON Cyril Fenick knew almost everything he needed to know to confirm his suspicions about Simon Blackstone.

He'd remembered Sally instantly, recalled the way he'd examined her hand and looked at the lines that life and fate had inscribed there. Even then, on that earlier occasion, he'd seen something else, something more sinister, but had brushed it aside. It was too faint and its message too fanciful for him to explore further. Yet he'd known she would return.

So, when she told him of Simon, a deeper meaning had begun to emerge. It was clear that there were sinister powers assembling and that their evil was inexorably focused on the young man who fled from them into a world in which he, himself, was the stranger. Cyril also realized that the young man, and any who came close to him, were in great and immediate danger.

All day he had consulted the charts that hung on

his walls, had followed reference after obscure reference in the books that filled his shelves, and each turning confirmed a little more, every allusion leading steadily to the same fearful conclusion.

Of all the menaces that slowly took shape, there was one that whetted his own particular fear. It was written that he who informed must pay the penalty. This was the task that had fallen on Cyril's own shoulders. He, who had read the early signs, who had been selected by the girl as consultant, was doomed to tell everything he knew and, by this action, to be himself condemned. The thought filled Cyril with a cold and certain dread, and he began to drink.

He went to a triangular wooden cabinet in the corner of his study, took out a bottle of crème de menthe and a thick liqueur glass, found room for them on his overcrowded desk, and began to sip steadily at the fiery green liquid as he continued his investigations. He allowed nothing to interrupt him.

By early evening Cyril had begun his second bottle of crème de menthe and was thickly, stolidly, overwhelmingly drunk. Even so with the edge of reality blunted, everything he had discovered was clear in his mind. The stark facts were beyond question. Their fates were clearly prescribed. Only one item remained obscure, one final movement incomplete: Cyril knew where the Changeling Child had come from and, if unrestrained, where it would go, taking with it as many lives as possible. He knew what must be done to contain it and even how this might be accomplished, but he was uncertain where the final act was to be played, on what piece of ground the creature would need to be laid.

It was related to the Changeling's beginning, of this he was certain. The cycle must end where it had begun—that much was clear—but whether the location was associated with birth or possession, he did not know. None of the charts indicated the ultimate resting place.

As the afternoon died and the dark grew deeper, Cyril became more and more confused. His fingers grew clumsy with the lowering level in the bottle, his mind grew thicker, and the final piece of information became more and more elusive.

He became fretful, began to move books and charts with less control. Once a chart fell to the floor, and as he reached for it, one of the seven black cats put a foot on it and it tore. A stab of panic ran through Cyril's heavy body. His eyes returned to the chart, his fingers probed a direction, lost it, and began again. He reached for his drink and hurried it to his lips, spilling dark, sticky liquid over his paperwork.

The girl would return soon, and he would need to instruct her. Time was against him, and still he did not know where the final act was preordained to occur, where the Changeling must be restrained. But he was sure that if the creature were taken to any but the exact location, it would never be laid to rest. It would roam free and merciless forever. The knowledge filled him with dread.

Ray Clark arrived at The Half Moon a few minutes before opening time. It was cold and he hunched his shoulders against the weather, but the rain had ceased, and as he came up the three steps to the pub he could see Molly White moving about inside, turning on lights, filling the snug little bar with warmth and brightness.

She saw him and came to the door.

"Yeah," he said when she opened it. "A bit early. Hope you don't mind."

"Hello, sunshine." Molly glanced at the clock on the wall. "Keen to see this friend of yours, are you?"

"It's not that." Ray slipped in quickly. "Wanted a word with you first, if that's all right."

"You don't say." Molly touched her dyed-blond

hair; she'd redone it this afternoon specially. "What did you want to talk about?"

"This . . . friend"—Ray paused and rubbed his hands together uncertainly—"well, he's not that much of a friend, if you know what I mean."

"He owe you money or something?"

Ray grinned thankfully. "Yeah, he does actually." He couldn't believe his luck; tonight was going to go great. "As a matter of fact I give him a loan the other night. Quite a bit, and, ah, well, you know what it's like with money. I got to be a bit careful, that's all."

"That's why you want to make it a surprise?"

Ray nodded.

"All right, sunshine. I'll leave it up to you." Molly smiled at Ray's tight, scarred face. "Wouldn't want to cross you, dear. You could be a right little bugger if you wanted."

Ray grinned again. He'd got her, he could see. "I'll make this up to you, really I will," he said.

"Now how would you go about that?"

"I'll think of something." Ray moved fractionally closer; he could've danced, things were going so well. "You just leave that to me."

Molly laughed. "You'll be wanting one on the house next," she said.

"Yeah, well." Ray rubbed his hands together confidently. "I'll have a ale, if that's all we got time for."

"Get away with you." Molly walked round behind the bar, her hips moving jauntily; she reached for a half-pint and began drawing the beer.

"You take your drink and sit over there like a nice boy," she said, pointing to a table on the far side of the room. "When your friend comes in, you can talk to him. No, not that table, Alf and Myrtle sit there, the other one."

Presently Alf and Myrtle came in and ordered their drinks; then a group of Americans entered, cooing their admiration, and by the time they'd decided what they were going to have and Molly'd served them, the house was filling, and it was some time before she had a chance to glance across and see how the little toughie was doing.

They were together by then. She'd not seen the handsome feller come in she'd been so busy. Fred must have served them. Fact was, she hadn't seen him at all since yesterday morning. But he was back now and the two of them had their heads together. Hope it works out for them, she thought. And for me, she added with a smile. Then things got busy again and she didn't have time to think of anything.

When the Americans left and the place got a bit quieter, she looked across, thinking she might ask them over for a chat, but their table was deserted, the glasses standing silently facing each other; she noticed that the handsome feller had left a little of his whiskey undrunk.

Gone to sort out the money, she told herself, and wondered when they'd be back.

When Simon Blackstone came into The Half Moon, he did not at first notice Ray Clark. He'd left the flat and walked slowly to the mews, half hoping to see Sally on the way, to catch her before she reached the public house. But there'd been no sign of her, and although he'd loitered a minute or two beside the three stone steps that led up to the front door, she did not appear. He'd fixed his eyes on the entry to the mews, patiently waiting for the moment that did not arrive, and then he'd made his decision.

It was a decision that had begun to form when he was alone in Sally's rooms earlier—a decision that had become so positive, it had forced all others aside.

He had decided to continue alone.

There was no doubt that Sally was involved; the fact that she'd given him the silver bracelet told him more than either of them had been prepared to admit. The way she looked at him, the tenderness in her eyes and the gentleness of her touch indicated how much more she was prepared to give. And this began to terrify him.

There was no hiding now from what he knew of himself, from what the ghosts that dwelt in the photograph of the faceless child had whispered to him as he'd lain, curled and shaking, on the bed the evening before.

He was a monster, a Changeling Child, lost and doomed.

Yet, he still might save her—if he continued alone. And in doing so, he could repay her for everything she had done.

He entered The Half Moon to find the bar unexpectedly crowded. A wall of backs greeted him, and his first reaction was to go straight to the photographs. He had half-turned in that direction when a hand touched his arm and a voice he recognized said, "Evening, your Lordship. Don't tell me you've forgotten me already."

Simon stared at the wiry figure, at the familiar face, and remembered.

"Give you a lift, I did." Ray's hard lips cracked into an uncertain smile. "From down Tonbridge way."

"Of course." Simon held out his hand. "Forgive me, but your name escapes me."

Ray laughed. "Just the same," he said, shaking Simon's hand. "Not giving nothing away." He ushered Simon toward a table. "Ray, Ray Clark, remember?"

Simon nodded. His eyes went to the door, searching for Sally.

"Expecting someone then? I'm not interrupting nothing?"

"I am expecting someone," Simon replied, looking into Ray Clark's shifting eyes. "She said she'd be here when the inn opened, at six."

"Half five's opening time," Ray said knowingly. "Good-looking, is she?"

"Dark and quite beautiful," Simon replied evenly.

"Get away with you." Ray couldn't believe how well it was going. Found him first-off, got him alone; the rest would be a piece of cake. "Here, sit down." Ray indicated a chair. "We've got time for a chat before she gets here."

"Very well." Reluctantly Simon took the chair. He must appear normal; he must not draw attention to himself in any way at all. Turning to Ray he studied the scarred face, trying to recall exactly who it reminded him of, where he had seen it before, and what it contained.

"You, ah, been up to anything since you got back?" Ray began. He'd planned what he was going to say. "Anything special?"

"Not that I recall," Simon replied carefully.

"I like that." Ray shook his head in mock admiration. "Right from the start I liked the way you kept yourself to yourself. Real talent that is." He paused significantly. "Mind you, you've got more than a few talents up your sleeve, haven't you now, your Lordship?"

Simon frowned. "I'm afraid I do not take your meaning," he replied formally.

"No, well..." Ray grinned. "Here, why don't I get you something?" He indicated his glass. "Then we can have a nice quiet talk."

"What is there to talk—" Simon began, but Ray was already on his feet.

"What'll it be?" Ray asked. "A whiskey?" Simon nodded. He watched the wiry youth walk across to the bar and wondered again about the image that kept returning. He *had* seen the lean, bitter face before; it had hung above a white collar and a frayed black tie, but he could not recall where it fitted among the ghosts and shadows, in the mists of his sepulchral past.

"There you go." Ray placed a whiskey before Simon, sat with his ale, then leaned forward. "The thing is, your Lordship, there's a few questions I've been wanting to ask." He grinned. "You know, you could tell me something if you wanted to."

Simon listened cautiously; a threat was beginning to emerge.

"Think about it"—Ray drank a little beer—"the other night and all. Like, what you was doing when I picked you up on the side of the road."

"I beg your pardon?" Simon's tone was chilly.

"Now don't try that with me." Ray's voice hardened. "You know what I mean."

"Are you being impertinent?" Simon asked, his mind alert, all his senses wary. "For, if so, I shall leave."

Ray grinned tightly. "You stay where you are," he said. "I know a copper or two round here; bit bent, perhaps, but they know their stuff. Like me to hop round the corner and tell them a few things."

"What are you talking about?"

"You, mate. Let's see you act high and mighty then. Looking for you, they are. They mightn't know who their lad is yet, but they're looking for you, all right." Ray leaned away a little, his hands flat on the table. "Now, if you and me was to come to a little arrangement, there mightn't be any trouble at all. You scratch my back, and I won't say nothing about what you was doing running away the other night."

Simon contemplated the tight face before him coldly, understanding enough of what was being said but unable to pinpoint what this bitter little man really wanted.

"You do know what I'm talking about, old son." Ray's head came closer. "So don't try giving me no runaround."

"I think I shall go." Simon pushed his chair away from the table. The photographs could wait. "I do not like your manners in any way at all."

Ray's arm flashed out; he grabbed Simon's wrist. "Don't give me none of your bullshit," he hissed. He felt a black anger rising inside him; it pulsed for release. This ponce wasn't going to push him aside like the rest of them. Not when he'd worked so hard to get here, not when he'd found him after being in every pissy pub in Victoria. He wasn't going to take no more from no one, not ever again. "You just bloody sit and listen," he snarled. "Listen good and bloody proper."

"I have listened, and I do not completely understand what it is you want." Simon made a effort to release his arm, but it was tightly gripped; he waited. Be patient, he told himself, you cannot afford a further scene in here. "Please be good enough to let me go," he said quietly.

"You don't know what I'm on about?"

"I haven't the faintest idea."

"What about this then?" With his free hand Ray reached into his jacket and took out a newspaper section he'd torn from the *Sun*; he slapped it on the table. It showed a seminaked teenage girl that he'd begun to tattoo with a ballpoint pen; angrily he turned it over. On the other side was the report of the Tonbridge murder. "Eh?" he said fiercely into Simon's face. "What you got to say about this?"

Simon's mouth went dry.

Ray watched Simon carefully, saw the frown and the widening of the eyes and something he could not identify: the pale skin of Simon's face seemed to darken as if a new force was present. Ray increased his pressure on Simon's arm. "I got you now, old son."

Simon read the newspaper item slowly. He saw a burst of light, heard the roar of an earth-moving machine, and sensed a hand removing silver. Blood began to spill; there was a shrieking in his ears, and he knew he must escape.

"What you got to say for yourself now?" Ray whispered confidently; he'd got the reaction he wanted. "Still think you're Lord Muck?"

Simon shook his head and pushed the soiled piece of newspaper away. Raising his eyes he looked into the snarling little face before him. Then abruptly he wrenched his arm from Ray Clark's grip, left the table, and disappeared out the door of The Half Moon into the freezing air of the London night.

Ray followed as unobtrusively as possible. Outside he peered up the narrow mews and saw Simon standing absolutely still halfway along its cobbled surface. His head was back and his eyes were on the darkened sky, his hands were slightly upraised and held together as if he were praying; his whole attitude was that of a supplicant, of someone alone and desperately lost.

Ray stared at the figure, then spat on the pavement. He's a girl, he told himself. I knew there was something funny the minute I picked him up. He's having a cry. Ray hitched up his jeans and made his way quietly toward Simon.

Going to be easier than he thought, he calculated as he walked confidently up the mews. Going to enjoy myself, I am.

Just then the moon slid free from the edge of a dark and heavy cloud and shone down brilliantly to light his way.

Fourteen

SALLY LAWRENCE pushed the bell of Cyril Fenick's basement flat three times and waited. She was beginning to hope she'd made some mistake, that there was still time to leave before she heard what he had to say, when a light appeared in the hallway and shone dimly through the stained glass of the door. Then the door opened, and the thick figure of the mystical old man beckoned her inside.

"Come in, come in," Cyril rumbled. "I am almost ready for you."

"I..." Sally began to apologize but stopped as a cat rubbed its back against her legs. "Is that Sootums?" she asked nervously.

"Mr. Big," Cyril replied without looking. "I told you, I'm not very imaginative with names."

Sally glanced at Cyril's heavy features in the hall light; they were slightly flushed, and his breathing was noticeable. "You sure you're ready?" she asked.

"I mean, I could come back some other time if you wanted."

"I'm ready." Cyril led her into the study. "Sit down, my dear, and tell me—did you . . . give him what he wanted?"

"Yes."

"And his reaction?"

"It was . . ." Sally sat on the edge of one of the overstuffed chairs and watched Cyril take his place behind the littered desk. "He said it made him feel . . . protected."

"Well, that is at least something."

"It means you're right."

"There was never any doubt of that; not in my mind, anyway." Cyril watched the girl through half-closed lids. "What else has occurred?"

Sally moved her shoulders helplessly. "When I got back last night, he was having nightmares. He wouldn't tell me what they were but . . . well, when I woke him, he . . . he shouted at me. He told me to leave him alone."

"He was not referring to you," Cyril replied. "You have nothing to fear."

"How can you say that?" Sally began quickly, then paused as she watched Cyril Fenick lift a glass from the tangle of material on his desk and sip from it delicately. "Would you like a drink, my dear?" the fat man inquired politely.

Sally shook her head.

"You don't mind if I do?" Cyril poured himself more crème de menthe. "I have had an extremely busy day. I've been alone, you understand. I told Eric not to bother me. I needed to be alone to concentrate on your . . . problem, so forgive me if I relax a little."

It was then that Sally realized the degree of Cyril's drunkenness. In a way she was grateful for his condition; it would make what she knew he was about to tell her less credible, would remove some of the reality from what he said.

"What...?" Sally began, then swallowed. "What have you found out?"

Cyril sat back in his chair and stared over the desktop; he must discover from her as much as he could, must try to draw it from her without her knowing what it was he lacked.

"He is a Changeling," Cyril said abruptly, his voice deepening. "Born on a day that didn't exist. The first time. Didn't I tell you that before?"

Sally shook her head.

"Where is he from? Do you know?"

"From?" Sally was caught in confusion. "I don't understand."

Cyril smiled a strained smile. He was being too precipitate, his own need forcing him. "Let me explain," he added, watching Sally carefully. "Let me try to help you understand what...what sort of a person your Simon is."

Sally sat back in the chair uncertainly.

"There are strange forces at work in this world," Cyril went on. "Forces we will never understand. Even I, who believe and who have seen something of the mysteries that surround us, will never exactly know how powerful they can be." He sipped more crème de menthe. "Am I making myself clear?" he asked.

Sally shook her head hopelessly.

"There was a calendar," Cyril continued, following another of his thickly entangled trains of thought. "A calendar that was calculated by a Greek philosopher named Callippus. He based it on one already in existence but which contained an error. The first calendar was Meton's, and it concerned itself with coincidental patterns of the moon. The coming together every nineteen years of a full moon on the same day on the same week of the same month." Cyril blinked. "Do you follow me?" he asked.

Sally closed her eyes. "Yes," she lied, realizing he was too drunk to stop, hoping that once he was past this explanation he might tell her what had to be done.

"Good." Cyril nodded to himself encouragingly. "But in altering the Cycle of Meton, Callippus made an error of his own. A lesser error but a significant one nonetheless." He raised a didactic finger. "Every five hundred and fifty-three years a day is lost. Gone. Never to be recovered, and it is believed that those born on that particular day are also irretrievably lost."

"But..."

"You might well ask what an ancient Greek calendar dealing with the moon has to do with this day and age." Cyril emptied his glass. He had the impression he was explaining things rather well. "And the answer to that is, *everything*. There are those who live by that calendar. There are those whose beliefs are shaped by the errors that calendar contains. It depends who they are and where they are and under what circumstances their powers are exerted." He paused, his hand on its way to the bottle. "Where does Simon come from?"

"He said..." Sally fought to gain some order from her confusion. "He said...the country, but he didn't say where."

"What country?"

"Well, this, I guess."

"Not...another country?"

"I don't know." Sally pressed her hands together urgently. "He told me something about...about being in Bavaria once, when he was a child."

"Ah." Cyril poured more green liquid. "A grave area for such beliefs." He recapped the bottle slowly. "A nonexistent day means a nonfulfilled soul. An empty soul. One ripe for possession, and in parts of Bavaria, who knows what fiend might have taken advantage of the poor, unprotected child."

"Hey, wait a minute." Sally struggled forward in the enveloping chair. "This...I mean, this is crazy."

166

Cyril's eyes turned to her solemnly. "I wish that it were," he said with slow, drunken melancholy. "I wish that I could agree with you, but that is not the case." He sighed deeply, and his eyes reddened with the presence of tears. "We are involved with something more sinister than you could ever imagine," he continued mournfully. "All of us. Even those who may not know it yet. We are all part of it." He put a hand to his heart. "Even I, who only pronounced the findings—even for me the involvement is inescapable."

"Oh, come on."

"Do not mock me." Cyril's voice gained force. "You have seen what effect the silver bracelet had. You must have realized that the manner in which it was accepted indicated its *need*."

"I..." Sally swallowed, torn between the theatrics of the drunken old man and what her own eyes had witnessed. "There's got to be something else... something that makes more sense."

"It all makes fearful sense." Cyril wiped his eyes. "That is the most dreadful fact of all. From what you have told me and from what these ancient references contain"—he swept his hand over the books and charts laid out on his desk—"there can be no doubt that the only logical conclusion I can come to is that your Simon is a Changeling, a Child of the Moon." Cyril's head went back. "One and the same, really," he added, as though speaking to himself. "Depending on how often the creature's been disinterred." His gaze returned to Sally. "Anyway, as such, he must be destroyed before he takes life from us all."

"*Destroyed*?"

"Yes, my dear, destroyed." Cyril drank more crème de menthe. He could feel oblivion at his elbow and knew he would need to instruct this girl as rapidly and as clearly as he could. "But, that does not necessarily mean elimination. It may be accomplished by restricting him, restraining him, returning him to the place from whence he came."

Aghast, Sally stared at Cyril.

"As the silver binds, as the metal of the moon protects, so will... will the place in which he was possessed." Cyril faltered. This was the detail he had not been able to establish. Whether the Changeling had to be returned to his birth site or to the location on which his soulless body had been filled with an alien force, Cyril did not know. "He has to be... to be taken back," he finished lamely.

"Where?" Sally whispered. "What has to be done when we get there?"

"An accident released him, and an accident will return him," Cyril replied obscurely. "That much is written."

"You've got to tell me more." Sally curled her hands into fists; she held herself steady. She watched the fat man's eyes glaze and listened to his ramblings. She knew she must get as much from him as possible before he collapsed.

"Listen to me." The thin intensity of Sally's voice caused Cyril Fenick to shake his head to clear it; he straightened himself in his chair. "Why... what would... anything want with Simon?"

"Eh?"

"This... this alien force, what does it want?"

"Ah, good question." Cyril wiped his lips with the back of his hand. "There are several answers," he went on, almost academically. "Some say it has to do with a blind vengeance, a hatred of all living things. Others"—he reached clumsily for a book on his desk and carelessly turned its pages—"others suggest such acts are an intrinsic part of the demon world, but I"—Cyril lifted his head and stared unblinkingly at Sally—"I believe it has something to do with rank."

"Rank?"

"Yes, a rising upward, a challenge to the pecking

168

order of the underworld. Here..." Cyril's unsteady
fingers groped for a chart, but Sally's voice cut him
short.

"Oh, for Christ's sake!" she shouted, "stop it...
stop this. Just please tell me what has to be done."
She leaned toward the sorcerer. "Tell me what *I* have
to do."

Cyril's mouth slackened; he swallowed.

"He must be returned to where he came from."

"Where...exactly?"

"He—" Cyril hiccupped. "He will know."

"Tell me where." Sally stood and leaned over the
desk. "Where's he got to go?"

"Where he came from."

"And what then?"

"He must be..." Cyril felt his eyelids closing. "He
must be made to stay."

"How?" Sally leaned over the sagging head; her
voice rose. "How? Tell me how."

Cyril sighed softly. "An accident released—"

Sally was on the point of screaming. She took the
old man by the shoulder and shook him, and his head
rolled. "God damn you, tell me what I've got to know."

"A child will change your life." Cyril opened his
eyes very wide and looked up. "I told you that once."

"You're drunk." Sally turned away. The study
menaced her. The charts on the walls, the books, the
littered desk all seemed to threaten. "You're drunk,"
she repeated to reinforce herself. "I don't believe you.
You've been lying to me all along."

"No." Cyril sat upright. The words came out in a
shout. "Believe me, I implore you. You must believe
what I say."

"No." Sally picked up her bag. "I don't want to
hear any more. I—"

"Listen." Cyril's arms spread like a man on a cross.
"Hear me this last time. You will see a change in
him, a change so final that all your disbeliefs will
die, and then, and then, my girl, you will know what

169

I have told you is the truth. Then you will know that this Simon of yours, this Changeling Child, this creature of the moon I have warned you of, must be fastened forever. Must be held in place by whatever means are possible *before he kills again*. Yes, before he kills again." Cyril watched Sally's face blanch. "Because each time he kills, each time this creature claims another victim, he alters. He moves one stage further through his own life cycle, moves one step closer to the shape of the beast that has taken his soul. He will continue his degradation until he becomes the monster itself, and then there will be no stopping him. Nothing will contain him then; no force will ever be powerful enough to restrain him once he reaches that objective. Your Simon will be no more. Nothing of him will exist; he will be replaced entirely by this...this beast of darkness." Cyril paused, breathing heavily. "That is why it must be done soon, my dear. That is why you must take him away, return him to where it was...it happened." He pressed the palms of his hands together imploringly. "Please, please say you will do what you can to restrain him."

Sally had a burning desire to tear herself away, to shed herself of everything the study contained, to reject the drunken old man and the fateful words she knew she must hear.

"Please...return him to—"

"All right." Sally moved toward the door. Her foot brushed a cat and she stopped. "I'll do it," she said to make him stop. "I'll take him home again."

"Home?" Cyril's head sunk to the desk. "Home may not be where he has to go."

"Bavaria then." Sally continued her journey to the door. "I've got some money saved. I'll take him there."

"That may also...fail. The right place—"

"We'll find it." Sally could feel her heart beating wildly; she could no longer breathe in the closed air of the apartment. She must get out, she must get away, she must clear her head and think about what had to be done. "I'll talk to him. I'll find out where." She could hear her own voice babbling. "Don't worry, I'll check it out."

"Don't worry..." Cyril's head went down to the chart-covered desk. Something like a whimper escaped his fleshy lips. "Don't worry, she'll check it out. On this we must rely...." Cyril Fenick had nothing more to say. He collapsed among the litter on his desk, breathing in a deep, steady rhythm. A cat leaped silently onto the desk beside him and began to lick its paws.

Quickly Sally turned and hurried from the room. She ran along the narrow hallway with its light dimly burning, pulled open the door of the basement flat, and stumbled up the steps onto the pavement. Her heart was racing; her mind was like a machine that had gone out of control. Lights flashed in the corners of her eyes, nothing was distinct, nothing seemed to make sense anymore. In spite of what she had seen, no matter how Simon had behaved, and regardless of the fact that it was she who had gone to the fortune-teller for help, nothing would make her accept what Cyril had just told her. She could not, in any manner that had anything to do with sanity, believe what he'd had to say.

Sally stood on the cold pavement and drew city-smelling air into her lungs. She watched a taxi cruise slowly past. She saw people and heard the distant call of voices, and one word rang fatally in her ears; it shouted through her entire being.

Destroyed.

Sally shook her head. She forced herself homeward, walked toward the lights of the Underground at Sloane Square. She knew only that she must return and talk to Simon. Her Simon. Her beautiful, gentle Simon, who had held her, who had trusted her, who had made love to her. She hurried on, shaking her head as she went, the suggestion unthinkable. "*Before he kills again*," Cyril had said. Sally shuddered and was afraid she was going to be sick.

She went into the windswept hall of the station and bought a ticket to Victoria from a black man who looked at her strangely. She ran down the steps, holding her cape so that she did not fall, stood on the platform and waited in the cavernous air for the train to carry her back to the square.

They would go to Bavaria; she *would* take him away. She had money and a credit card her father guaranteed. They would return to where he'd been happy as a child, leaving behind everything that had happened here. There was really nothing to fear.

Sally began to rationalize Simon's behavior, to find excuses for the details that had worried her, the differences that, in the beginning, had sent her to Cyril Fenick. There were lots of things that made sense.

No sane person could accept the raving of a drunk fortune-teller, Sally said to herself as the gray shape of an underground train swung into sight at the far end of the platform. My God, when he talks about destruction and killing and changes, how can you take him seriously?

No. Sally shook her head. The gray train ground toward her, people on the platform began to surge forward. Sally closed her eyes. Who was she fooling? she thought. Every word Cyril Fenick spoke was the truth.

She opened her eyes and looked down at the shining black rails, the train was almost upon her. For a sad and desperate moment she thought of throwing herself beneath the approaching machine, to find her own darkness, to end everything before it became too extreme. Then someone bumped into her, and the moment was gone.

Sally found herself in the carriage, holding onto a strap on her way back to Victoria; about her was the warmth of bodies and the smell of cigarette smoke.

She turned her head to stare at a watch on a passenger's wrist. It indicated six-thirty, and with a shock, she realized she was late for her meeting with Simon. She wondered, sickeningly, if he would wait for her.

She looked up and caught her own reflection in the darkened windows. Her face was the color of chalk.

Fifteen

RAY CLARK walked down the mews toward the solitary figure of Simon Blackstone with slow, arrogant confidence. He'd have some fun with this one, he told himself. Even if the ponce didn't have nothing to do with the driver in Tonbridge, he'd have a bit of a laugh pushing him about. He wondered if he should've brought his bicycle chain but dismissed the idea. He didn't need anything with this girl. What was the wanker doing now? Crying or praying? Ray grinned. He'd have something to cry about by the time Mad Ray'd finished with him.

Simon heard footsteps and turned; he watched Ray approach. He began to recognize the face that held the memories which went beyond his grave. "What do you want of me?" he asked.

"Depends what you've got, squire," Ray replied, and snickered.

Simon looked down at the face; the anger had gone

from it; now it displayed only malevolence. "Do you require money?"

"Wouldn't've thought you'd had a lot of that." Ray spat on the cobblestones. "Don't look to me like much of a carrier."

"Then why do you pester me?"

Ray shook his head in mock wonder. "I got to give it to you, your Lordship," he said. "You got a way of putting things that's different."

"Leave me alone." Simon turned his head away; he would avoid this confrontation if he could, would do his best to hold back the terrible force that threatened to break him. "I do not wish to converse with you any longer."

"And who you think you're talking to?" Ray's fist flashed out and struck Simon in the stomach. Simon's mouth opened in shock and pain. But his eyes began to glow with the power that was growing within him.

"You're not with them toffy friends of yours now, mate. You're with me. You'll do like I say."

"You..." Simon found it almost impossible to breathe. "You struck me. From you... the first blow."

"That's the way I do business." Ray's fist darted out again and caught Simon in the ribs. Simon backed away. "It shows you who I am, you understand."

"No." Simon found himself forced against a wall. His ribs were painful, it was agony to breathe, but every particle of his being was alive with fury, with outrage demanding to be released.

"What you need, old son," Ray said, his fists stabbing and biting, "is something to remember me by." He thrust his face forward, pointing to the scar, holding the half-remembered visage close to Simon. "See that, your Lordship? That's me trademark."

Ray's face shone gleefully in the moonlight, and Simon recognized it completely. It rose from the sewers of his memory, reeking of his terrifying past.

"I've..." In spite of his pain Simon saw a shuttered

room in a mountain village, a man with a frayed collar and a black tie. There were coffins about the walls, and a dark lid hung above him, ready to close. "I've seen you before."

"What you trying to pull?" Ray blinked. "'Course you seen me before."

"In the undertaker's."

"What?" Ray drew back his fist. The ponce was cracking up. Be screaming in a minute. The best thing to do was get it over with. He made a cutting blow toward Simon's mouth. Simon's hands tried to block it, and the silver bracelet glittered in the eerie light.

"Hello," Ray said with new interest. "What you got there?" He reached forward and took hold of the cross between thumb and forefinger. "Now, that's a bit of class, that is. How'd you like to give it to your old mate?"

"No." Simon's voice became even darker. "That you will never have."

"Well, bugger me. The girl's going to protect her jewels. That's what I like, a bit of a struggle."

"Go," Simon said. He felt the power within whistle like a knife. "Go while you still have the opportunity."

"I will and all," Ray Clark said, "when you give me the bracelet."

"Go now."

"Not for a minute, mate."

"Then die."

The metamorphosis had begun. No man would steal his silver; none of their challenges would remain unchecked. His eyes widened, and he stared down at the would-be thief with a cold fury. The wrist from which the bracelet hung began to distort grotesquely, to grow and thicken. The whole hand turned black. Horny nails on the ends of clawlike fingers sprang forth and dug deep into the grasping fist of

Ray Clark. Blood ran darkly down the smaller man's arm as the hand of the beast began its deadly work.

Ray felt his knees sagging. He fell to a crouching position on the cobbled mews, moaning as the unbearable pain shot up his arm in stabbing, fiery needles. But what was worse was the sight of the claw that gripped him. It was coarse and gnarled, thick with black hair and bulging with the power of some crazed animal.

"You would steal my silver," Simon said in a voice that was not his own. "You would confront me!"

"No, really," Ray whispered as his knees scrabbled on the stonework. The claw-hand released him. Ray stared at his bloodied fist and was about to scuttle down the mews when he felt the sharp nails catch him in the throat. He began to drown in a gush of his own warm blood. The last thing he saw was Simon Blackstone's face staring down in relentless fury. The red eyes sprang outward, the lips were drawn back, and wolflike teeth protruded. From the throat came a fiery growl that seemed to sear the air.

Simon held him for a few moments, shaking the body once or twice like a dog until there was no response, then dropped it. "You tried to contain me once," the ancient tone of the animal hissed. "Now the debt is paid."

The claw-hand disappeared, and Simon Blackstone began the second of his transformations. He seemed to shrink slightly, and his figure grew a little frail. He lifted his hands and rubbed his face. When he took them away, his features were those of a middle-aged man. Fine lines radiated from the corners of his eyes; his cheeks had thinned and his lips were more pronounced. A deep frown furrowed his forehead and his rich copper-colored hair was thinner now and streaked with gray. In the space of a few seconds he had aged a further thirty years.

Simon looked about him, blinked at the street lamp, glanced at the sign of The Half Moon, at the yellow sickle against the blue-black sky, and nodded as if recalling it from another phase, another time. He brushed his hands against the material of his anorak, which hung on him more loosely now, and proceeded slowly up the mews. When he arrived at the end of the street, he turned and began to walk toward the apartment in the old house above the tree-filled square. He traveled like a man in a dream.

Albert Scot heard of the death of Ray Clark three hours after it occurred. He was seated in the living room of his mother's two-storied cottage rereading his notes when the telephone in the hallway rang. He lifted his head half-expectantly and stared at a glass-fronted cabinet that contained a collection of Staffordshire highwaymen. A moment later his mother called him.

It was Chris Wilkinson phoning from London. "Thought you'd like to know," he began, "there's been another of your Ripper murders. Up here." Chris's voice contained little of the flippancy the words suggested. "Victoria, to be exact."

"When?"

"Six-thirty. Body wasn't found for twenty minutes or so. It happened in a mews." Chris coughed. "Someone coming out of a pub tripped over it. American, in fact."

"The body?"

"The tripper." Chris's voice lightened. "Anyway, I thought you'd better know. Seemed to me the same MO as your lorry driver."

"Bulldozer," Albert corrected automatically. "Was the throat attacked?"

"Something dreadful." Chris's voice went away from the mouthpiece; he spoke rapidly to another person and then he was back. "I've just been given some photos. The throat's been ripped to pieces. And a hand, it looks as if it's been crushed."

"Who was the victim?"

"Ray Clark. Aged twenty-four. Lived not far from where he died. Council flats near Dolphin Square."

"Anything known?"

"Oh, yes, lots." There was the sound of Chris Wilkinson's fingers flicking paper. "Been in and out of bother all his life. No surprise he was done, really. Thought you'd like to know, though."

"Was he another driver?"

"He was, as a matter of fact. Does a run a couple of times a week down to his uncle's hardware store the other side of Tonbridge. Almost a neighbor of yours?"

"And the night...?"

"Right with you, captain," Chris replied before Albert's sentence was complete. "The night of the Tonbridge killing he was down there. Got home late, his mother says." Chris paused. "Got home *after* your ... tractor driver was done."

"Thank you," Albert said. He became aware of a faint buzzing noise. "Anyone have any idea who might be responsible?"

"He'd been making inquiries at this pub I told you about. Said he was after a young feller who owed him money. The publican's wife's got lots to say. Just keep your distance, that's all."

"What do you mean?"

"You'll see. I'll hold her for you. Thinking of coming up?"

"Yes." Albert looked at his watch. "I'll be there by eleven." He listened; the buzzing was getting louder. "They were seen together then?"

"The victim and the feller he was after? Yes, just after opening time. Got quite a good description, really."

"What was he wearing? The feller you think might have done it? Anorak and blue jeans?"

"Well, well." Chris was impressed. "You've not been wasting your time down there, have you? Know him, do you?"

"I know the gear," Albert replied. "About what age, did anyone say?"

"Young. Early twenties. Very good-looking by all accounts. Been seen with a pretty, dark girl who looks like a gypsy. They shouldn't be difficult to spot."

"If they're still together," Albert said, half to himself. "Anything else?"

"Something odd," Chris replied, his voice thoughtful. "Publican's wife had quite a chat with the handsome feller yesterday. Seems he's interested in old photographs. The pub's full of them. Instead of horse brasses it's got Victorian photos. Couple of them took his fancy. One of a woman playing croquet. The other of the same woman with a man and a boy in a sailor suit. I can't think—"

"*What!*" Albert's voice came like a pistol shot. "What was the boy wearing?"

"Uh, oh, a sailor suit. That mean anything?"

"Yes," Albert whispered. He felt the skin on his face prickle; something cold passed close to him and the buzzing in his ears grew louder. It wasn't interference on the line, it was within him; it was a response echoing throughout his body. "Yes," he replied. "It means a great deal."

"Right then." Chris sounded a little uncertain. "Anything else you want me to do?"

"Get an artist down to the pub," Albert replied. He found it difficult to keep his voice even. The process had caught him: whatever his grandfather had attempted to warn him of all those years ago in the kitchen was now beside him. He heard its presence as keenly as the howling of a wind. "See if he can rough up something on the handsome chummy and his girl friend."

"Will do. What else? Like me to send constables round knocking on doors, asking questions?"

"Let's wait till we get the sketches." Albert looked at his watch again. "See you in an hour."

"Think you'll make it that quickly?"

"If I break a few laws."

"Not like you, Albert."

"Sod off," Albert replied, but there was no vigor in the words. "And thanks, you've really helped."

After he'd spoken to Chris, Albert Scot rang the Chief Constable for Tonbridge. The elderly policeman was preparing for bed, and when Albert told him what had happened and what he intended to do, the Chief Constable murmured his agreement. "You'll be back of course," he added.

"Yes, sir, I think so."

"Oh, you'll be back all right." The Chief Constable's voice was sure. He was doing rather well, this grandson from London. Hard to get to know, but his brain seemed to function. "Kearsley," he said as if thinking aloud. "You'll check on him while you're up there?"

"Yes, it's already crossed my mind."

"Some sort of note, something like that." The Chief Constable reached for a nightcap he'd poured himself from the bottle of Glen Grant that stood beside the telephone. "Funny, you know, that nothing was ever found."

"Yes," Albert replied very carefully. "When you think of what he knew."

"Quite." The Chief Constable sipped malt whiskey and felt a satisfaction that did not come solely from the spirits. It had been worthwhile waiting; the timing had to be exactly right. "Mind you," he went on casually, "who knows how carefully they looked in those days."

"There wouldn't have been a personal file? Nothing like that?" Albert fought himself to be patient. "A dossier that mightn't have had anything to do with police work?"

"Now that's a thought." The Chief Constable sounded as if it had just occurred to him. "Be worthwhile looking into."

Albert agreed.

"Elizabeth Crone. Archives Room. Funny old girl but knows the place backward. If there's anything she'll find it for you. Mention my name." The Chief Constable drank a little more whiskey. "Say it has to do with my...hobby."

"Very good, sir." Albert wanted to ask more but sensed it would not be wise. The elderly policeman was trying to erase a stain that went back too far for it even to be admitted. He was using Albert to restore a confidence that had a great deal more to account for than uncertainties among his staff. There were names to be cleared; there were ghosts to be laid to rest that reached back eighty years or more. "I'll talk to Miss Crone in the morning."

"Excellent." The Chief Constable coughed discreetly. "And do be careful, Scot," he said in an avuncular tone. "In every sense of the word."

"I will," Albert replied quietly. "Don't worry about that, sir."

"Not worried. Just thought I'd mention it, that's all."

"Thank you, sir. For everything."

"Not at all, Scot. I'm glad we understand each other."

Albert replaced the receiver and turned to find his mother watching him; her small, neat frame was perfectly motionless, but her sharp eyes glittered in the uneven light of the hallway. For a moment Albert could think of nothing to say.

"So you're going." Mrs. Scot broke the silence. "At last."

"You, ah, heard the conversation."

"Every word."

"Then you'll know—"

"Take it," Mrs. Scot interrupted.

"What?" Albert asked, knowing even as he asked but seeking confirmation. "Take what?"

"He said you'd know what it was for." Mrs. Scot's eyes did not move. "Take it."

Albert swallowed. "Who else . . . knows?" he asked softly.

Mrs. Scot shrugged. "Impossible to say. Those who are part of it, those who have lived with it, people like Bates who involved themselves." She watched her son steadily. "They will all help you if they can."

"Why didn't you tell me before?"

"Ye gods." Mrs. Scot moved, and the mood was broken. She opened the door of a closet under the stairs and took out Albert's raincoat. "Would you have believed a word of it? You, a policeman? You'd have thought I was senile or something." She smiled a bright, determined smile and gave him his coat, ducked back into the closet, and returned carrying the pistol—wrapped in its soft black cloth. She handed it to him and added, "You'd have had me put away."

Albert did not reply. He unwrapped the pistol and examined it; the single cartridge with its silver bullet was in the chamber, the hammer half-cocked. He put it into his raincoat pocket and encountered the packet of cigarettes. He removed the cigarettes, looked at them for a second or two, then threw them into a wastepaper basket that stood in the hallway.

"You'll be all right," Mrs. Scot said.

Albert nodded; he felt strangely free. For reasons that had nothing to do with sanity or logic he felt like a man on a crusade.

"Be careful, nevertheless."

"Bates said the same thing."

Mrs. Scot nodded. "I heard him." She straightened the collar of her son's coat; he turned to speak to her when the telephone rang again.

Without hesitation Albert answered it.

"Is that you, Albert?" It was the slightly nasal voice of Constable Hooper on the line. "Sorry to disturb you this time of night, but—"

"That's all right. I was on my way to London, it's just as well you called."

"I hadn't heard you were . . . off?"

"There's been another murder," Albert explained. "In London." He listened. The buzzing was back, alerting him. "What did you call about?"

"A lab report." Hooper's tone was awkward. "I didn't see it for a bit. I was poking around here trying to sort out some paperwork, and I came across it. It was probably sent down some time this afternoon."

"What's it say?"

"It's, well, it's a bit uncertain."

"Any identification?"

"Not yet. They've asked a funny question, though. They want to know if the hairs came from"—Hooper hesitated and Albert heard him swallow—"came from some sort of fossil, sir. Something that's been pre-served. They say there's nothing alive like that to-day."

Albert listened and his purpose was clear. There was no fear in him, but he knew what had to be done. Where the encounter would take place and under what circumstances seemed unimportant. He was certain that the forces which had lain dormant all his life had come into play. What his grandfather knew, what the German inspector had come to Ton-bridge for, and why the English inspector had shot himself would all soon be revealed.

"Did you hear me, sir?" Constable Hooper's voice sounded worried.

"Yes," Albert Scot replied softly. "I heard you."

He replaced the receiver and turned to his mother. She had not moved. Her bright eyes were fixed on him; her head was still, as if listening.

"They will all help you, Albert," she said softly. "There are many who want you to succeed."

"How many?"

"We'll never know."

"How long..." Albert began, then paused to clear his throat. "How long have you known?"

Mrs. Scot smiled her wintry smile. "Always, I sup-pose," she replied.

"But, you waited until now?"

"I had to. We all had to. Even you."

Albert said nothing more. She was right; always there had been something that had separated him, made him feel apart, different from anyone he had ever met, and only now had its full presence made itself known. The alertness he felt, the buzzing on the telephone, the sense of significant departure, told him the final moments had begun.

Very quickly he leaned forward and kissed his mother's unmoving cheek, then went to the door and opened it to the outside cold and the windswept, uncollected leaves.

Sixteen

SALLY LAWRENCE did not recognize the middle-aged man who came to the door of her apartment at the sound of her key in the lock. He was just suddenly there, opening the door, standing to one side politely to allow her to pass. She stared at the lined, distinguished face, the faded, copper-colored hair, and peered into the gently smiling eyes, feeling as if she had been confronted with the counterfeit of someone she'd known.

Then he spoke. "I regret not waiting for you," he said. "But you seemed to be late and I...had to leave."

With a shock that left her wide-eyed and staring, Sally recognized the voice as Simon's. The realization almost crippled her. "My God," she whispered, unable to contain her stupefaction. "It's you."

"Yes." Simon spoke as if there had been no change in his appearance. "I tried looking for you. I was afraid you might have met with an accident."

Sally nodded dumbly. She moved away, trying not

to look, attempting to control the rising panic that threatened to make her turn and flee from this travesty of the Simon she had known.

"I am glad to see you." He smiled gently. "The public house was very full, and I doubt if you would have enjoyed yourself. We are better off here, alone together."

"Yes," Sally whispered, willing herself to remain, willing her voice to sound normal, fighting desperately the shock that ran through her in icy waves.

You will see a change in him, Cyril Fenick had said. *A change so final that all your disbeliefs will die. Each time he kills, he alters.* The chilling words rang clearly. She looked at Simon, at the lined face, the stooped shoulders, the graying hair, and she turned her eyes away.

"I missed you, but it was terribly crowded, quite uncomfortable," he said pleasantly.

Sally swallowed. My God, she told herself, be normal, pretend that nothing has happened. *He will move one step closer to the beast that has taken his soul.* She heard the old sorcerer's voice, and her stomach rose in protest; quickly she put a hand to her mouth.

"Are you all right?" Simon came closer; he touched her arm solicitously. "Nothing has distressed you?"

"I..." Sally moved away, took off her cape but did not know where to put it. "I'm a little hot. The Underground was crowded and I was late. I almost ran to The Half Moon and then around here." She breathed deeply, fighting for control. "I'm just a little ...hot."

"Shall I get you a glass of cold water?"

"Yes," Sally replied quickly.

Simon peered at her anxiously, then went into the tiny kitchen.

Sally was overtaken by a desperate desire to run down the stairs and telephone Cyril Fenick. She'd already made the first step toward the door when she realized how futile it would be. The fat old man was drunk. He would not hear the telephone ring, and even if he did, there was nothing more he could tell her. She was alone now; whatever she did would determine the destiny of them all.

Simon came back from the kitchen and gave Sally a glass of tap water. She drank a little, walked to the bed, sat on the edge of it, and breathed evenly, determined that the shock would pass. "Thank you," she said after a moment. "That helped."

"Would you like a little more?"

"No." Sally shook her head and swallowed. "Have you..." she began, "have you had a good day?" The triteness of the words stuck in her throat, but she could think of nothing else to say.

"Well, in a way." Simon sat in a chair facing her, seating himself neatly, adjusting his jeans as if they were the best flannel. "Although, as I say, I had to leave the public house. There was a young man there whom I found most offensive."

"What happened?"

"Nothing very much. He was rude, that was all." Simon smiled, and his face creased into a map of tiny lines. "I found it easier to leave. A little cowardly, perhaps, but much better in the long run, don't you agree?"

Sally nodded. He'd become his own parent. His manner, his mood, his delivery were all that of middle age. She found it impossible to believe that the polite man seated before her was the enthusiastic youth who had counted ducks in the park, who had eaten chestnuts with unabashed enjoyment, who had made love to her in this very room. Yet no alternative was possible: this was the same person, trapped in his black hole of endless change, doomed by an evil over which he had no control.

"So I simply left," Simon went on. "There was no scene."

He doesn't know, Sally realized with horror. He

hasn't any real idea of what he's done or what's happening to him. She knew now where his nightmares came from; they were the truth seeking escape; they were the animal within trying to gain a greater possession.

She pressed her hands into the bed on which she sat and managed to control her twitching fingers. "I have been thinking..." she began, speaking slowly, forcing herself to be still, determined to maintain a pretense of normality. She must fabricate something to cling to; otherwise she would go out of her mind. "I have been thinking, that we should go away for a while. Somewhere different. Someplace else, for a holiday."

"Must we?" Simon's voice was curiously removed from reality. "I was beginning to like it here. Where on earth would you want to go?"

"Bavaria," Sally replied abruptly. "You told me once you were happy there. As a child."

"Bavaria?" Simon leaned back in his chair. He saw the bleak outline of a mountain village against the background of snow. The air was frozen, and the roadway rang to the sound of his boot heels. Mountain mist swirled above the tree line; ice encrusted the buildings. A wisp of memory began to return. "Well, yes, I do recall visiting Bavaria once. Although it does seem to be a very long time ago."

"You were going to ski. You told me you were going to ski." Sally's words were uneven. "Only it was too...cold. Don't you remember that?"

"Yes, yes of course." An image flickered through the inner eye. There had been a further change. The crone's words were in his ears; he heard her warning and knew with pain that he had been turned again. Simon looked down at his hands. He touched the silver bracelet this pretty girl had given him, and memory began to invade.

In a dark alleyway leading from a public house, an undertaker had died. A mean and sinister man had been punished for his avarice. Simon studied his hands and read the lines of time on them; he felt his skin and understood that he had been transported one step further toward the shape he was to become. His eyes went up to the girl, and he wondered what she knew and if she were still attempting to protect him. If so, he pitied her and regretted the fact that he needed her so intensely.

He had loved her once, he recalled painfully, but that, also, was a long time ago. She was more of a daughter to him now. "Yes," he said, as if his mind had not wandered at all. "I do remember how cold it was in Bavaria."

"Wouldn't you like to go back?"

"Back?" Simon smiled gently. "I wonder."

"To...to where you were happy." It took all of Sally's concentration to continue calmly. *He must be returned,* Cyril Fenick had said. *He must be made to stay.* "Wouldn't you...wouldn't you like to go back there?"

"It might be very pleasant." Simon looked at Sally cautiously. "I've had a strange time of it lately," he said in the voice of a man who is wary of committing himself. "Been out of sorts, if you take my meaning. It might be just what I need, to get away for a bit. Will you accompany me?" he asked.

"Yes," Sally whispered. She pressed her fingers against her palms, willing them to be still. She held in the pain she wanted to release, held back the tears that welled up behind her eyes. My God, he was so sad, so pitifully alone. She *was* all he had, and in spite of the horror of the change in him, in spite of what else he might become, she could not desert him now. "Yes," she managed to say. "I'll come with you."

"That would be extremely kind. When do you think we should begin?" He relaxed a little and kept his eyes from his hands. "I must say—"

"Now," Sally interrupted impulsively. "Tonight."

"Tonight?"

"Yes, the sooner... the sooner the better."

Simon shook his head. "Surely there's not that great a hurry," he said evenly. "Let's plan our journey this evening and then, perhaps tomorrow, we could set off."

"All right," Sally agreed with greater control. "Let's wait until tomorrow. There's no real rush." She could not keep her eyes from him. She could not avoid wondering what evil had been committed to cause so profound a change. He who had been a lover was now someone to deal with as though he were ill or infirm. Steadfastly she held her mind on the present. "I'll... I'll call a travel agent I know," she went on. "We should be able to catch a flight in the morning."

"I beg your pardon?"

"From Heathrow, I guess," Sally continued. "It'd fly to Munich. Someplace like that."

"Are you suggesting that we actually fly?" Simon smiled an indulgent smile. "Surely you're making fun of me?"

"No, I mean..." Sally stopped. What was it Cyril had said the first time she'd seen him? Something about being out of touch? It was stupid of her to have forgotten so rapidly. She began again. "What I was going to say was we'll go by train. We'll catch one at Victoria. That'll take us down to Dover or wherever the ferry leaves from." She forced a wavering smile to ease him, to calm herself, to make the charade acceptable. "Once we're on the other side of the Channel we'll take a train or something. That sound all right to you?"

"That sounds perfect." Simon sat back in his chair and looked at Sally with great and sincere fondness. "Won't it be fun to go away together? Won't we have a wonderful time?"

"Yes." Sally closed her eyes and knew in that moment that she was committed to a greater extent than ever before. This man who was smiling at her

191

with such tenderness had become her total responsibility. That which began with a chance meeting late at night, which had turned from a love affair to a nightmare, was hers alone to bear. "It'll be great going away together," she said with pain in her heart. "We'll have a ... terrific time."

Molly White told the two detective sergeants all she could remember about the little toughie and the pretty boy she'd seen him with—for the second time that night.

Well, she'd not exactly told them both before; she'd told the lean, healthy-looking one and then his podgy friend came in and he'd wanted to hear the whole thing again. She was getting a bit sick of it, actually. Fred had gone to bed leaving her on her own, and now it was something like one o'clock in the morning and neither of them looked like going. *They* didn't have to leap out of bed at sparrow fart and start getting the place ready for the day's trade. Molly wondered, for a minute, what effect the murder would have on turnover and decided it wouldn't be bad. Things like that interested people; they'd be chocabloc for days.

"When did you first notice the suspect?" the podgy one asked. "Was it only recently?"

"I hadn't set eyes on either of them before yesterday." Molly put a hand over her mouth and yawned. "No, that's not true; the good-looking feller came in the evening before. With his girl."

Albert looked at the sketches of Simon and Sally the police artist had made from Molly's description; both were reasonably accurate. "She wore a dark cape, that what you said?" he asked softly.

Molly nodded. "I'm sure you know the type, dear," she replied.

"Any one else see them?"

"Alf and Myrtle. Thought they were hippies, Myrtle did." Molly looked at Chris. "But I've told you that, haven't I, love? Remember."

"Yes." Chris smiled. "I'm sorry you've had to go over the whole thing again, but it's Albert's case. He had to hear for himself."

"Yes, well, he would, wouldn't he?" Molly pushed her tired hair into place. He wasn't bad-looking, this thin feller; he had one of them bony faces she quite liked. He looked fit, as well. Quite a lot of go in him, she wouldn't be surprised. "Was there anything else, do you think, he'd like to hear again?"

"I'm sorry," Albert apologized without looking up from the sketches. "I know it's late."

"It's the morning, you see, dear." Molly lit another cigarette. "It's me who makes the start." She looked at Chris significantly. "Fred's not well; he stays in bed of a morning." She drew smoke into her lungs. "He's not up to much at all these days."

"Tell me what he was wearing," Albert said. "Go over that once more and then we'll leave you alone."

"Very kind of you, I'm sure." Molly flashed a half-smile at Chris. "Anorak and jeans, I believe I said."

"Shoes?"

"Well, now, I can't say that I noticed, really."

"You'd notice," Albert said without rancor. "You have an eye for detail."

Molly frowned. "Was it them—what do they call them—that American word, sneakers? That's it, he was wearing sneakers. Everyone has them these days."

Albert nodded. "And under the anorak?" he asked softly.

"One of them turtle necks, dark blue. That I did see."

Albert looked straight at Molly. "Pretty drab for a person of his taste, wouldn't you say?"

"You know, the same thing struck me." She blew a little smoke at Albert. He had a twinkle in his eye, this podgy one; there was something going on. "It wasn't the sort of gear that, well, went with his personality, if you know what I mean."

"How would you describe his personality?"

"I thought he was queer at first, myself. When I first saw him, standing outside in the rain, I thought he was another of them that lives round the corner. He's in those adverts on the telly—oh, what's it for, you know the one I mean, very pretty. Always got that big dog with the spots."

"What changed your mind?"

"Eh? Oh, I don't know, dear. Perhaps it was just the way he acted with me." Molly tapped ash from her cigarette. "You can tell, you know, straightaway."

"Would you like to show me the photos?"

"The, ah . . . you mean the ones he got so excited about?" He was hard to keep up with, this podgy feller; you had to have your wits about you. On the whole she preferred the lean one herself. Molly smiled inwardly. What a thing to even think, she thought. She turned to Chris. "Be a love and show him where they are," she said. "I'm all in, and that's the truth."

Albert stared at the photographs for a long and silent time; he studied the one of the woman alone, leaning on her croquet mallet, looking past the camera into what could have been either past or future. Then he bent and examined the sepia-tinted group of three; the woman, the man, and the faceless child in the sailor suit. The boy seemed to have been about seven or eight, but his features were lost completely in the slip of light, the turning away from the present at the moment the image was recorded.

Albert fixed his eyes on the group for what seemed to be an eternity. Chris waited patiently beside him, glancing across at Molly once to see her dozing, her arms on the bar, her head resting on them uncomfortably. When Albert finally stood upright, his eyes had a distant look. The antique sailor suit was identical to the shredded garment in the storeroom of the police station at Tonbridge; the molded shape in the padded casket was the size of the boy in the photograph, but the features of the child were absent. The force he was destined to meet gave him nothing to recognize it by.

"Where's the body?" he asked Chris.

"Westminster Hospital." Chris looked at his watch. "You want to see it tonight?"

"What's it doing there?"

"It's only round the corner from here. Someone from the pub called the ambulance. Before anyone knew it, they were there, and the body admitted." Chris shrugged. "Now they're stuck with it."

"Poor sods." Albert started for the door. "Let's get over there then."

Their voices woke Molly; she lifted her head. "Going, are you?" she asked hopefully.

"Thank you for all your help." Chris went over to her. "I'm sorry we've kept you up so late."

"That's all right, love." A piece of Molly's hair seemed to have come out of place; she pushed it back. "Come by anytime, have one on me."

Chris smiled. He just might do that, he told himself; he liked her. "If I get the chance."

As they left the pub Albert handed the sketches of Simon and Sally to a uniformed constable. "Get this on the wire," he said quietly. "I want every airport, ferry terminal, bus and rail station to have one by morning."

Albert drove to Westminster Hospital in the plain green Vauxhall he'd brought up from Tonbridge. It had begun to rain again, and the roadway was black and shining in the lights from the vehicle. This part of London was sleeping now; night had drawn its cover over the city.

The hospital was a blaze of light and activity. The two detective sergeants went in through the Casualty Department where victims of wet roads and motorcycles, the spilling out of public houses, the tailings of the day's domestic violence had come for repair.

Chris led Albert through the seeming chaos with the air of someone who had seen too much of it before, went to the reception desk, and asked a black nurse in a white uniform to be shown to the morgue. Presently a young porter with a spotted face arrived and led them away through a maze of white-walled, linoleum-covered corridors. When they arrived, both men pulled their collars a little tighter about their throats as if anticipating the coolness that awaited them within.

"Who was it again?" the porter asked. "You got a name?"

Chris Wilkinson gave him the details.

"Oh, yeah. I remember him coming in." The porter made a gruesome face. He showed them into the morgue. "Round the back here."

The detectives followed until they came to a gray, refrigerated cabinet with chromium fittings. They watched the porter unlock the door and swing it open; cold air poured out to greet them. The porter hummed tunelessly while he consulted the names on the numbered units, then he reached for the bottom one and pulled it out. The remains of Ray Clark rolled toward them creakingly on unevenly oiled bearings and stared sightlessly upward.

"Bit of a mess, isn't he?" the porter said to no one in particular. "Don't usually see them that bad."

Neither detective replied.

Albert bent and looked at the throat. The wound was black, the flesh about it blue-white; it seemed to have been ripped open as if something metal had dug in and then sprung away. Black blood smeared the chest; on the face was a look of inordinate terror.

"What happened to him?" The porter was picking at a pimple on the back of his neck. "Get hit with a chain saw or something?"

"Something like that," Chris replied.

"Scared the shit out of him, didn't it?"

Chris nodded. "Just be quiet for a bit, lad," he advised.

"Suit yourself," the porter replied, and explored the tenderness he'd created on his neck. "Just being friendly."

Albert reached forward and took a coarse black hair from the wound in the throat; he found another in the crushed flesh of the hand and placed them both carefully between two blank pages of his notebook. He stood upright. "That'll do," he said, and turned toward the door.

"Yeah?" The porter seemed surprised. "Right." He replaced the body and slammed the cabinet shut.

"Anything else you'd like to see?" Chris asked as they retraced the corridors back to Casualty.

Albert shook his head.

"What do you make of it?"

For a few paces Albert didn't reply. Then he said, "It's the same as the one in Tonbridge." His voice was low; it did not carry to the porter.

"What did it?"

Albert shook his head very slowly. "You'd never believe me," he said, and his reply was final. He walked along the corridor, his eyes on the linoleum squares at his feet. As he moved he was aware of the weight of the pistol in his raincoat pocket. Instinctively his hand went to the weapon.

The Return

Seventeen

IN SALLY LAWRENCE'S APARTMENT above the tree-lined square there was a chill, a heaviness, that filled the air. None of the lightness, none of the passion remained. Sally was afraid to think of it. Simon appeared to have forgotten it even existed. As he prepared himself for sleep on the divan in the corner, Sally brought him a final cup of tea. He looked at her curiously, then leaned forward and kissed her softly on the cheek, and for a second or two while his lips brushed her, he seemed to recall something closer. Then, abruptly, he stepped away, smiled, and took his tea.

While he removed his outer garments and climbed into the divan, Sally prepared her own bed and noticed that he still wore the red socks and the dark blue knickers she had given him. It seemed wrong now, that he should continue to wear them; it seemed mockingly out of place. Sally closed her eyes tightly to hold back a return of the panic that had overcome her when she'd opened the door earlier and seen the terrifying change in him for the first time. Now the sight of those intimate garments, so lightly given to so different a being, filled her with misery.

Immediately she hurried into the bathroom to clean her teeth and scrub her face with cold water. She delayed as long as possible and, when she returned to the main room, Simon was asleep. She approached the divan, as she'd done the night of his arrival, and looked down, at the lined features, the thinning, graying hair. She closed her eyes and turned away. There was no hiding from the facts that surrounded her.

Sally slept badly and awakened early, feeling drained, feeling as if she were suffering from jet lag. Her skin seemed too sensitive, the lights too bright; each movement she made was clumsy and unsure. As she reached for the clock on the table beside her bed, she knocked it onto the floor. She looked across to the huddled figure of Simon and was relieved to see that he remained asleep.

Quietly she took a long bath and washed her hair, drying it slowly, keeping herself apart. She changed every article of clothing, glancing at Simon from time to time as she did so. He remained unmoving; he lay on his back, breathing softly through his nose like an old man, his lined face relaxed on the pillow.

Sally thought of trying to wake him but hesitated. He was a stranger to her now, and she decided to leave him alone. She could fill in another hour or so by calling a travel agent and by going down to the corner shop to buy something for a meal before they set out on their unknown journey.

Anything, she thought, instead of facing him again.

Quickly she left the apartment.

The call to the travel agent took little time. There were many trains from Victoria to Dover; there were many ferries to Calais. Both journeys would take about two hours, the agent told her, advising her to avoid the rush hour. But that was all, he added, it wasn't even worthwhile for him to make a ferry booking this time of year. It would be just as easy for her to go to the office when she got to Dover and pick up the tickets direct. He made it seem all very simple.

Sally left her building and walked slowly round the square to the corner shop where they were talking about a murder.

The shop, a delicatessen run by a Cypriot, had only one customer. The owner shrugged and moved his hands eloquently as he listened to the woman who was in the middle of a conversation about a youth who had been killed in a nearby mews the night before.

At first Sally barely listened, but as the woman made minor purchase after minor purchase and continued her chatter, what she was saying slowly filtered into Sally's consciousness.

It was when the woman said, "I hear they're looking round here. Door to door, they said on the telly," that Sally felt a touch of involvement.

"I hear that, too," the Cypriot replied as he wrapped a piece of cheese. "You want anything else?"

"No." The woman took the cheese. "Well, some of them crackers. No," she added as the Cypriot reached for a pack. "The others, those are too salty. Yes," she went on as if the conversation had been without interruption, "skin heads, I heard it was. Fighting outside of a pub. Dreadful, you know, what goes on nowadays."

"The, ah, the pub," Sally could not avoid asking, willing her voice to be still. "Do you know it's name?"

"Name?" The woman noticed Sally for the first time; she looked with disapproval at the long, dark hair and the cape. "I don't think they said what it was called." Her voice was indifferent.

"The 'Arf Moon," the Cypriot replied casually. "You want anything else, Mrs. Duggan?"

Sally heard the words and froze. The name of the public house went through her like a knife. She saw a fat old man surrounded by cats talking about the transformation after each killing.

The death in the mews had brought about the change; of that she was certain as she stood paralyzed, listening to the ordinary voices and the unnatural hammering of her heart, feeling the nails in her fingers bite into the palms of her hands.

Finally the woman left, and with immense effort Sally roused herself and managed to purchase a pound of sausages and a packet of instant mashed potatoes. She bought the items quickly, holding her head forward so that the swing of her hair covered her face. She thought only of getting away without being noticed, without leaving an impression to be recalled later.

She walked rapidly back to the square, going indirectly, taking a road that led away from her apartment and then another that would complete her return. As she rounded the second corner she saw two policemen walking toward her on the far side of the street.

For a second her heart stopped. She felt her mouth open with the beginnings of a scream; her hand went toward her cape to lift its hem, and she turned as if to bolt from the twin dark shapes coming toward her in the cold midmorning air. But she held her panic, forced herself to stare into a shop window; her own image was in the glass, and its presence gave her strength. She looked steadfastly at herself and saw the policemen pass behind her. She let her breath out to look up to an artificially smiling model inviting her to forget the difficult days of her calendar by using a certain tampon.

Oh, Jesus, Sally thought, aware of a frenzied desire to laugh. She felt the muscles about her mouth begin to pull back into an uncontrollable smile.

No, she said to herself, holding on. Stop it. Once you start you'll never stop. Stop. Stop it now, for Christ's sake. Oh, Jesus, please ... stop it.

She did. She walked back to her apartment, moving one leaden foot after the other, deliberately making herself return to face a responsibility that was hers alone.

When she entered the flat, she found Simon awake. He was sitting up in the divan beating dust from his red socks on the back of a chair. Specks spun about him in the thin light that came through the window, giving an air of further unreality.

"Hello," he said, his voice sluggish. "I was beginning to wonder what had become of you." He put his hand to his mouth to cover a yawn. "We're off today, isn't that so?"

"Yes," Sally replied, her words uneven. "We ... we should go as soon as we can."

"Of course, of course." Simon pulled the socks onto his feet and looked about him. "A bathrobe?" he muttered. "Did I have a bathrobe?"

"Here, use this." Sally handed him her cape, her head spinning. She would leave it behind, she thought. She'd wear a jacket and a skirt, pull her hair back, and put on dark glasses. She'd do whatever was necessary to alter her appearance. She'd change herself as he had changed, realizing that even if the police knew Simon was responsible for the death in the mews, he'd be difficult to identify now. "Would you ... would you like something to eat?" She forced herself to sound reasonable as she went into the kitchen.

"That would be splendid." Simon rubbed his eyes sleepily. "I do love a good breakfast."

"I'll ... I'll get started."

"What is there?"

"Sausages and mashed potatoes. I went to the shop

on the corner. That's where I was when you woke up."

"Well, well." Simon smiled with pure delight. "How wonderful." He sniffed the air in anticipation. "I'll go and clean up. It won't take a moment." He shook his head in wonder. "Sausages and mash for breakfast, what a very thoughtful girl you are."

He went away humming a tune Sally had never heard before.

She closed her eyes and pressed her hands to her face. She felt her body begin to tremble and leaned against the sink and shook, tears streaming down her cheeks. In an effort to halt the spasms that ran through her body, she wrapped her arms about herself, holding on desperately. She felt her knees weaken and realized that any moment she would fall. It was useless, she knew, as her control lessened; she couldn't do it alone.

And then, from the square, she heard a cry of pure and simple joy. It was the child she had seen the morning after Simon's arrival, playing with the same dachshund on the leaf-littered grass. The voice rose up as if it were for her ears alone; it came as a personal call, and it saved her.

She listened, and it came again; she watched the child run as the absurdly shaped dog scrambled after; she saw the child turn its head and stumble and almost fall.

Instinctively Sally's hands went out as if to prevent the child from falling, and it was then that she realized that she'd stopped shaking. She knew then that she would be able to continue, to take Simon wherever he had to go and to do whatever had to done in order to help him. Because he needed her; because without her he would be doomed; because without her he would fall.

She wiped her eyes, took a frying pan from a hook on the wall, and began to prepare the sausages. Behind her she heard the door of the bathroom open and the sound of Simon approach.

"Not ready yet?" Simon asked from the doorway, adjusting his pullover. "I'm famished."

"It...it won't take a minute."

"Would you like me to peel the potatoes?"

"No." Sally reached for the packet, her hand steady. "They're instant."

"Instant?" Simon's eyes opened in surprise. "How quaint."

He watched her continue, and he hoped she'd remain. He was torn between need and a desire to preserve.

It was essential, he knew, to keep her apart, or as apart as he was able.

Perhaps, later, he could abandon her along the way, leave her before the next of them arrived. Sooner or later they would all arrive to challenge, to attempt to steal, to try to deprive him of what he possessed.

He looked at her as she bent over the stove, cooking the sausages, preparing the strange potatoes, and his heart turned cold at the thought of what he was doing, of the danger he could not avoid leading her into.

He must wait, he told himself, remain calm, and hope there would be a moment when an alternative to what he was doing was offered, when an opportunity rose to set her free before she was utterly damned. In the meantime his need for her guidance was as great as ever.

In his untidy flat at Swiss Cottage, Albert Scot was late in beginning the day. His sleep had been restless; he had lain awake for long periods seeing the body of Ray Clark in the cabinet of the morgue at Westminster Hospital, the wound in the throat gaping as if it were issuing a challenge. The killing worse than the one in Tonbridge, more savage; it contained a greater degree of rage and hatred. Albert wondered again what motive lay behind it and could think of nothing that made any sense.

A dozen ideas came to mind, some simple, some outrageous, but none satisfied. He could imagine nothing that involved an infant's torn garment, a few unidentified hairs, and a wound so grotesque he could not put it from mind, whose horror robbed him of sleep.

By the time he finally climbed out of bed, shaved, and dressed, it was almost eleven o'clock. He was hungry but could not face preparing anything. He decided to take the Vauxhall into Scotland Yard and get something from the canteen. He picked up his raincoat and was aware of the weight of the pistol. It was uncomfortably reassuring. He took a final look about the disarray of his flat and shook his head in disapproval. He was glad his mother was not here to comment. He locked the door behind him and wondered when he would return; something told him it would not be for a while.

New Scotland Yard seemed absurdly normal when he arrived. He parked the car and went up in the lift, walked through the bullpen, past the sergeants and the clerks and the woman constables, one or two of whom nodded at him casually, as if he'd never been away. He went into his office and looked at his desk; it contained nothing that had anything to do with either of the deaths. Without even removing his raincoat, he turned and left again and went down the tiled stairs to the canteen in the basement.

It was almost empty. The tea was still hot, but there were no bacon sandwiches. Albert bought a tomato and cheese sandwich, wrapped in plastic, which tasted as if it had been prepared under water. He sat with it alone at a table and wondered why he was wasting time in an almost deserted canteen playing with a sandwich he no longer had any taste for. He knew the answer even before the question was properly formed.

He was afraid to go to the Archives Room, afraid there might not be a file to find, afraid what such a file might contain. It could tell him everything or nothing or too little of either. Finally he pushed away the remains of the sandwich, drank the rest of his tea, and made his way slowly to a long, high-ceilinged room whose countless shelves contained mountains of multicolored folders and whose air always smelled of dust.

Elizabeth Crone was a spinster wedded to the records she presided over. She was of an indeterminate age, with gray hair and bosoms that threatened to escape the dowdy garment that covered them. She looked up at Albert as he approached her desk, and blinked at him sternly.

Albert introduced himself, but it made no impression. She had been dealing with detective sergeants for over thirty years and was yet to meet one who knew precisely what he required. This untidy, dumpy fellow was no different. She could tell immediately that he was going to ask for something that would take a week to locate, and then he'd discover it was not what he wanted at all.

"This isn't going to be easy," Albert began, contritely. "It has to do with an Inspector Peter Kearsley. He was with us here a long time ago."

"Dates?"

Albert shook his head slowly. "I don't have them," he said apologetically. "But he died in the early part of this century." Albert paused. "He shot himself, I believe."

"Hmmp. Well, that's something." Miss Crone peered over the tops of her half-spectacles. "Sit down, his name should be on a list somewhere."

Albert sat on a hard, straight-backed chair, put

his hands on his lap, and waited as Miss Crone rose from behind her desk and sailed down one of the archive-lined corridors. Albert heard the sounds of pages being turned and then Miss Crone reappeared.

"Nineteen hundred and five," she said precisely. "Died by his own hand. What was it you wanted to know about him?"

"Everything."

"Good Gracious." Miss Crone almost smiled. "You do want a lot, don't you. I'll do what I can, of course, but it'll take at least a week to prepare."

"I need it today."

"Impossible." Miss Crone returned to her desk. "Absolutely out of the question."

"I'm sorry." Albert moved his hands apologetically. "But I must have it today." He paused, then added, "If it's any help, Chief Constable Bates told me to tell you it's to do with a hobby of his."

"Ernie?" Miss Crone's smile became real. "The old codger. What on earth's he up to now?"

"We're working on something together. I can't tell you much about it, but this information could be critical. Really, it's very important."

Miss Crone thought a moment. Her eyes went to a wall clock with black hands and Roman numerals. "Come back at three," she said abruptly. "I'll see what I can do." She looked at Albert sternly. "Off you go. You'll only hold me up sitting around here." She watched Albert retreat from the Archives Room. "Ernie," she repeated, with quiet animation, "you old devil."

Albert returned to his office and inquired about Chris Wilkinson, only to find that his lean colleague had gone to St. Albans. Albert called in one of his detective constables and sent him off to the laboratory with the hairs he had taken from Ray Clark's wounds in the Westminster Hospital Morgue; he told the man he wanted them handled by the same technician who'd worked on the material from Tonbridge; he asked for an assessment to be phoned through to him as soon as possible.

Then he took off his raincoat, hung it carefully on the back of his chair, and began to type a preliminary report on each of the two murders, supplying all the facts as he knew them, including none of his opinions. In this manner he filled in the time until a quarter to three and then, taking his raincoat with him, went back to the Archives Room and stood sheepishly before Elizabeth Crone, feeling like a schoolboy.

"You're early." Miss Crone's eyes flicked to the clock on the wall. "You're also very fortunate," she said, reaching for three brown manila folders marked by the passage of time: they had pale borders where they'd protruded from the dusty shelves. "Especially with this." She lifted the thinnest, least-handled file. "It should have been burned years ago."

Albert's mouth dried. The folder had *"P. Kearsley. Personal."* written in a copperplate script on its top right-hand corner.

"Wrongly filed during the war," Elizabeth Crone continued. "The *last* war, that is. Almost anything else like this was caught by an incendiary bomb. Burned to pieces." She looked at Albert over her glasses. "You're a very lucky young man."

Albert reached for the file.

"Sign here." Elizabeth Crone turned a ledger in his direction and watched him add his signature. "Sign for all three, if you don't mind."

Albert looked at the other two folders. One was Kearsley's record, the other a résumé of his cases; Albert took them all. "Have you been through these?" he asked carefully.

"Certainly not." Miss Crone's voice was hostile.

Albert apologized profusely, thanked Elizabeth Crone, and returned to his office. He replaced the raincoat over the back of the chair, closed the door, and with a feeling of curious certainty, opened Inspector Peter Kearsley's personal file.

It was not an official record; that was obvious from the moment he looked into it. There were no printed forms, nothing that appeared to have anything to do with either routine or duty. There were several old photographs of a tall, rather elegant inspector, in and out of uniform, which Albert assumed was Kearsley. There was a theater program dated 1896 which was signed in one corner: My deepest and most sincere thanks, Lucille. There was a calling card with an elaborate Egyptian border belonging to a Mrs. Fitzgerald, which had nothing written on it at all.

Albert examined each piece as it came to him in order, turning it over in his surprisingly long and elegant fingers, looking at it from every angle and then placing it aside until he came to the next. In this manner he arrived at the telegram.

It had been sent to Inspector Kearsley on December 30, 1897, by an Inspector Leopold Fuchs of the Munich Municipal Police. It was on a faded blue form, and the message was handwritten. It said: PLEASE WIRE ME ALL INFORMATION YOU ARE ABLE TO SUPPLY REGARDING EDMUND AND ANNA BLACKSTONE LATELY OF TONBRIDGE KENT AND THEIR SON SIMON STOP MYSELF ARRIVING DOVER TOMORROW EVENING STOP SCHMIT OF MY OFFICE HAS MY SCHEDULE STOP YOU MAY CONTACT ME THROUGH HIM. STOP

Albert read the telegram until he knew it by heart. He laid it carefully on his desk, got up, walked round his office, and returned to his chair and read it yet another time. He turned it over and looked at its other side; nothing was written there. The telegram was simple and direct, and it filled him with such a clear sense of linkage that it brought a smile to his pudgy face. It connected a German belt buckle to a ripped sailor suit. It began to explain why Tonbridge might be the center of the violence he had witnessed and gave him a name. Above everything it gave him a name.

His fingers a little damp with excitement, Albert put the telegram aside and then came to the report.

At first he did not recognize it as anything. It lay facedown in the folder so that, for a moment, he believed he had come to the end of the documentation and a few blank pages was all that remained in the file. Then he turned one over and saw the embossed crest of The George Hotel, Tonbridge, saw the spiky writing, the stilted English, the elongated German s's, and he knew, before he even read a sentence, that this was what Inspector Leopold Fuchs had written to Kearsley the night before his disappearance. It was the report that had been handed to Albert's grandfather on the morning the German Inspector had gone off into the early mists, never to be seen or heard of again.

That's what the Chief Constable had told him in the Conservative Association Rooms, Albert recalled, before any mention of the report had been made. What else had been said—something about looking at old maps, ordering a carriage? Fuchs had been investigating a series of European murders; he'd gone to Tonbridge to check information that might have helped him discover why three people had died of particularly ugly neck wounds. He must have been close to a solution, and it had killed him. His bones had been discovered beside the decayed wooden casket the bulldozer driver had dug up before he also had died in the same hideous manner.

Now all that remained of the German inspector was a solid-brass belt buckle with an eagle on its facing. That and this report, Albert thought, as his hands collected the closely written pages, which he had given to my grandfather, who read it before he passed it on, and who also knew everything.

With a mounting sense of excitement Albert Scot began to go through Leopold Fuchs' final recording.

Eighteen

SALLY LAWRENCE and Simon Blackstone caught the
3:53 p.m. from Victoria to Dover.

In spite of Sally's desire to leave as soon as possible, Simon dawdled over his sausages and mashed
potatoes. He chewed each mouthful with slow, determined enjoyment; he drank two cups of tea with
a lingering appreciation. He gave the impression of
being quite content to remain where he was.

After eating he fussed over what luggage they
should take, caused further delay by searching her
apartment fruitlessly for clothing he did not possess.
When Sally finally offered him another pair of socks
and knickers, he accepted them without interest, as
if they were not what he was seeking.

He watched from the bathroom door while she
altered her appearance. It seemed that the disguise
she adopted for their journey gave him a peculiar
satisfaction. He approved the stern way in which she
parted her hair and drew it back on her skull; he

nodded wisely at her choice of sunglasses. But most of the time he acted like a man with something else in mind as he dealt with detail after detail.

Finally, however, they were ready to leave. Sally locked her apartment door and dropped the key into her purse, wondering with a touch of panic when she would use it again. She led the way down the narrow flights of stairs to the entrance of the building and peered cautiously out into the beginnings of the cold winter evening.

"What are you looking for?" Simon asked.

"Nothing," Sally replied, her eyes searching for police. "Come on."

"Should we hire a cab?"

"No. It's not far. And we've only got one bag."

But once in the great and bustling hall of Victoria Station, Simon Blackstone's bearing altered. His manner became tense; he peered about him as if expecting someone he knew. A fat, young porter, eating a Mars Bar, went past, and Simon craned furtively to examine the youth's features, seemingly fearful of being recognized.

"What's the matter?" Sally asked uneasily. By the barriers leading to the platforms were groups of uniformed police. "You... you worried about something?"

"I... I am merely being cautious," Simon replied, acknowledging for the first time that he might have a reason. "But, do not worry, the man is going now."

"Who was he?"

"I'm not sure." Simon's eyes went round the great, bustling hall jammed with people. There was no denying the presences in this vast and knowing place. "I... was just being cautious."

All morning, in the relative safety of the rooms above the square, he had managed to contain himself, and the voices had not intruded. They were there, he had sensed them, but the silver and the presence of the girl had forced them to keep their distance.

216

But here, out in the open, he heard their muted snarls—he could almost feel the movements of their passing.

Surreptitiously he touched the bracelet about his wrist and looked about him carefully.

It was this place, he realized, here in the open, busy hall of the station, that he was once again exposed. Threats and menaces were all about him, issuing their dark challenges.

He knew now, almost certainly, what lay ahead.

Twin endings beckoned; two clear alternatives stood before him. One of them would bring a captive peace, a form of rest; the other stretched downward through blood and death and destruction to a bottomless pit in which there was no salvation. He saw the twin endings clearly—and was incapable of making the slightest effort to decide his destination.

"Let's get the tickets." Sally's voice interrupted abruptly. "There's a train in ten minutes."

"Yes..." Simon whispered; he breathed deeply. "I wonder if you'd mind taking my arm?" he asked.

"Come on." Sally linked her arm through his. "The ticket office is over here."

She led him across to it and, with her credit card, bought first-class singles to Dover. She reasoned there would be less likelihood of their being disturbed in a first-class compartment. Then, with the first pricklings of new fear, she walked him toward the ticket collector who stood at the head of the Dover platform. Two police constables, one male, one female, were standing there also.

Sally did not speak, nor did Simon say anything as they drew closer to the barrier. Her heart began to beat rapidly; there was tension in Simon's arm. The woman constable turned and glanced at them casually and then looked away. The policeman lifted his eyes and quietly observed Simon, then he, too, stared in another direction. As they came level with the collector Sally handed him the tickets; he looked at them, punched them, and returned them without any interest at all.

Sally continued, Simon with her, seeming what they appeared to be: a middle-aged man and a studious young woman, father and daughter possibly, on their way home after a day in London.

They found an empty compartment, took their seats and sat silently, waiting for the train to thread its way out of the station. They avoided looking at each other and gazed out of the window at the billboards, the graffiti, the movements of people—anything that might take their minds from themselves.

Later, when the train was winding southeast out of the city, past packed houses with little lights in their windows and the occasional glimpse of a woman in a kitchen at work on an evening meal, Simon let out his breath, turned and smiled at Sally, and said, "I must thank you again, awfully, for what you're doing."

"That's . . . that's all right," Sally replied, her tone uncertain; the strain of passing the barriers, of boarding the train, had left her drained. She stared at the tiny lines about his eyes that deepened when he spoke.

"Will we ski, do you think?" Simon asked unexpectedly. "Do you think that might be possible?" he added, maintaining his role.

Sally nodded dumbly.

"It's just what I need, a trip like this." Simon settled himself back in his seat. "I have been a bit under the weather lately. It will be jolly nice to have a break."

Sally could no longer bear to look at him. She turned her gaze away, wondering how much longer the pretense could be maintained, wondering for what length of time they could continue to avoid so much that needed to be said.

Before they'd gone to their different beds the previous evening, Simon had mentioned the name of the village in Bavaria he'd been to as a child, but although Sally possessed a map of that part of the country, it was not marked. It was somewhere near Kempten, Simon thought, yet he had been unable to find it, either. So they'd begun without knowing where they were going, disguising the true reasons for their departure, treating the event as if it were some sort of unspoken pleasure.

But the hard facts of reality must soon intrude. They had passed the first barriers and were out of London. Sally believed their changed appearances would enable them to leave the country, and she's heard that a journey to France could be made without a passport, providing a return ticket was purchased. Even so, they would cross the Channel and proceed from there, but sooner or later they would encounter a frontier where the passage would not be easy. Then the bitter truth would arise, and Sally wondered if either of them would have any idea how to face it.

Take him back, Cyril Fenick had said, but she did not know where. *Make him stay,* the fat old man had implored in his thick, drunken voice, but she did not know how.

Sally looked at Simon now as he sat back in the comfort of his seat. His eyes were beginning to close; his lined face was calm. She hoped he would sleep the entire journey. She turned away to stare out at the dwindling city, the dark countryside coming up. Sheep, like white pebbles, dotted the black-green hillsides; lights in the distance shone like faint expectations of hope.

When Albert Scot had finished reading the German inspector's report for the second time, he was sweating. In spite of the relative lack of heating in his office, he'd had to remove his jacket and push up the sleeves of his roll-necked pullover. Cold sweat ran down his sides, and his neck seemed to be wrapped in a steamy towel, for the German's spiky writing carried a message so surprising, so macabre, it burned through him like a flame.

The bewildering chain of events that had led Inspector Fuchs halfway across Europe to the Kentish market town of Tonbridge were clear and absolutely terrifying; they instilled in Albert a sense of involvement so absolute that he marveled at its sureness.

Albert knew everything that had happened now, knew why the bulldozer driver had been killed and how; he knew why the van driver, whose route took him through Tonbridge, had his throat torn out in a darkened mews beside a public house that contained a collection of photographs a hundred years old. Albert now understood why the German inspector, himself, had died; he knew also what had to be done immediately, before any further victims fell to the creature who roamed, somewhere loose and free, with a dark-haired girl beside him.

For one fact emerged searingly above all others; in itself it was absolutely vital: *Simon Blackstone must not be permitted to return to the Bavarian village, for, once there, his power would become complete. He would be invincible.*

He and Albert were opposing forces now, had become so in the past eighty or more years while the sinister fruits of the original deed matured in the earth beside the Tonbridge river. They were two sides of the same triangle, one evil, one good. When the final confrontation came, only one of them would survive.

Albert pushed the report away and stood before his desk; he began to pace his office, trying to decide his next move.

Whether Simon Blackstone was still in London or had escaped was impossible to determine; no information had come in. Only one phone call had interrupted Albert's reading, and that had been from the laboratory technician who had been given the hairs from Ray Clark's wounds. He'd rung to say they were the same as those from Tonbridge, but so far no identification had been made. He would have said more, but Albert cut him short. From what he had read of Inspector Fuchs' report, he now knew why the hairs would never be identified.

Albert paused in his pacing, and found himself beside his raincoat, which was hanging from the back of his chair; automatically he reached out and lifted the garment, feeling the weight of his grandfather's gift. He had no doubt now why it had been left to him.

It was his to use when he found his enemy, and he wondered suddenly what it was he was looking for. There had already been one alteration in the creature's appearance—the split sailor suit had belonged to a child; the stolen clothes that Simon wore were those of an adult. And now, after the second killing, if the process continued, what could he expect?

Albert bent over his desk and flicked, once again, through the report. What was it Fuchs had said? *The child's hand and arm retained the form of the beast. Each time he killed, the distortion grew.*

But clearly, that transformation no longer applied. Whatever had occurred in the eighty-odd years the creature had been held in its coffin, that manifestation was not now *permanently* displayed. Albert tried to recall everything the woman in The Half Moon had told him; she'd said nothing about any deformation. She'd been close to Simon, and it was his beauty that had impressed her most of all. She'd seen him touch the photographs and would have reported any distortion of the hands.

Albert leaned over his desk, thinking; the child had become a man, and perhaps it had aged again. Albert closed his eyes. If so, what was he searching for now? He did not know. He could only guess, and that was a game he could not afford to play.

Sweat began to roll over Albert's ribs again. He had no way of knowing what either of them looked like now. He must wait and hope that someone somewhere would recognize something that might lead him to the far side of the triangle, to Simon Blackstone, the Moonchild, the Changeling, and his gypsy companion.

Albert returned slowly to his chair. He sat with his elbows on his desk, his head in his hands. Concentrate, he told himself. There are powers on both sides; call on those that might assist you, bring them into being. He closed his eyes and focused into darkness; he willed himself into a void.

Small fires appeared in the corners of his eyes; there was a sudden rush, and a wave of light went through and past him, and he had the sensation of floating in a weightless vacuum, of being suspended with neither shape nor substance, existing solely as a seeking instrument.

He forced himself into a world unknown, to voyage in a living, isolated state. He could see himself now, see his bulky body seated at the desk, unmoving. He continued outward, past shapes and unknown faces, through rooms he had not seen before, in and out of alleyways he did not recognize. He traveled as the images about him became obscure, until he found himself moving through mist and cloud, the beginnings of heat, the fringes of darkness, and from somewhere came the sound of chanting. Ahead of him now he became aware of a new light, a clear, distant signal, and slowly, unfailingly, he groped his way toward it.

Fifteen minutes later the telephone rang.

For a moment Albert was unable to respond; he had gone so deeply into his concentration that he heard the jangling of its tone as if from a distance. Slowly it grew louder and louder until it intruded completely, and then he opened his eyes and picked up the receiver.

The call was from a Detective Constable Lazenby in Dover who thought he'd seen the couple that was in the sketch he'd been sent. He wasn't sure, he said diffidently, but he thought it might be worthwhile reporting.

"Where?" Albert asked, immediately alert.

"At the station, sir," the distant voice replied. "It was because there were the two of them that caught my attention. But they were some ways away. I can't be sure."

"What did they look like?"

"Well, it's that that worries me, sir. It could have been her, all right, but he was older, you see. More middle-aged than the sketches showed."

"*What?*"

"Older." Lazenby hesitated. "I hope I'm not bothering you, sir. But it was the distance, you see. At first I was sure, but when I got a bit closer he was, well, he was older. You know, lines and things; going gray. She wasn't so different. Hair pulled back. Dark glasses, that sort of thing. But him, well...."

"Did they see you?"

"I don't think so, sir."

"What were they wearing?"

"Ho was the same, sir. That's what I was trying to say. He was wearing—"

"What did she have on?"

"A jacket and skirt, sir. Tartan, I think it was, but dark, you know. Sort of Black Watch, if you know what I mean."

"Write down a clear description." Albert felt a current go through him. The faint buzzing was there again; he knew what it was now: he was closing in. "Phone that description to the ferry offices, bus stations, taxi ranks, anywhere you can think of. Do it now. Do it quickly. And be sure they understand. Is that clear?"

"Yes, sir." Lazenby swallowed. He felt as though he'd just been sentenced. "Right away, sir."

"Don't dither. Be precise. And for God's sake be sure they understand."

Albert put down the receiver and stared at it with a sensation of disbelief. He would never know why the call had come, what series of coincidences or accidents or chance happenings had brought him the information when he needed it most; he would never know if his small voyage of pure concentration had had any effect or not, and for the moment it did not matter; he had direction now and a view of the change in the shape of his enemy. He was moving again.

Albert stood and pulled on his jacket. He lifted his raincoat from the back of the chair. He completed two steps toward the door and then turned, scooped Fuchs' report and the telegram off his desk, and stuffed them into a jacket pocket. He walked out through the bullpen and went down to the Vauxhall he had brought from Tonbridge and headed for Dover.

He did not tell anyone where he was going.

Nineteen

JIMMY SINGER saw them coming. The next ferry was due to leave for Calais at 8:15 p.m. and he knew, even before they came to his window in the Dover Cross-Channel Ferry Building on the pier, who they were.

Less than five minutes earlier a police officer had called, his voice urgent, his words filled with importance. They'd got it wrong, the officer said, when they sent out the sketches earlier in the day. They weren't looking for a young feller at all; it was the girl and her father they were after. The old chap was close to sixty and she wore sunglasses now and had her hair drawn back in a bun. The old man was going gray, the policeman explained; he had lines and bags and walked with a bit of a shuffle. London had blown it, the officer assured Jimmy Singer; they'd mucked it up. He didn't say what the couple were wanted for, and he didn't want anything done. Just watch out for them, he'd asked, and report back quick if you spot anything.

Jimmy Singer had taken the message and hadn't passed it on. Very quietly, while no one was looking, he'd gone to the pinboard where the police sketches had been put on display and taken them down. He'd make the alterations first, he told himself, if anyone asked; he'd get it right before the information went out of mind. But he'd keep it to himself if he got the chance. This couple could be just what he was looking for.

Jimmy was in trouble. Well, it wasn't big trouble—he'd had problems like this before—but the Novice Hurdle at Sandown Park had really put him in it. His horse couldn't have lost; on paper it just couldn't be beaten, it stood out from the rest of the field like a pair of dog's balls, and Jimmy'd bet heavily on it running away with the race. But somehow it had lost, and he was up to his credit limit with both his bookmakers. He had no idea where the money was coming from.

Until he saw them coming. The middle-aged chap and his daughter, looking at even fifty yards away as if they had something to hide.

Jimmy glanced down at the changes he had made to the sketches: he'd cut the girl's hair back and put on sunglasses; it could have been a photograph. It'd been a bit harder with the old chap; he had more lines than Jimmy had added. And was more refined-looking as well. Just the sort of person who wouldn't give any trouble, the sort of rundown gent who'd probably got off with the whole of the pension fund, the sort of feller who'd pay up with no fuss at all.

They came straight up to his window and asked for tickets, just as he knew they would. The 8:15 p.m., twenty-four-hour returns. That threw him for a moment until he saw through it; it was only a fiddle to give the impression they weren't running away at all. The daughter paid with a credit card. Jimmy had it checked while he watched them; nothing wrong with the card. It was a pity the police hadn't been able to give names as well as descriptions, but they'd more than likely have got them wrong as well, the way they were handling the case.

"What time did you say we could go on board?" It was the girl asking. American accent. Jimmy made a note of that on the sketch. "Was it half an hour before?"

"That's right, miss." Jimmy glanced at his watch. "You've got a little over forty minutes to fill in." He smiled, and his handlebar mustache moved genially. "The canteen's just over there if you'd like a cup of tea." He paused, then said, "There's plenty of time for ... *anything*." He emphasized the last word significantly, staring at the man as he spoke. "And I wouldn't muck about if I were you, squire," he added with just a touch of menace.

Sally's eyes went swiftly to the heavily built man behind the ticket counter. She didn't trust him; she didn't like the way his little eyes moved. He filled her with sudden panic.

Don't lose control now, she told herself. Don't show anything. Slowly she let out her breath and turned to Simon. "Wouldn't you like a cup of tea?" she asked as evenly as her tension would allow.

"Yes," Simon replied in a voice that did not seem to be his own. "I should like a cup of tea very much indeed."

Sally stared at him, frightened by what she saw, dismayed by the change in his being. He stood upright; his eyes were bright and determined, and his whole body gave the impression of expecting a confrontation. *He had come to life again.*

"Simon?" Sally breathed the name as if it had no meaning. "What...?"

"This person requires something." Simon stared levelly at the greedy face before him and knew that the opportunity he had almost given up hoping for had arrived. This overeager man had provided it willingly; his unspoken demand was clear.

Simon would go with it; he would follow this new challenger, would allow himself to be led away from the girl and her goodness and the danger he exposed her to.

Perhaps, that way, he would save her.

This hungry ticket seller, with the curiously familiar handlebar mustache, could take responsibility for the direction in which Simon Blackstone went, and its outcome would be no more than he deserved.

Simon smiled a brief, wintery smile. "I must find out what this person wants," he said.

"Wants?" Sally's eyes went from one to the other; from the face she didn't trust, to the one she suddenly had no desire to part from. "What does he want?"

"That is something I must find out."

"Simon..."

"Please," Simon said softly, looking at her tenderly. "It is something I must do alone."

Impatiently Jimmy Singer leaned forward. The old gent was nobody's fool; he knew he'd been recognized, but the girl was wasting precious time. "Why don't you run along, duckie," Jimmy said to Sally, keeping his voice low. "Your daddy and I have something serious to discuss." His little eyes went to Simon. "Wouldn't you say so, old man?"

"Yes." There was a distinct shift in Simon's bearing. The skin on his face seemed to be darkening, and he looked as if he needed to shave. "We have much to talk about."

"No." The small cry came from Sally; she did not know what the interchange meant, but it filled her with an overpowering fear for them all. "No, please, let's go and get a cup of tea. Come on, we don't have to wait all that long." She put her hand on Simon's arm and was astounded by the strength she felt below the cloth, the muscles that suddenly seemed to have come alive. "Please..."

Simon turned to her and smiled a gentle smile of comfort and farewell. He took both her hands in his and said, "Don't wait for me, Sally. Go alone to the tea room. I will be with you as soon as I am able, but I must deal with this person before I can accompany you."

"Deal...?" Sally swallowed. "What do you mean?"

"He wants something from us, something I must attend to."

"No," Sally said, but the word was lost; she saw a harshness in Simon's eyes she had not witnessed before.

"Run along, girlie. You heard what he said," Jimmy interrupted.

"I'll wait here," Sally said.

"No." Simon shook his head. "There is absolutely no need."

Sally looked at the heavily built man with the old-fashioned mustache; he was placing a CLOSED sign in front of the ticket counter. "Where are you going?"

"Not far," Simon replied. He looked at her with love and gratitude. "I shall be with you shortly. Goodbye."

Sally watched them go, saw Simon walk beside the seedy-looking man with the soiled jacket and the crumpled trousers. They paused for a moment, their heads together; the man with the mustache did the speaking. Simon listened, nodded once, and then disappeared with him round a corner of the corridor. Sally waited only a second then followed, but they were gone. There were doors leading off into further offices, a metal grille at the top of black iron steps that went down to a pebbled shore. Sally stood peering at the top of the steps, but in the darkness there was no one to be seen.

Slowly, she turned and went into the canteen; she ordered two cups of tea, which came in white plastic containers so thin that the hot liquid burned through to her fingers; she added sugar to the one for Simon, then carried them to a plastic-topped table and sat with her eyes on the corridor waiting for him to reappear.

Albert Scot glanced at his watch as he drove through the outskirts of Dover. It was almost eight-thirty, but he'd done well in spite of the wet roads and the evening traffic. He'd driven fast and skillfully, and only once had a traffic policeman on a motorcycle started after him, his siren howling, his red light flashing. Albert had pulled over immediately and spoken to the officer; after that the motorcycle led the way until the lights of Dover appeared, then it swung off. Albert waved at the rider and went on, driving steadily toward the port.

Once in Dover he headed for the Central Police Station to question Detective Constable Lazenby further. He hoped there would be other information in by now, especially from the ferries.

Whatever happened, Albert was certain that Simon Blackstone would attempt to cross the Channel. No matter what means he used or how devious he appeared, that would be his intent, and it must not be permitted, for once on the other side of the water, the creature within would have full control.

From the German inspector's report Albert knew Simon must be taken back to Tonbridge, to the spot on which he was born, and retained there. Nowhere else would do; to allow him to escape from the English shores would be to see the beginnings of interminable disaster.

Albert drove through the town on wet roadways where ice was beginning to form in gutters. This part of Kent could be bleaker than Scotland; at times the sea itself froze solid. Albert drove as rapidly as he was able, but the traffic had condensed and his progress was agonizingly slow.

He turned a corner and saw the blue light of the

police sign in the wet and glistening distance. He made his way toward it as a car swerved in front of him. Albert wrenched his steering wheel, missing the vehicle by inches. Tension hummed through him like a charge of high voltage electricity. He was in Dover—and close—and something told him Simon had not yet left. The air itself seemed to buzz about him, alive with information. He, and his enemy, were together and nearing, almost within each other's orbit.

Simon Blackstone's mind was clear; he understood what he had to do. All his bitter memory returned, arming him, providing the knowledge he needed. Now that he had been able to leave the girl safely, nothing seemed to be important any longer.

She, who he had held in his arms, who had shown him tenderness and passion, and something so completely unselfish that he would retain it in his memory forever wherever he went and whatever he became, would be spared by what he was about to undertake.

He followed the shape of Jimmy Singer, knowing who it was who led him. The face was familiar; he had recognized it immediately. He had seen this portly figure with the handlebar mustache once before. To find it again was not surprising; they would all return to challenge him; they would all appear, seeking proof of what he was.

Each time he ascended they would be revived, the old circles would be formed, the contests restaged. Each time he would need to show them that he alone was the strongest, that the beast within was Master of them all.

Simon knew who this one was. A ticket-seller, but earlier he had been the Guardian, who, in the guise of a German inspector, had followed him all the way across Europe more than eighty years ago, until they had died together—the last time.

He'd been a weak, imperfect boy then, incapable of resisting light, who'd had to be carried across the Continent in a sealed casket with the lid held shut by a silver latch. An inept boy, only his arm bearing the stamp of the beast.

It was different now, now that he was in his prime, at the height of his powers, inviolate. Now he alone would survive, and soon his great and overwhelming force would break completely free. He would continue as he had been destined to continue from the moment, almost a century ago, when the power had entered his empty soul and his eternity had been defined.

He followed the challenger down the iron steps until they came to the pebbled shore, then walked back beneath the pier that ran out toward the sea. From the walkway Simon could see black water swirling. At the end of the pier rode vessels of great proportion; they reminded him of ancient castles. Here it was cold, his breath turned white, his ears tingled, but cold meant nothing to him now. Power surged through him close to the surface; it was ready to break.

"I think you know what I'm after, old man." Jimmy Singer stopped. In the faint glow of filtered lighting he turned to Simon. "So, let's not waste any time. It's bloody cold out here."

"What do you want of me?" Simon's voice was low and harsh; it seemed to come from a long way away.

"I want to help you, old man. For a fee."

"You would steal my silver?"

"Oh, for Christ's sake ... what are you, some sort of out-of-work actor?" Jimmy reached out and took a firm hold of Simon's pullover; he twisted it, expecting to see fear in the old chap's eyes, and was surprised by the intensity of the gaze he received. "Listen, how much have you got?"

"You would challenge me? You would steal?"

"I, ah, I wouldn't call it stealing, old man." Jimmy

relinquished his grip. "Let's just put it down as a loan."

"I do not lend," Simon said, and the voice of the beast whispered harshly; it rose from the black mists of the past. "I take."

"What the hell are you talking about?"

"You will know. It is time."

"Listen to me, you bloody old idiot." Jimmy moved fractionally away. The man was clearly crazy. Perhaps he was wanted for something more serious than robbing a pension fund, something nasty. His voice weakened a little. "I don't want much. Just enough to see me through."

Simon did not appear to be listening. His eyes were still, his body did not move, and yet he seemed to swell, to increase within himself, to extend his clothing until he more than filled it, until it stretched tightly over his muscled frame. He stared at Jimmy Singer as if he were inspecting a token from the past.

Very slowly he extended a knotted forearm; from the wrist hung the chain of linked silver hearts, and the cross dangled, catching what little light there was. "Take it," Simon said in a terrifying whisper.

"What?" Jimmy's eyes caught the bracelet.

"It is worth more than you will ever know. *Take it*."

"Well, if you insist." Jimmy reached for the bracelet as the wrist that wore it moved toward his throat. Jimmy's eyes opened wide as he saw the alteration begin, the flesh of the arm darken, the hair begin to grow. He tried to push the arm and the bracelet away; he grabbed at the hand, and his mouth opened in cold, crippling fear as the claw thrust his own hand aside. "No," he heard himself babbling. "No, it's all right, old man. You keep it, I'll manage."

His pitiable, futile words were silenced by the claw on his throat. Its deadly nails bit deep. Blood spurted and life fled. Jimmy's arms flailed for a second or two, beating weakly against the impossible strength that forced itself upon him and tore his throat away. His legs collapsed and he hung for a moment, held upright by the strength that had killed him.

Then Simon dropped him, and Jimmy fell, empty and still, to the walkway.

Simon looked down at the corpse at his feet as the final metamorphosis began. "We died *together* last time, Guardian," he hissed. "Now I alone am free."

Simon's body thickened, filled, and shrank; within seconds what had been a man became shorter, broader, closer to the earth from which it had sprung. Simon lifted his hands and covered his face as the moon, high above the pier, moved clear for an instant from scudding clouds. It shone over the landscape, the white Dover cliffs, the freezing sea, with a full and swelling light, and then it went in again, spun back behind its running cover.

When Simon took his hands away, he was unrecognizable. His face had become simian, and it bore the stamp of the wolf: the teeth had lengthened, the lips about them were drawn back, the eyes had grown dark and small and glittered beneath their lowering brows. Only the hair remained in its fullness, but it was white now, pale as snow, and it grew from the dark flesh of the skull like a bizarre halo of distorted light.

But it was not only the face that had returned to the beast; the whole body had been transformed. The hands were coarse and sinewed; black hair grew from their backs, the nails remained in the shape of spines; dark, heavy veins pulsed along the forearms, their visible force fearsome. There was little left of Simon that was in any way human. What, so little time ago, had been a gracefully handsome young man was now a warped, shuffling brute.

It turned away from its latest victim, took a shambling step toward the light that filtered from beyond the darkness of the pier, blinked, and held one distorted hand over its eyes. A ray of light caught the little silver cross as it dangled from the linked-heart bracelet. Then the creature backed away, scraping its feet, now free of their shoes, and scrabbled beneath the pier into the blackness.

Twenty

DETECTIVE CONSTABLE J. LAZENBY, who had telephoned Albert Scot with the sighting of Simon and Sally, waited in the Dover Police Station for Albert to arrive. He stepped briskly forward when the short, untidy figure of the man from London burst through the main entrance, obviously looking for someone.

"Detective Sergeant Scot?" Lazenby inquired. He was a tall blond man with a soft country accent. "I've been expecting you, sir."

"You're the one who phoned me?"

"Yes, sir."

"Did that information get out?"

"Yes, sir. I called the ferry companies myself. One of the other constables covered the bus stations and the taxis. I think we've talked to everyone possible." Lazenby pointed to a door leading away from the main lobby. "Why don't you come through here, sir? There's tea, or coffee if you'd prefer. It's perishing tonight. We've not had cold like this all winter."

"You've had no reports in? No one's called?"

"No, sir. But do come in through here. It's warmer, and we'll hear what's going on as well." He smiled a slow, friendly smile. "It's where the telex is, sir. And the radio. You'll keep in touch."

"Thank you." Albert realized he must sound unnecessarily impatient. The tall blond detective appeared to be handling things well. The information had gone out; now there was nothing to do but wait. "I'm sorry," he said, half-apologetically. "But it's important that we get these people."

"I understand, sir." Lazenby opened the door to the Communications Room. "May I ask what they're wanted for?"

Albert hesitated fractionally. "A man was killed last night in London." His tone was abrupt. "We think these two might be able to help us."

"I see. Would you prefer tea or coffee, sir?"

"Oh? Coffee." Albert glanced at his watch. "What time's the next boat?"

"To where, sir?" Lazenby poured coffee from a clear glass percolator. "France or Holland or Belgium?"

"France."

"Car or passenger, sir?"

"Passenger."

"I'll have a look, sir." Detective Constable Lazenby handed Albert coffee in a thick white mug. "In the meantime drink that. I've put sugar in it. I can see you're worried, and the drive down from London can't have been much fun on a night like this, but just wait here a moment while I go and check on the timetables."

Albert smiled briefly; he took the mug and sat in a steel-framed chair. "Thank you," he said sincerely. "I didn't mean to come on strong."

"It's the big city, sir," Lazenby said, heading for the door. "It has that effect on everyone."

Albert sipped the hot, sweet drink and waited. He was in the corner of a long, narrow room in which two policemen sat, one wearing headphones. Upright radio receivers, transmitters, and a telex machine filled one wall; detailed maps of Dover and the surrounding parts of Kent another. Neither officer took any notice of Albert as he waited, willing a call to come in.

After a few moments Detective Constable Lazenby returned, a slip of paper in one hand. "There's a boat to Calais at 8:15 p.m.," he said, looking at his watch. "That's in just over half an hour. They'd be going aboard now, sir, if that's the one they're taking."

"Is it the only one they could take?"

"Yes, sir. Unless they were waiting—"

"They wouldn't wait." Albert put aside his half-empty coffee mug. "Where's it sail from?"

"The Admiralty Pier, sir. West end of the harbor. Shall I ask the lads to put a call out? There'll be a car somewhere in the vicinity."

Albert shook his head. "I have a car." He looked up at Lazenby. "Do you want to come along?"

"Yes, sir." Lazenby reached for a mackintosh and a cloth cap. "I'd like that."

"Let's go then." Albert began to open the door when the police officer wearing the headphones looked up. "Jack," he called, speaking to Lazenby, "there's a funny one just come in. Might have something to do with what you're dealing with."

"Now what could that be?" Lazenby asked.

"Young couple, looking for a quiet place," the police officer began and grinned. "God help them in this cold. They went along under Admiralty Pier and found a pair of feet sticking out of the dark. They thought it might only be a drunk, but even so, they let us know."

"Admiralty Pier?" It was Albert who asked the question. "Where the ferries sail from?"

"Yes, sir."

"We'll take it." Albert was already moving. "Get

238

an ambulance down there," he added tightly. "We're going to need it."

He opened the door and went out through the police station entrance, Detective Constable Lazenby at his heels; by the time they reached the Vauxhall both were running.

Detective Constable Lazenby recognized what remained of Jimmy Singer immediately. He stared down at the limp figure with its mutilated throat, and for a moment he thought he was going to be sick. "Holy Jesus," he muttered. "What... what happened to him?"

"He's like the others," Albert replied without explanation. "You know who he is?"

Lazenby nodded but did not speak.

"Talk to the ambulance men," Albert instructed. "Get him to the morgue."

"Yes, sir." Lazenby tried to look away, but his eyes were fixed on the throat; he had never seen such a wound. "Whoever did this, sir," he said, his voice dry, "must've hated him something awful."

"Yes." Albert bent, pulled up Jimmy's shirt until it covered the open, hideous wreckage. "Who was he?"

"He... he worked in the ferry office." Lazenby looked away at last. "I've had to talk to him once or twice." He shrugged and licked his lips, recovering. "Little things, you know. Missing property, stuff like that. He always owed someone. He never had any luck with the horses."

"He didn't have much tonight." Albert pushed his hands into his raincoat pockets, feeling for his grandfather's pistol. "They must have gone to him for their tickets."

"Should we have a look on board, sir? She won't have left yet."

"No." Albert was certain. "They won't be going now." He turned the beam of the flashlight he carried upward: reinforced concrete disappeared into blackness; seaweed and shell-encrusted pillars ran down to dark, oily water; no life seemed present. "Let's go up and have a look at the office where the poor sod worked."

"Yes, sir." Lazenby's voice was stronger. "There are steps just round the corner." He peered at Albert. "I don't suppose there's any point trying to find the couple who reported the body? They might have seen something?"

"We'd never find them. They didn't leave a name." Albert turned and began back along the walkway to the light at the foot of the iron stairs. "Anyway," he added, almost to himself, "the less they know the better."

Albert waited while Lazenby spoke to the ambulance men. He watched the breath of the driver and his assistant plume and billow as they replied; he had never felt such cold. It cut through his flesh like a scalpel and seemed to reinforce everything he knew.

One glimpse of the body had been enough; no examination of the wound would have yielded more. And from somewhere the steady, high-voltage buzzing continued, telling him that Simon Blackstone was not on the ferry. He was close, and they were both aware of it.

The time of encounter was approaching.

"If you're ready to go up now, sir"—Lazenby was at Albert's elbow—"we'll see what the other clerk, Jock McLeod's, got to say for himself."

"Yes," Albert replied. "I'm ready."

Jock McLeod could tell them very little.

He'd noticed Jimmy was busy when a Spanish gentleman had come to his own counter. It'd had taken him a long time to deal with the foreigner. It might have been easier if the gent had been French or German; he didn't have much of a problem with those languages, but Spanish was way beyond him.

So he'd been busy, and when he'd finished, he'd looked around, and the CLOSED sign was up and Jimmy'd disappeared. Frankly Jock thought he'd been caught short. They'd had lunch together in an Indian restaurant and, well, meals can be dodgy in places like that even if they do cost a bit less. So he'd waited and waited, and handled the whole bloody lot for the 20:15 to Calais, which fortunately wasn't too much on account of the weather. What's more, he had no idea where Jimmy might have gone. He'd checked the loos and there'd been no sign of him. He couldn't think what the silly old "See You Next Tuesday" might've got up to.

Albert didn't tell him. He listened with mounting impatience to the thin Scottish accent; finally he held up a hand, and McLeod stopped with a blink.

"That his over there?" Albert asked, indicating a thin deal desk near Jimmy's ticket counter.

Jock nodded.

"He worked between there and the window?"

Jock nodded again.

"Take a few notes. Get his address," Albert told Lazenby. "Wait for me here." He went over to Jimmy's desk.

"Who's he?" Jock asked quietly, mouthing the words. "Big shot or something?"

"London Murder Squad," Lazenby replied heavily, taking a notebook from his mackintosh pocket. "Now, let's have that all again."

Albert went rapidly through Jimmy's desk. Apart from material relating to his work, and a number of racing journals, there was little of importance. Albert left the desk, walked to the counter, and almost immediately found the copy of the police sketch Jimmy had altered after he'd talked to Lazenby on the telephone. As Albert looked at the changes he felt a sudden warmth of excitement flush through him. As he read the word *American* Jimmy had scrawled beside Sally's portrait, he heard his mother's voice. "They will all help you if they can."

Albert returned to Jock McLeod. "Is there a waiting room nearby?" he asked.

"There's a canteen, sir." Jock's voice was respectful. "Just round the corner."

"Stay here." Albert spoke to Lazenby. "I won't be long."

Lazenby nodded; he was not sure what was happening, but suddenly he found he had a great deal of faith in the short, untidy detective from London. The man was certain, and that was enough. Ever since the flashlight beam had shown the most hideous wound he had ever seen, Lazenby realized that what they were dealing with was beyond his experience, so, without any aspect of doubt or even curiosity, he nodded briskly and returned his attention to the wide-eyed Jock McLeod.

Sally sat in the canteen in the ferry building, her eyes fixed on the entrance; she waited, as she'd done for the past forty minutes, for Simon's return, but there had been no sign of him.

The tea in the thin plastic cups had grown cold. Other passengers had assembled and were now beginning to drift in the direction of the boat to Calais; soon they'd settle themselves on board, waiting for the ship to move and the lights of England to dwindle. She watched them go, clutching the tickets in her hand tightly, as if their presence would assure that she and Simon would soon be on their way.

But she knew, as she held them, that she was fooling herself. "Good-bye" he'd said as he parted from her to follow the ticket-seller. He'd said it once before, the morning he'd remained in her apartment, and she'd returned to find him inextricably altered. He'd known then, as she knew now, that they'd reached a point of no return, that their contact would never be the same again.

She did not notice Albert Scot enter the canteen. By now she had almost relinquished any hope. The truth was near; it nudged and it muttered. She turned her eyes downward in order to avoid its presence. Albert recognized her immediately and walked slowly around the whole canteen, watching her closely. When he came to the refreshments counter he stopped, purchased a cup of tea, then went to a table behind Sally, his eyes not leaving her downcast head. He took one sip of tea and pushed it aside.

Taking the sketch from a raincoat pocket, he studied it. It featured the girl exactly: the generous mouth, the high-cheekboned face, the dark hair pulled unnaturally back in a bun. She was innocent. He realized that merely by looking at her: the hopeless slope of her shoulders, the resigned angle of her head, her pathetic stillness told him how little she knew.

Albert turned his head, listening to the buzzing. Blackstone was somewhere not too distant, but he was neither in the canteen nor within reach of it. Albert sensed a presence, but it was too far away to cause concern.

Presently he left his table and walked toward Sally; he stood beside her for a second or two, looking down at the nape of her bent neck. It seemed so utterly vulnerable.

"He's not coming," Albert said quietly. "There's no point in waiting any longer."

Sally lifted her head and took off her sunglasses. She saw a rumpled man with enlightened eyes and a face that was creased with sympathy. She was unable to speak.

"Do you mind if I sit down?"

Sally shrugged; she felt as if she were in a vast, unending vacuum. She watched the untidy man sit before her.

"What do you want?" she whispered.

"I'm a policeman," Albert began, and saw that

there was no reaction. "And I know what has to be done."

"Done?"

"I am part of it."

"No." Sally's eyes went to the untasted cups of tea. "You can't be. Not a...policeman."

"Where were you taking him?"

Sally closed her eyes. "Away," she whispered.

"Where?"

"To the mountains. To a village." Sally sat in her own darkness; it was not difficult to respond to the voice of the stranger. "He said he'd been happy there when he was a child."

"Tonbridge," Albert said, as if he were correcting a simple error. "He must go back to Tonbridge."

"He didn't say anything about that."

"What did he tell you about himself?"

Sally opened her eyes wearily; they were blue-gray, Albert noticed, with small flecks of hazel. He was strongly aware of her attraction as he watched her shake her head.

"What were you going to do when you got there?" Albert asked, studying the girl. "How were you going to stop him?"

"What has he done?" Sally thought it strange that she could accept this man who called himself a policeman so readily, but it was a miracle to be no longer alone.

"When did you see him last?"

"He went to talk to that...that man who sold us the tickets." Sally lifted her hand, presenting tickets like worn promises. "I think he knew who we were. I think he wanted money or something."

"You've been here ever since?"

"Simon said he wouldn't be long, he said he was coming. He told me to wait for him here." Sally's eyes went from the tickets to a clock above the canteen entrance. "It's late," she said sadly, as if she had only just acknowledged the passage of time. "We're not going to make it."

"If he didn't tell you anything about himself," Albert began, his voice soft, his eyes not missing anything, "how did you know where to go?"

"I didn't say that." Sally hung between silence and response. She was afraid of sounding disloyal, and yet the presence of sympathy was almost overwhelmingly tempting. It would be such a relief to be rid of it all. "He told me he'd run away from home but he ...he didn't say where...home was."

"He had no socks?" Albert placed the remark carefully. They'd remained beside the drunken sleeper together with his undergarments; their rejection showed a certain fastidiousness. "That's right, isn't it? You had to give him a pair."

"Yes." Sally was suddenly very still. "What else *do* you know?"

"Everything," Albert replied simply.

"Do...do you know that he's changed?"

"Yes." Albert saw the throat that had been dragged from the ticket clerk. "And will have again."

"Oh, Jesus..." Sally's voice was suddenly a murmur. "What...what will he look like now?"

Albert swallowed. "We won't know," he said, his own tone uneasy. "Until we find him."

"We?"

"Yes. We should do it together."

Sally could no longer bear to look into the stranger's eyes. She bent her head again and found herself staring at the crumpled tickets. Very slowly she began tearing them to shreds. "Do you know Cyril Fenick?" she asked after a moment.

Albert shook his head.

"Who are you?" Sally eyes remained on the rubbish she was creating. "How do you know so much?"

Albert leaned forward. "What did he call him?" he asked softly. "This Fenick? What did he say he was?"

"A Changeling." Sally's voice could barely be heard. "A Child of the Moon."

"They used the term Moonchild," Albert said softly. "Eighty-five years ago."

"He's that...old?"

"Older. No one knows when it began."

"He said..." Sally turned her gaze upward so that she spoke to the polystyrene ceiling, to the strip of neon overhead. "Cyril Fenick told me that an accident released him and that...that an accident would return him. I thought he meant Bavaria, where Simon was when he was little. But Fenick didn't really know; he was drunk when I saw him the last time. I don't think he could face it sober."

"What else did he say?"

Sally told him everything. There was no alternative. He was sympathetic and informed, and while he remained anonymous, it was not difficult to tell him everything she knew. She kept her eyes on the pale gray patches of plastic insulation in the brightly lit ceiling. She spoke steadily, in short clear sentences, and was surprised at how easily it all came out.

Albert listened silently, watching the long, vulnerable neck as the words here issued; her Adam's apple moved when she swallowed. Between her statements Albert could hear how grateful she was to be able to share.

"Did you know what he'd done?" Albert asked when the girl seemed to stop. "Outside The Half Moon?"

"No. I mean, I guessed. I was in a shop and I heard them talking. And, he'd changed. Fenick said he'd... change. He said that's how I'd know, but it was too late then, I was...involved with him." Sally lowered her head and looked fully into Albert's eyes. "I... loved him," she said. "I did, before...before he changed." She sighed with great sadness. "I love him still," she whispered.

"Will you help me?"

Sally's gaze remained steady. "What do you want me to do?" she asked.

"He must be taken back to Tonbridge."

"For . . . an accident?"

"We'll see."

"What has to be done?"

Albert didn't tell her. "We must find him first," he said. "Do you think he'll try to leave the country alone?"

"No." Sally thought of Simon in her apartment in the London square. "He won't go anywhere on his own." She recalled his behavior after he'd killed in the mews. "He'll find somewhere and then he'll sleep. Last night, after we'd talked of leaving, that's all he wanted to do."

"Will you help me?"

Very slowly Sally Lawrence nodded. "What will he look like now?" she asked.

Albert stood and held out his hand. "Come on," he said softly. "We've got to find him. Tonight. Before it gets light."

Sally took the outstretched hand, Albert helped her to her feet, knowing that she would be both benefit and burden.

Between them they shared all there was to know

Twenty-one

~

WHAT REMAINED of Simon Blackstone awoke in the chamber of night. Freezing air drifted about him, the cement on which he crouched was like a glacier, and the black hair which now grew from his nostrils contained particles of ice.

He did not know how long he'd been where he was or what had brought him to this frightful place. The sour smell of an oily sea, of dead creatures washed up on an unclean shore, was all about him. In the distance was the sound of a siren screaming.

The beast now possessed him almost entirely. He hung between the frightful power that was his for the calling and a dazed and murky appreciation of what he might have been, before it had sown its deadly seeds in his vacant soul.

Physically he had altered completely. His body was knotted and covered with hair; sinewy wrists and clawed hands protruded from the shredded arms of his pullover; his apelike feet extended from the remnants of his jeans. The anorak had been lost somewhere between the confrontation on the walkway and this angle of concrete in which he lay above the swirl of the ugly sea.

His face was black, and the bones of his skull seemed to press through the flesh; his wolflike teeth showed permanently; his mane of dirty white hair lay matted and thick. Only in the small red eyes was there something of the child, the youth, the man who had been seeking a future path that did not lead downward, an ending that was not filled with rage.

What Simon had become lifted its head and sniffed the sullen air. There were images in the ice: a woman leaned on a croquet mallet; a handsome man held a razor strop; there was a girl who looked like a gypsy. Of them all, she was the clearest; of them all, it was her innocent face he saw most vividly.

For a moment the creature's brain cleared.

He had tried to save her, he recalled, passed her responsibility of guiding him to someone who had accepted it greedily, who now lay dead behind him. What remained of the human being within the beast wondered if that act had been enough, if the girl had, in fact, been excluded. He hoped so. He grunted as his mind began to darken once again. She had given him herself, she had dreamed with him, she had planned with him—and they had almost succeeded.

They would have voyaged together to the nameless village in the lost mountains if it had not been for the Guardian. He had come again, as he'd come before, when it suited him best, and each time he had given his life to prevent an escape.

The last had been when the casket containing the Moonchild had burst as it was lowered into the hole in which the creature was doomed to remain. He, Simon, the Moonchild, would have broken free but for the intervention of the Guardian, who had held him and died with him and whose bones and belt buckle had remained beside him all those years.

What now remained of Simon Blackstone knew that there was no question of returning to the village, of going back as Master of them all. The second death of the Guardian had killed that black ambition. Now he lay huddled in a corner of ice, waiting, not knowing what for, certain only that there were others out there, seeking.

The creature moaned softly and thought again of the girl who had helped him, who had shown him the shape of peace, who had loved him once and, perhaps, loved him still. Suddenly he was aware of her presence. It came to him like fire through the ice-cold, biting air.

The creature's numb, questing face peered into the darkness. He moved clumsily in the niche in which he crouched as the animal force surged back to overwhelm him, to suppress everything else. He felt his rage return like thunder as he heard the sound of distant movements; he waited.

When they came, he would be ready for them, whoever they were. He no longer thought of the girl.

Albert Scot led Sally back to the ticket office where he found Detective Constable Lazenby standing alone; Jock McLeod had already returned to his counter and was dealing with traffic for the next ferry.

The Dover policeman shifted his feet when he saw Albert approach; his eyes went questioningly to the elfin, dark-haired girl. "Sir?" Lazenby asked. "There's no sign of the gent then?"

Albert shook his head. "She's agreed to help," he said quietly.

"I see, sir." Lazenby waited. He trusted the crumpled detective. It was a long time since he'd encountered anyone who inspired such respect. "Do you want me to remain here or..." Lazenby hesitated, unsure of what he was asking. "Or would you like me to accompany you on the search? It's all the same to me, if you understand what I'm saying."

Albert looked up at the tall blond man with the open, country face and felt a surge of gratitude. "Thank you," he replied softly.

"You finished with him, sir?" Lazenby nodded toward Jock McLeod. "I've taken the liberty of telling him we'll call him when we need him. But, if you'd like someone to mind him for a bit..."

Albert shook his head. "He's not important," he said.

"The other one's gone." Lazenby's eyes went to Sally's stiff face and away again. "I suppose you heard the ambulance?"

Albert did not reply; he'd heard nothing but Sally's voice in the hollowness of the canteen.

"Well, sir"—Lazenby stood very still—"where do you think we should start?"

"He'll be sleeping." It was Sally who spoke, her voice a whisper. "By now he'll be sleeping."

"It's no night for that outdoors, Miss...?" Lazenby's inquiry was respectful.

Sally told him her name.

"The cold, Miss Lawrence, it's perishing. We'd better start with the hotels along the waterfront. You think he might have gone to one of those?"

Sally looked at Albert. "He doesn't know, does he?" she said; the tone of her voice was despairing.

"Not yet." Albert turned to Lazenby. "We're not sure what we're looking for," he began.

"Sir?"

"It's unlike anything you'll have dealt with... ever."

"I'm...I'm beginning to understand that."

"He'll be hiding," Sally said. She could not bring herself to explain; she hoped only that when the time came, one of them would know what to do. "In the dark," she added, her words like small, cold stones. "Away from everything."

251

"Should we try the breakwaters, sir?" Lazenby stood upright and waited. "Along the seafront there's places where... something might hide."

"Yes," said Albert, "let's get started."

They went out into the raw cold, down the metal steps where Jimmy Singer had led Simon Blackstone, and felt the metal shift with their weight; they stood for a moment in the pool of light and heard the rattle of the sea as it lapped the pebbled beach. They walked away from Admiralty Pier, along the seafront where the lowering tide had left breakwaters like beached whales at intervals along the cove. They went away from the ice cavern in which the Changeling lay, they went along the low-lit, awkward shoreline beneath a wall of wet, encrusted concrete. They walked carefully and silently, filled with their singular fears, their eyes following the thin beams of flashlights that went, seemingly of their own accord, to each deepening of blackness, to every irregularity they encountered.

They found no sign of any living creature; there was not even a crab amongst the sea litter thrown up along the coastline. They saw bottles and cans and sheets of plastic; they encountered spars and splinters and once the body of a decaying dog, but nowhere was there any sign of life.

The cold stung and pierced, numbed their feet and hands, burned their nostrils, and brought tears to their searching eyes; it seemed to still them before they took a further step. It was the only life force along the stretch of desolate coast.

"He's not here, sir," said Lazenby after what seemed an interminable time. "I have the feeling we're not going to find anything along here tonight."

"No." Albert lifted his head. The buzzing was growing fainter. "We've come too far."

"He'll be sleeping," Sally said woodenly, as if they should have paid more attention to her earlier. "He'll have found somewhere to sleep."

Together they turned and began to trudge back toward the pier, stepping through the trash, climbing over the sullen breakwaters, going back to where they'd begun.

This time they searched beneath the pier. As they walked slowly along the pathway their flashlights picked up the patch of blood, now covered with sand an ambulance man had thoughtfully provided, which marked the place of Jimmy Singer's death. Nothing moved apart from the flow of the sea, the drifting weed about the giant pillars, and the slime that marked the coming and going of the tide. Their breath billowed in the freezing air; their footsteps rang empty and hollow as they continued from one side to the other without sight of what remained of Simon Blackstone.

"He's not here, either," Lazenby said. "Where should we try next, sir?"

"He's here." Albert looked back into the dark. "I'm sure of it now." He'd felt something as they'd passed beneath the pier, a buzzing in his ears, a distinct, inescapable call. Its presence had increased and then begun to fade; he knew now precisely where to look. "I'll show you."

"Yes, sir." For the first time Lazenby sounded doubtful. "Back there again, you say?"

Albert nodded and began once more along the walkway. After a second or two Lazenby, pulling his cloth cap more firmly onto his head, went with him. Sally accompanied wordlessly.

Albert, his head turned very slightly to one side as if listening, the flashlight steady in his hand, walked surely until he came to a pillar beneath the center of the pier. He stopped, closed his eyes, and concentrated; the buzzing rang throughout his head, rampant as a hive of bees. He turned the torch light upward.

It revealed a groin of concrete, the edge of a wider support that protruded some eighteen inches on either side of a beam. On it, in a faint film of frost, were twin lines of claw marks, as if something had leapt at the hiding place.

Albert stepped a pace or two backward, the flashlight not moving from the spot above his head. The skin of his entire body shrank suddenly, as if every particle of him was attempting to withdraw from what he knew he was foredoomed to see. His body was issuing a warning: flee or prepare to die.

He saw the first of the movements, a twitch in the darkness just beyond the reach of the torchbeam, the faintest stirring of shadow on shadow, as if the darkness itself had shifted. Then eyes above him opened.

Albert knew a moment of perfect blinding fear; sweat sprang from him in spite of the cold, the torch in his hand trembled, and he opened his mouth to cry but no sound came.

It took every ounce of courage he possessed to remain and watch the eyes stare down at him in red and bitter hatred, to burn through him in fury.

With enormous effort Albert held his fear as the black lips lifted, as the teeth sprang in the light and the wolf-snarl came from the animal above. He heard the breaths of the others pull in, the uncertain movements of their feet on the walkway as they waited for him to decide. Their terror gave him strength. His hand steadied, the beating of his heart slowly resumed, and he lifted his head and cleared his throat.

"Simon Blackstone," he said, his own voice a growl. "I have come to take you home." The words echoed throughout the hollow beneath the pier like a sounding in a grave.

Above him the teeth drew back and a claw-hand extended down toward the offending light; from it dangled the silver bracelet. The cross jumped in the flashlight's beam.

"Oh, my God," cried Sally, and her call released them.

The sinewed arm and the bracelet went back into

darkness. Albert felt a surge of power; his hand was about his grandfather's pistol. Lazenby came closer.

"Is that, sir..." Lazenby swallowed, not believing what he had seen. "Is that what we've been looking for?"

"Yes," said Albert.

"That's what...did for him, the chap from the ticket counter?"

"He has killed them all."

"Then, sir"—Lazenby sounded uncertain—"I'd better go for help."

"There is no need," said Albert. "He'll come with us."

"It's not him anymore," Sally whispered, staring up into the red eyes, the black lips above the threatening teeth. "There's nothing left of...Simon."

"It's what he's always been, beneath the skin. Each time he's killed, the beast has come closer to the surface." Albert held the flashlight steady; beside him he felt the girl's pain leap. "You know that," he added softly. "Fenick must have told you."

"He's..." Sally's voice was a whisper; in her mind's eye was the glint of silver, the stamp of identity. "...he's wearing it."

"The bracelet?" Albert knew the importance of silver. "Did you give it to him?"

"Fenick had it...he said it would...bind him."

"It will."

"What...?" Sally attempted to face a truth. "What do we have to do?"

"Take him home." Albert's words went upward; his voice lifted. "You know that, don't you, Simon? We're here to take you home."

"You're..." Lazenby took a step closer. "You're not thinking of actually handling that, sir?"

"He'll come with us." As Albert spoke, the eyes above moved quickly from one side to the other, as if in search of escape. "He knows he must go back."

"You're sure of that?"

"I'm sure."

"But, after what he did." In spite of himself Lazenby shivered. "That wound, sir, the man's throat was, well, you saw for yourself."

"They were enemies," Albert said simply. "We are his friends."

Lazenby stared at Albert in open disbelief.

"We will not hurt him," Albert continued in the same simple tone. "He knows who we are."

Lazenby took a deep breath. "In that case, sir..." he said, and stepped closer to the ledge above.

His height enabled him to reach the concrete shelf. He lifted a cautious hand to explore the possibility of grasping the creature and urging it from its hiding place. But he'd not completed half the distance when, with a slashing blow blurred by the flashlight beam, the arm of the Changeling flashed down. There was a crash of ripping material, a cry from Lazenby, and the curling snarl of a beast at bay. Blood ran down Lazenby's arm.

There was scuffling, as if what remained of Simon Blackstone might spring from the ledge. Then Sally's voice cut through all other sound. "Simon," she said clearly. "*I'm* here, Simon. It's me. Don't be afraid, I'll help you."

Immediately there was silence beneath the pier, a deep, still silence broken only by the lapping of seawater against the encrusted piles.

"No, miss." Lazenby grasped his torn arm. "Don't get close. Those claws, they're like razors."

"He will not harm *me*," Sally replied, repeating Cyril Fenick's words, believing them because there was nothing else to believe. "He knows *I* am here to help him."

Lazenby lifted his bloodied arm. "Look what he did to me."

"He doesn't know you," Sally replied. "He doesn't trust anyone but me." She turned to Albert. "He's frightened of you," she went on, a sureness in her

256

voice. Of them all she alone could approach, could do what needed to be done. "If you leave me with him he'll come down."

"Miss Lawrence..." Lazenby began, but Sally continued.

"Wait for me," she commanded, "at the foot of the stairs." She paused, then added, "We won't be long."

"Do you want a torch?" asked Lazenby hesitantly.

"No."

"Are you...?" Albert looked into her determined eyes. "Are you sure?"

"I am. Leave us alone."

Albert nodded and, without looking back, walked away. Lazenby's eyes went from the detective to the girl; he would never be able to explain this to anyone. He said nothing, and followed.

When they reached the pool of light at the bottom of the metal staircase, Albert stopped. "Let me look at your arm." His voice was expressionless.

"It's all right, sir."

"Does it hurt?"

"Yes, sir, but it will be all right."

"You think we're mad, don't you?"

"Well, yes and no, sir." Lazenby licked his chilled lips nervously. "Do you think you could tell me some of it, just for my own satisfaction, if you understand what I mean."

"I can't." Albert looked up at the big honest face, at the doubt in the eyes; pain had given new lines to the mouth. "Not now."

"I see, sir." Emptiness remained in Lazenby's voice. He coughed awkwardly. "I'm a religious man, myself, and some of that mightn't take too much talking about, but this, this is...different."

"Is it?" Albert looked away.

"Yes, sir." Lazenby waited, staring at Albert's closed face. "Do you think she'll get him to come out, sir?" he asked after a while.

Albert's eyes flicked back quickly.

"I mean, she mightn't." Lazenby looked past Albert to the black entrance of the walkway beneath the pier. "Have you considered that, sir?"

Albert did not reply.

"That... that thing in there's not human. She'd be no match for it if, well, you know what I mean. I think we should send for a marksman, sir. Someone with a high-powered rifle."

Albert tried not to listen. He stood perfectly still in the invading cold. He knew that if he began to acknowledge what Lazenby was saying, his own determination would dissolve, and with it, everything would be lost. He waited, using the intense cold as a weapon, forcing himself against it, excluding everything else.

"I think we've reached a stage," Lazenby began again. "I mean, with all respect, sir, I think the time's come to call in some of the others. You've done your best, you've found him and, well, we tried, didn't we?" He touched his wounded arm. "But there comes a time when no one can expect... I mean, sir, she's been in there alone with it for more than ten minutes now. Anything could have happened."

Albert forced himself to be still.

Lazenby could not stop. "If you don't mind, sir"—he coughed slightly to ease the decision—"I think I'll just go back upstairs and use the phone. I won't make a fuss about it, but I'll ask a couple of the lads to come down with a rifle, just in case, you know. So that there's more than the two of us should there..." Lazenby's voice died away. He stared at a hint of movement in the darkness of the walkway.

Neither of them spoke. They remained fixed, their eyes boring the blackness, hoping for something they did not dare believe.

Slowly, as if coming through a fog, the figure of Sally Lawrence appeared. At first it seemed she was alone—there was no sign of anyone or anything with her—then they saw that she walked with one hand behind her. As she emerged farther into the light it became clear that she led the Changeling by the silver chain she had once placed about his wrist.

As soon as he was certain Albert ran forward. "Stop," he said quietly but forcefully. "Don't come out any farther. Someone might see."

Sally waited; behind her the creature halted like a dog on a lead.

"Holy Jesus," said Lazenby, moving closer. "I'd never have credited it."

"Get the car." Albert handed Lazenby the keys. "Bring it round to the promenade." He paused. "Can you drive with that arm?

"Yes, sir." Lazenby's voice was a mixture of awe and relief. "I'll manage." He pointed up to the sea wall above. "There's some steps about fifty yards along there. I'll bring the car round to the top." He left, grateful for something to do.

Albert turned back to Sally; he opened his mouth to speak, but the distress in her eyes stopped him. He saw strength and determination and the saddest, most heart-rending despair he had ever witnessed. It filled him with pain merely to know it existed. It caused his own eyes to moisten, and he was obliged to look away

"My God," he whispered, but the words were for himself alone. "What did she have to do?"

They waited, a small unmoving tableau in the devouring cold: Sally held her head up. Albert looked across the dark sea. The shambling figure remained where it had paused, almost asleep.

Presently they heard Lazenby calling and, together, went up the stone steps and from there to the car.

Sally led the Changeling by the wrist. She entered the back of the car and the half-clad, dark, and hairy figure followed, one hand held to its eyes as if even the faint light from the street was more than it could bear. Only once did it look at Albert, and then the

259

red eyes focused for a moment in puzzlement, in question, as if it would know more of the power the short, untidy policeman held. After that it curled in a corner of the backseat beside Sally and gave the impression of knowing nothing of its surroundings.

Lazenby stood uncertainly as Albert got into the driver's seat. "Would you like me to come along with you, sir?" he asked quietly.

"No." Albert started the motor. "We must do this alone." He looked out at the tall, confused detective. "Thank you," he said simply. "Now get someone to look at that arm."

"Yes, sir." Lazenby paused. "The, ah, report, sir? What would you like me to do about it?"

"Nothing."

"Nothing, sir?"

"Not yet. I'll be in touch with you later. But in the meantime I'd appreciate it if you didn't say anything to anyone."

"I see." Lazenby nodded. "Then you be careful, sir. It's quiet now." His eyes went to the creature in the back of the car. "But it mightn't always be like that."

"Thank you." Instinctively Albert checked the weight of the pistol in his raincoat pocket; its presence was essential. "I'll be careful."

"Yes, sir." Detective Constable Lazenby stepped away from the car. "Good night, sir."

"Good night."

Albert put the Vauxhall into gear and drove away. He turned the car in a westerly direction and headed for Tonbridge.

Behind him Sally was silent. The Changeling stirred uneasily.

Twenty-two

FOR OVER AN HOUR Sally Lawrence held the silver-linked bracelet between thumb and forefinger while Simon slept restlessly beside her. She still thought of him as Simon, no matter how he'd altered, no matter what he'd done. To her he would remain the lost young man she'd befriended, the lover she had held. He was someone with whom she'd shared a love that had not faltered in spite of the changes and the terrors and the threats that surrounded it. It was the kernel of that love which gave her the strength she needed to endure.

She sat rigidly upright in the backseat of the lurching car, staring past the shape of Albert Scot hunched over the wheel. She watched the patch of light, thrown forward by the headlamps, move ahead over cold, black, winding asphalt. She stared steadfastly, willing time to absorb her, trying not to think of what would happen when they arrived at their destination. But she began to wonder if the short, untidy policeman really knew what lay in front of them and how this bleak and frightening journey through the night would end. She regretted he had not told her more. She *must* know more, what lay ahead, what had to be done to be rid of the nightmare. Desperation began to throb through her head like migraine.

Finally she could contain herself no longer and asked, in a voice that was far too loud, "What do we do when we get there? What will happen? Do you know?"

"Yes," Albert replied immediately. He did not know how much he could tell her, how much she would be able to take. "I know."

"Tell me..." Sally controlled her voice. "My God, please tell me, what's going to... happen."

"It will end."

"How? Do you know how?"

"We must go to where he was buried last time. We must return him to his grave."

"*No.*" The word was instinctive. Sally would not allow herself to imagine what Albert's suggestion meant. "We can't—"

"Didn't Fenick tell you what had to be done?" Albert interrupted. The girl's distress was piercingly harsh. "Didn't he say he had to go back?"

"He... he didn't say anything. I mean, he didn't tell me exactly what was going to happen."

"Perhaps he'll stay there." Albert tried to sound as if he believed it. "When he gets back, maybe he'll ... want to return."

"Do you think so?"

"It's possible." For the first time in days Albert felt the need for a cigarette. "We'll... we'll have to see."

"He... Simon asked me to bind him with silver." Sally's voice held a desperate hope. "Do you think that might keep him where he has to stay?"

Albert glanced over his shoulder to see the bracelet held loosely in her fingers.

"That's why he's quiet now," Sally went on. "That's why I gave it to him. It keeps him quiet."

Albert did not reply. The weight of the pistol with its single silver bullet hung in his raincoat pocket; each time they swung round a bend he was aware of its company.

"Do you think it would work?" Sally could not stop herself. "Did it work last time?"

Albert cleared his throat. "Last time there was a Guardian," he said steadily, "someone to keep him in place. It was a German inspector called Fuchs. He didn't know it, but that's what brought him to Tonbridge. He was destined to die with the...Moonchild, to be buried with him, to keep him there."

"How...how did Simon get out?" The conversation helped. Whatever she learned it would be better than just sitting in the dark, waiting.

"They're tearing up the area he was buried in to put in a car park. A bulldozer driver dug up the coffin." Albert paused very slightly. "He's dead, too."

"An accident released him." Sally's voice was brittle. "That's what Cyril Fenick said."

"Yes. Digging him up was an...accident."

"Is that what got you involved?" Sally found it was becoming easier. Talking to the back of Albert's head had the same anonymity as speaking to plastic squares in the ceiling of the ferry canteen.

"Yes," Albert replied, his eyes on the road. "But it began before that. My grandfather helped the German inspector. Fuchs wrote a long report, describing everything he'd discovered, the night before he died. He gave it to my grandfather to send to an inspector they both knew in London." Albert changed gear, and the motor rose as it ground up a hill. "My grandfather read it before he posted it. It...it involved him then."

"What did he tell you?"

"Practically nothing. He was a very old man when I knew him, but I found the report. I read it today. It spoke about what happened last time, what had to be done then." Albert swallowed. "It will be the same now."

"Will it?" Sally's voice dropped to a whisper.

Albert nodded.

"Who...?" Sally could barely force herself to shape the question. "*Who will be the Guardian this time?*"

Albert felt her words go through him like fragments of glass.

The same thought had occurred to him frequently in the past hours; each time he'd put it aside. He had no answer, and there was no point thinking about it. Each would do what had to be done; nothing of their fates could be avoided. But the bleakness of the girl's tone and the directness of her question was too demanding; he must tell her something.

"There may not be a Guardian this time," Albert said, keeping his tone even. "Many things have altered. It's not the same as it was before. Last time Simon remained a child; he didn't grow at all. Only his arm was affected. But it's different now, this time; with each killing he's aged twenty or thirty years, and now ... well, you know what he's become. It's not the same."

"You said it was." Sally's voice rose; she could not control it. "When we get there, you said it would be the same."

"Please." Albert found himself shouting also. "Some of it, maybe, but certain things *have* altered. He's met you this time, that's different."

"*Am I the Guardian?*"

"I don't know. Please believe me. I don't know." Albert felt the car racing; he slowed it down deliberately and lowered the level of his voice. "I promise you," he said more evenly. "I don't know anything about that part of it at all."

"No one does." Sally whispered the words, forcing

herself to be still. "Even you... even you can't explain why there's all this violence."

"I..." Albert cleared his throat. "I can't explain all of it, but I do know that these manifestations occur much more frequently than any of us realize."

"Not like this." Sally's voice was cold; she could not look at Simon, who sat quietly beside her. "Not this way."

"They come in many forms."

"Does it...?" Sally closed her eyes tightly. "Does it have a name?" Anything, she thought, to deny.

"Yes, it's called lyncanthropy. A human adoption of a wolf form... a sort of possession."

"That... that doesn't explain it." There was contempt in Sally's voice. "That's just a... word."

"Maybe there's no explanation," Albert went on levelly. "These forces, powers, whatever you like to call them, are with us. They have always been with us. Sometimes they're good and sometimes they're evil. No one can ever tell."

"Until it's too late." Sally gripped the bracelet; suddenly she held Simon more firmly. "Is that what you're trying to tell me?"

"Yes," said Albert. "Until you meet it."

"But—"

"There aren't any buts," Albert interrupted quietly. "It could happen to any of us. We're all still so primitive. It was only in the last century that they stopped hammering stakes through the hearts of suicide victims to keep demons away."

"What happened last time?" Sally asked abruptly. "What did he do?"

"Simon?"

"Yes, Simon."

"He..." Albert gripped the wheel. "Do you really want to know?"

"Yes."

"He killed four people." Albert's voice remained steady. They did not have far to go now, less than half an hour; if he could keep her talking until they arrived it would be easier for them both. "He died, you see, as a child. He caught a fever in this Bavarian village and it... it seemed to kill him. His parents purchased a casket, and they were going to bring him home for burial, but he wasn't dead, not really; he was in a trance and whatever possessed him took control." Albert glanced at Sally in the rearview mirror; she listened intently.

"They traveled by coach and by train and by boat on their way back to Tonbridge," he continued. "And everywhere, at each stage of the journey, he was able to get out into the light. To get free. There was a coach crash, and the casket broke open. There was a railway man in France who opened it of his own accord. Even on the cross-Channel ferry there was someone else who tried to release him. It was the light he responded to then; it activated him. He was sensitive to light, any light; it brought out the... beast immediately." Albert glanced at the girl again. Her elfin face was still with listening; her eyes had not moved.

"And that's something else that's changed," Albert went on. "God knows what's caused these changes, but they've happened. Anyway, then, the light made him... kill."

"Who did he kill?" Sally's voice was as cold as the outside air.

"His governess," Albert replied, aware of the significance. "She was the first."

"Being close to him was no protection?"

"No." In spite of his efforts to keep control Albert felt the car begin to accelerate. "But you've got to realize that something happened in all the years he was in his grave. He's—my God, he's no longer a child."

"You sure he ever was?"

"Yes, when the bulldozer driver opened the coffin he *was* a child. I know." Albert's voice was becoming shrill again. He protested to her, to himself, to the creature who was listening. "I've seen the clothing he wore. It was a boy's sailor suit. It burst when he grew out of it. Really, it's not the same as it was before." He put both hands on the wheel and gripped it firmly. "This time there will be no need for a Guardian." He thought of the silver bullet in his grandfather's pistol. "This time he will...stay."

Sally closed her eyes. For nearly a century Simon had been torn with pain and misery; now it seemed that anything was worthwhile to save him from more. And, she was becoming aware, in herself, of an overpowering need for rest. "Who else did he kill?" she whispered.

"The coachman," Albert replied, fighting the speed of the car. "And the railwayman. Both were by the open casket when the light got in and the Moonchild killed them."

"And...he killed his Guardian?"

"Yes, he had to. Fuchs died with him in the grave."

"Perhaps he didn't die." The suddenness of Sally's thought filled the interior of the Vauxhall. "Simon came back; perhaps the Guardian has come back, too."

"We...we found his bones."

"Does that make any difference?"

"Yes." Albert found himself grappling with a force he didn't understand. His voice was uneven; the car raced ahead. "They were there in the grave."

"It's not bones we're talking about." Sally watched the highway pitch toward them; the white lines had become a blur. "Flesh and blood have nothing to do with it."

"It doesn't matter—"

"It does."

"Listen—"

"You're driving too fast." Sally's voice had become harsher; it held something deeper and darker than she had ever known. "You know that, don't you?"

Even she did not understand where the words came from. "You'll kill us all if you drive like this. There's ice on the road."

"What?" Albert half-turned, frightened by the sound behind him, desperate to know what had occurred. "What's that, who...?"

"There's ice ahead." The growl continued. "Look, there's a patch on the bend."

Albert's head jerked back. He only had time to see a sheet of blackness glinting in the headlamps before the tires hit it. He barely managed to swing the wheel into the skid before the car struck the ice and began to slide. He was aware of headlights spinning, of trees and bushes at the side of the road hurtling past, of a rising, grinding, enormous roar as the car seemed to break in two and the side of the road came up suddenly. There was the juddering of wheels on the embankment, a report as one of them burst. The steering wheel was torn from Albert's grasp. The last thing he remembered was his forehead breaking through the windscreen before the car lights were extinguished and the world went black.

Albert Scot had no idea how long he remained in a limbo of darkness, but it could not have been long, because when he became aware of the pain in his head, of warm blood running down past his right eye, the small tinklings that followed the accident had not yet ceased.

Very slowly, feeling for broken bones, he eased himself back into his seat. Apart from the gash on his forehead he appeared to be intact. His ribs hurt where they'd bent the steering wheel, one knee stung where it had hit the dashboard, his head throbbed steadily, but nothing was broken.

Then, with a feeling of sudden panic, he remembered those behind him and turned sharply, causing his breath to draw in quickly with pain, and stared into absolute, unyielding darkness. There was neither sound nor presence behind him. He felt, at once, frighteningly alone.

He turned away from the emptiness and, with mounting urgency, scrabbled in the glove compartment for a flashlight he knew was there. After a few seconds, he found it and switched it on, its beam cutting through the dust floating in the car. He turned it behind him and saw two pairs of eyes watching him unblinkingly. They glared back at him in the light that shook in his hand.

Albert opened his mouth and licked the dryness of his lips.

"It's all right," Sally said. Her voice had returned to normal. "We're still here."

"I..." Albert's throat blocked with the word; he coughed. "We hit some ice." He could think of nothing else to say.

"I know. I tried to warn you."

"Are you... are you all right?"

"We're both all right." Sally sounded as if she were speaking from a distance. "You're bleeding."

Albert touched his forehead.

"I... I couldn't avoid it." Albert watched her carefully, looking for some sign, something that might tell him where she stood, but could see nothing. He remembered the car racing of its own volition, the deep growl of her voice. Now she sat upright on the seat, the Changeling beside her, and stared at him levelly. "Has..." Albert found words difficult to form. "Is he... awake?"

"Yes," Sally replied. "Simon is awake." There was the faintest note of hostility in her voice. "Is the car still working?"

"I'll have to see."

"We'll wait here."

Painfully Albert got out of the Vauxhall, flashlight in hand. He walked round the vehicle, inspecting it. The off-side doors were dented and immovable; one tire was flat and the wheel buckled; the bonnet was knocked in where it had hit a tree and the headlight on that side was smashed. There was no way of knowing if the car would start again without getting back into the driving seat and turning the key, and Albert was suddenly aware of an overpowering reluctance to do so. He stood, the flashlight beam on the flattened wheel, one hand holding his ribcage, urging himself to return, to face whatever it was the vehicle contained, but no part of him responded.

The cold bit into his wounds, and began to sap his strength. It would be easy, he thought, to walk away; it would be so peaceful to close his eyes and sleep.

An owl hooted somewhere, and the clear, haunting call caused him to start. He could not default now—there were too many who had brought him here, too many who depended on him. Very slowly Albert went back to the car. He flicked the beam of light into the rear seat and, as he opened the door, two pairs of eyes, one normal, one fiercely red, watched him in parallel. Not a word was spoken.

Albert eased himself into the driver's seat. The steering wheel was bent where his ribs had been thrown against it and several switches on the dashboard had been broken by the crash of his knee, but the starter key was in position, and carefully holding his agonizing breath, he turned it and heard a slow whine from the motor.

Albert stopped and began again.

On the fourth attempt, with the battery faltering, the engine caught. Not all cylinders were firing; there was the constant slapping of something broken against the metal of the block, but it seemed there would be enough power to carry them the rest of their journey.

Albert turned the engine off. He reached for the light switch and found it was one of those broken by his knee. He flicked the stub of what remained, and the unsmashed headlamp glowed a dull and sickly yellow.

"I'll change the tire," Albert said, his voice unnaturally loud. "It will take a while."

"Do you want me to help you?"

"No." Albert's reply was instant. "Stay there. Keep him with you."

Sally's voice did not return from the dark.

It took Albert over half an hour to change the tire of the Vauxhall. Each effort was painful; each time he put his weight into undoing or resetting the nuts, it was agony. His breath went in and out of his damaged rib cage with stabs of fire. The cold gnawed his fingers, making them clumsy, causing him to drop the tire nuts again and again. There was a moment when the new tire, half in place, jammed, and the pain from the cold in his hands so intense that Albert almost failed. He allowed his head to fall forward against the battered metal of the car; he let the flashlight roll away into the frozen grasses by the side of the road.

He was about to yield when from somewhere came his mother's voice. He saw the sharp, birdlike face, the bright button eyes, and heard the clever voice saying, "He always said that, your grandfather did. He said you'd get there on your own." The voice grew louder. "Come on," it urged. "There's not all that far to go now. You can do it."

Albert found himself smiling. In the freezing air, the impossible pain in his fingers, blood congealing on his forehead, he found the corners of his lips twitching in an absurd smile. "Sod off," he whispered, and began to work again.

Somehow the new tire went into place. With movements that seemed endless, the tire-nuts were fitted and tightened. Then, leaving the ruined tire, the brace, and the jack in the grass by the side of the road, Albert climbed to his feet and went back to the driver's seat. He did not look behind him this time; he knew they were there. He started the motor, its crippled, uneven action vibrating the steering beneath his frozen fingers. He put the Vauxhall into gear, and, the single headlamp casting its weak and uncertain glow on the black strip of road before him, Albert resumed the limping journey onward to Tonbridge.

Outside, a mist began to rise, seeping upward out of frozen ground, binding the crippled vehicle and its occupants in wreaths of lapping gauze. Behind him Albert felt two pairs of eyes boring into the back of his neck like sharp, searing points of steel, but steadily he continued.

They began to descend to the town.

Then, in a moment of panic so intense that it caused him to shudder in his seat, Albert remembered his grandfather's pistol. It was gone, he was certain. He could not recall its reassuring weight in any instant since the accident; he wanted to open his mouth and shout, its need was so urgent. It took every effort that remained in his broken body to restrain himself, but quietly, so as not to indicate his loss to the others, he took one hand from the steering wheel and with fingers that burned—the circulation was returning—felt for the weapon.

It was not there. And then it was. It had been thrown forward and had caught in the lining of the raincoat pocket. It was still with him, and he allowed his hand to rest on it in comfort and in faith.

Slowly the agony began to ease. Finally Albert turned the car off the highway, and they began to crawl down the main street of Tonbridge, toward the swirling river mist at the bottom of the town, toward the open gash of the workings for the new car park where the Moonchild had been disentombed and the Changeling had been born.

The hearse was once more on its way.

Twenty-three

THE BEAST THAT LODGED in the soul of Simon Blackstone was aware of the dark end rising. He was aware
of familiar shackles in sodden earth. As comprehen-
sion began to beat through him, as it throbbed with
the steady rhythm of a drum, his mind came vividly
into focus.

He knew where they were now and why they were
going down through the town. He recognized the
power of the man who was conducting the vehicle.
It was ancient. It was formidable, and it had not ever
challenged him before. Once, a long time ago, he had
sensed it distantly, but the force had been oblique
and he'd ignored it; now it stood before him like a
door that must be smashed if he were to advance in
his chosen direction.

Yet, beside him was his friend; the innocent girl
remained. From the moment she had seen him, her
heart had gone out to him. She was strong, she had
done whatever she could at a time when it had been

needed most. She would do now what she believed he wanted—if she were guided correctly. For that was her only weakness: She did not know how to lead him in the direction his black heart preferred. The choice still lay between rage and power—and an impotent silence; to him the way was clear, but she would need to be piloted.

He had almost succeeded some miles from the town; then his strength had nearly brought her completely under control. She'd listened and she'd spoken; the driver had turned and they'd struck the ice. The vehicle had crashed as once before a coach along a country road had crashed and he had been thrown free; but this time it had not happened that way.

At the last moment, in the instant when the world spun about them and darkness closed in with a roar, she had renewed her grip on the bracelet; the fingers that had almost released him had tightened, and he was once again held.

It did not matter.

He, the beast that occupied body and soul of Simon Blackstone, the Moonchild, the Changeling, would be given a further opportunity. That which had occurred earlier was only a test, a probing, to see if the girl would respond—and the indications had been good. When the critical moment came, she would do what he wanted.

He lifted his head and sniffed the air. It was familiar. He knew every turn of this town, every tiny detail; he'd lain beneath this earth for over eighty years, through the waxing of a thousand moons, sensing the changes, aware of the alterations, waiting for the opportunity to escape, which had finally been given to him by a workman who had become greedy. Who had seen a silver lock and desired it. Greed had been the undoing of them all: the undertaker who became the scar-faced youth; the Guardian who had become a ticket-seller, yet who remained a Guardian still. And, as far as the others who lay before him were concerned, they would also fail because of their greed—it would be their ultimate undoing.

The beast that ruled the body and soul of Simon Blackstone waited; he had time.

And yet, within the same creature, sharing the same form, while the beast planned, a fragment of the heart of the copper-haired youth with the handsome features rebelled. From somewhere deeper but not yet destroyed, an aspect of initial goodness turned in protest. What remained of Simon, the young and tender lover, fought against the evil that squatted on his soul as the Vauxhall drove down into Tonbridge.

There was no indication of life in the town. Street lamps burned, but that was all. Houses were dark and silent and shuttered. No one moved; nothing broke the stillness, apart from the drifting, curling mist that rose up from the lowlands by the river as if to welcome him, the true Simon, back to the eerie cycle: conceived, born, to be interred above and below the same piece of earth.

That is what had been said last time and should be said again—unless those he relied on were not strong enough or brave enough to see him to his ending. He depended on them completely now, this girl beside him and the man who drove; he hoped they understood.

They must not be guided by the beast.

They must not be diverted, they must take him back to the place he had come from and restrain him there.

If he, and the creature who lodged in his soul, were restricted together, then what remained of his own innocence might be preserved. And the beast would be held.

And the girl he had loved?

The tiny flickerings of what was left of the innocence of Simon Blackstone squirmed and struggled...and listened as from somewhere a soft and ghostly voice whispered bravely that she could still be spared *if she walked away.*

The voice was clear. If she, the elfin girl who had saved him once and could do so again, were to leave him in his resting place and walk away, she would survive.

But how? he wondered as his small flame began to die and the power of the beast rose afresh. How could he ever let her know what she had to do?

The Changeling sat alert beside the girl. There was fire in his nostrils; his red eyes burned. He looked about him furtively.

Gently, so that if discovered it might be taken for a movement of the vehicle, he eased his left wrist away from the girl's fingers. Immediately she tightened her grip on the bracelet, and he was still.

It did not matter, he told himself, the time was not yet ripe. Soon the opportunity would come, and then she would respond in his favor. Then she would be with him forever.

He waited, dominant now, counting his time as the car crawled along the road at the bottom of the town. It made its way toward the mud and the turned earth, the stacks of concrete blocks, the mounds of sand and gravel, and the jungle of reinforcing steel, all of which stood upright in the ill-lit, watchmanless night.

For no one remained here after dark now. Since the death of the bulldozer driver, not even dogs patrolled this wasteland of construction material.

This was as it should be, the creature thought: ready for him to begin his final confrontation.

Sally sat upright in the limping car. Uneasily she leaned forward and peered past the shape of the policeman; he drove with only one hand now, the other held his ribs, which obviously gave him pain. She regretted his injuries but could do nothing to help;

he'd driven too fast, and black ice had caused the damage. She remembered trying to warn him, but it had had no effect.

But that was past now, she told herself. It was what lay ahead that mattered; she'd survived and she'd continue. Her sole responsibility was Simon; she would do whatever was required to return him to where he must remain—nothing else mattered. It was what he wanted, she believed, and she would see him to his rest.

Unless... Sally paused in her thinking, a sudden thought touching her, as if something new had entered her mind. She shook her head wearily. No, she must continue.

And once there... Again she felt a new thought tugging. Once there it would be... complete.

No. Again she shook her head. *He must go...back?*

Resolutely she held the bracelet.

She peered out of the car, seeking some indication that the frightful journey was almost done; she stared at the dark and alien landscape, searching for some relief from the desolation that threatened to sap her strength.

"Have you been here before?" she asked Albert suddenly, to break the silence that numbed her, to put aside the new thought that intruded. "Do you know where to go?"

"Yes." Albert's voice was hoarse. "I've seen where he came from."

"Is it far?" She must keep talking. "Tell me, is it far?"

"No. We are close." Albert swallowed; his body ached. "How...is he?"

"He knows." Sally lowered her voice. "He knows where we are."

"You're holding him?"

"I have the bracelet in my hand." Sally leaned a little closer. "It will keep him when we get there," she said, as if to convince herself. "The silver will be enough."

"Yes," Albert replied, his mind on another form of the metal. "It will be enough." He changed gears downward; the car was beginning to falter as if it, too, knew the end was nearing. "Last time there was a silver clasp on the coffin. That was enough."

"Until ... the accident?"

Albert nodded.

"Last time"—Sally voiced a question that had lain unanswered in her mind for almost all of the silent journey—"there was a report that explained everything." She paused. "It was sent to an English policeman, but nothing was done. Why?" Her voice rose slightly. "Why didn't they do something to prevent any ... accidents?"

"He didn't show it to anyone."

"Why not?"

"He killed himself."

"He didn't destroy it?"

"He destroyed himself instead."

"I see." Sally let out a long breath; she understood. What had occurred so long ago seemed to justify everything she now believed. "That's what the Guardian had to do, too," she said quietly. "Perhaps that's what we all must do."

"What do you mean?"

"We can't escape; none of us who has had anything to do with him will ever get away." Sally's voice became very still. "We must do whatever we have to ... to make sure there aren't any more accidents after this."

Albert opened his mouth but said nothing. She spoke the truth. No matter who he took with him, whatever price need be paid, the Changeling must be locked here forever—nothing else was acceptable. Albert felt sudden pain at the depths of the girl's understanding.

"It's all right," Sally continued, as if she'd read

his thoughts. "I don't mind, I feel quite calm about it. It will be such a relief when it's over."

Albert shivered and stared ahead. Through filtered, misty yellow light the wire gates of the building site came into view; one of them stood half-open as if expecting the vehicle and its contents. "We're here," he whispered.

With the words the Changeling's restlessness increased. He leaned forward and began to shudder; deep, low moans came from the back of his throat; his bright red eyes flickered from side to side, looking for an outlet, seeking an avenue of escape. The hand that carried the silver bracelet, still in Sally's fingers, remained quiet, but the other began to claw at the car's upholstery, to tear great gashes in the fabric.

"What's he doing?" Albert called, his eyes on the gate. The car would not go through.

"He knows. Hurry."

"I'll have to open the gate."

"Don't leave us."

"There's no room."

"Break it down."

Albert eased the car forward; it came up to the wire gate and pressed. There was the sound of scraping metal, the twanging of wire as the barrier began to slide away in the mud. Albert pushed the accelerator, and the car jumped, the gate opened, and the remaining headlamp went out. The car ground forward in the uneasy dark, in the little light from naked bulbs strung about the site, through the mist that rubbed against them.

"Hurry," Sally said.

Albert felt the creature behind him increase in agitation. The beast reached forward and gripped the seat behind Albert's head; talons dug into the headrest, and as the creature shook, hard, chilling vibrations shuddered through Albert's pain-racked body, taking his breath away, making it impossible

279

for him to see the track in the uneven light. Misty, swirling stacks and mounds seemed to block the landscape through which they crawled.

For a moment Albert lost his bearings and hung on the steering, allowing the car to carry him forward on its own until he recognized the beginnings of the trench the bulldozer had dug. The machine itself stood silent in the frozen mud; behind it, towering above the basement trench, was a structure Albert had not seen before—a high, massive wall filled the foundation trench the bulldozer driver had dug before he died. Nothing had halted the constructor's plans: the holding wall had been erected; cement had been poured that afternoon. The wall ran all the way to the corner where the coffin had been excavated; it almost obscured the place to which the Changeling must be returned.

Albert stared at it, trying to make out its detail, wondering what more there could be to overcome. Behind him the beast became still. He ceased his rocking of the driver's seat; his wolflike face lifted, and he stared at the new wall as if recognizing the beginnings of defeat.

"Are we here?" Sally whispered.

Albert nodded. He opened his door and eased through it.

"*We'll* get out now." Sally's words were precise; she forced herself on, toward the ending. "He'll be all right," she said determinedly. "As long as I'm with him."

Sally turned to the creature beside her. As if he were still the gentle youth who had held her, she placed a hand on the Changeling's arm. "Come on, Simon," she said gently, "we must go now."

The creature turned his red and restless eyes toward Sally questioningly and slowly removed his hand from the headrest; shreds of fabric hung from his claws. His moans became softer, more like the plea of some small animal seeking comfort, and he hunched toward her, allowing his black forehead and the mane of matted, whitened hair to rest against her shoulder.

Sally took a firm hold of the bracelet and led Simon out and away from the car.

"Where do we go?" she asked.

Albert held one hand to his damaged ribs; the other was deep in the raincoat pocket clutching the pistol. He limped toward the trench, his feet sliding on the frozen mud. "Here," he said.

"Come on," Sally urged Simon. "It's not far."

The Changeling moaned and peered from side to side; he pulled away from Sally, and the bracelet stretched between them.

"Simon." Sally's voice trembled, almost faltered. "Come along. I'll . . . I'll look after you. Don't worry, you're still my baby."

The Changeling turned his red eyes toward her; their expression was lost and pleading, their confusion pitiable. Albert watched, then looked away. The scene was too macabre, too poignant. It filled him with the saddest horror he had ever known.

There were movements beside him, and he dared not turn his head to witness them. He forced his eyes to travel the length of the wall of wet cement. A single unshaded globe burned at the far end of the wall; it sparkled in the frozen air. Black water stains ran down the wooden boarding which held the wet cement in place. Spikes of reinforcing steel protruded from the structure; some were hooked, some were straight, and to them the sequential phases of wall would be linked until the whole gray concrete edifice was complete, ready to house its vehicles.

Albert held his eyes on it, listening to the small sounds beside him, thinking how bizarre it was that the creature should be returned here, to be buried beneath this concrete, and how fitting.

"Where do we go?" Sally asked.

"There," Albert replied without looking back. "Where the light is."

They moved a step or two farther and then Sally asked, "This wall, was it here before?"

"No," Albert replied. "It's just been erected."

"Will it make any difference?" Sally's tone was uncertain. "Weren't they digging when they found Simon?"

"That was in the corner," Albert explained, listening to the crunching footsteps following his own. "It hasn't been covered over."

"But we must... we must have the exact place, isn't that right? Didn't you say so? That's what Cyril Fenick said, it had to be the right place." She had to force the words from her frozen lips. She thought only of each word as she formed it; she held back the pain and the terror that threatened to disarm her. She kept herself going by speaking. "Isn't that... so?" she stammered. "It... has to be the... right place."

"It is." Albert's voice was weary. "Believe me, it is. It's the right place. I've been here before." He looked ahead. Part of the hole at the end of the bulldozer's run was visible; a section of the cavity that had contained the casket remained outside the wall. Albert hoped desperately it would be enough, that the symbol was of greater value than the cavern itself. Somehow he would bury what remained of Simon Blackstone after the silver bullet had completed its task. Some way or another he must be able to cover the monstrosity, however frozen the earth, however monumental the effort, until professionals could be sent down to finish the job, to fill in more earth, to pour more concrete, to make sure the creature was not ever disentombed again, no matter how fixed it might seem to be, no matter how extinguished its evil may appear.

The small procession came to a halt at the end of the wall. There, amongst the hooks of steel, the heavy wooden shuttering, were the remains of the hole in the earth in which Simon Blackstone had lain so long. Albert stared at it in recognition; Sally viewed it with fear and relief; the Changeling's excited, coal-red eyes saw it with a mounting fury, a deep and wretched loathing. His hunched black body began to shake.

He shook in rage and impotence, shuddered with fury as his clawed feet crunched ice beneath them; he swung his burning eyes toward Albert, and the hooked fingers of his right hand curled, ready to strike while the other, the hand still linked to Sally, trembled with such intensity that the silver bracelet tinkled in the cold and bitter air.

This was his moment; now he must prevail be-cause... He shook his dark, matted head angrily, in mounting confusion. Because the girl was not re-sponding to his wishes. She had begun to think of freeing him—he had seen it in her eyes—but now ...now his power did not seem as effective.

She was evading him.

At the same time, within his twisted body the old tired forces he believed he had defeated were rising up again. From somewhere came the voice of the child, the words of the young man, the actions of the middle-aged companion who had tried to abandon the girl once but had failed. They rose about him, frail as leaves in the wind, attempting to divert her in these final moments.

No, he shouted to himself. No, not now. Not ever. Rage, he told himself, hurl your rage, fling it at them. Rage against this dying...

Turning to Sally, he curled back his lips and snarled.

"*Simon.*" Sally's voice was a plea. "*You must stay here. It's where you came from.*"

The growl rose in the Changeling's throat; the challenge of the beast was bursting for release. His shaking increasing, he turned from the hole to bolt into the surrounding darkness. Only the slender silver chain held him in place, prevented him from escaping into the wasteland of stone and cement that lay on either side.

"My God..." Sally felt the bracelet almost plucked from her fingers. "He's so... frightened."

"Move away," shouted Albert.

"I can't."

"You must." Albert had taken the pistol from his raincoat pocket; he held it behind him. "Get clear."

"I can't... I'm holding him."

"Put the bracelet over that." Albert pointed to a hook of reinforcing steel. "It will hold him."

With fingers that shook as much as the chain they held, Sally reached for the iron hook. Pain flooded every part of her being as she looped the entwined hearts over the protruding steel. She saw the silver cross dangle and watched Simon's arm follow the power of the bracelet and allow the linkage with the steel to be made. He stared at her dumbly until her fingers left him, until he was no longer aware of their touch on the chain, then his outrage burst like an outpouring of thunder.

The black flesh appeared to darken even more, the nostrils spread, the lips lifted away from the challenging teeth, every muscle in the squat body swelled until it stood distinct, tumescent with fire and anger. The free hand swept, its claws whined through the brittle air, reaching for Albert; the other, the hand chained with silver, the metal of the moon, rattled against its bindings.

"Get away." Albert shouted to Sally. His voice was filled with dread. "You've got to get clear."

"I can't go."

"You must."

"No."

Albert took the pistol from behind him. It was cocked and the hammer back ready to fire. He lifted it and aimed, but Sally remained with her back to him, her eyes on the monster. Albert shifted his

284

weight onto his damaged knee, but it would no longer sustain him; it seared with pain. All his wounds were suddenly agonizing and began to bleed afresh. To breathe was almost impossible. Blood ran down his forehead into one eye; his knee began to sag beneath him.

"Please..." Albert shouted as a thick cloud above him opened and the moon shone down in full, spreading its light over the whole of the building site, issuing strength to its creature trapped below. "There is no time."

"For what?" Sally turned and saw the pistol. "Oh, my God, no."

"I have to."

"No." Sally held out her arms. "I won't let you."

"It's silver." Albert's words hurled themselves at the girl. "The bullet. My grandfather left it. He knew. It's the only thing that will stop him. Please, it must be used."

As Sally's mouth opened, the Changeling began to shriek. It began as a low, deep hiss of rage, and it built upon itself, fed by the great force of the moon above it, until it reached a scream that threatened to destroy all that lay within range merely by its power alone. Sally opened her mouth, but her words were lost in the violent sound behind her.

Albert yelled into the fury of the frozen air. Holding himself against his pain, he stumbled to one side. In the light from above he could see part of the Changeling's face. It was turned toward him, the lips pulled back, the wolf teeth glistening. The free hand slashed in his direction. "I will," Albert cried out. "I must!"

He steadied the pistol, his finger on the trigger. The girl lurched toward him, her face distorted with possessive wrath. The Changeling tore at the silver that bound him, fighting for a last chance to survive. Albert pulled the trigger. He saw the barrel leveled at the raging head. He heard the explosion as Sally's hand reached him and the pistol was knocked away.

They tumbled headlong onto the ice-bound mud to slide from the Changeling, who was shrieking as he ripped at the silver that shackled him to the hook of steel.

All knew that in a matter of seconds he would be free. All heard the whimper of their own ending; each smelled the sulphur in the air.

Yet it was not the silver but the steel that gave. The bracelet remained intact, but the rod onto which it was linked tore from its moorings, bringing with it a tangle of linked metal, a splintering of boards. The wet concrete wall began to tumble.

Once begun there was no stopping it. The shuttering cracked from side to side; the steel bent like chicken wire; the wet, heavy, endless sludge, with a force that seemed greater than its mass, oozed from its bindings and slid down into the trench at its feet. Its relentless power was paralyzing.

Sally was the first to move. She climbed to her hands and knees and looked about her. Wet cement crawled toward her; it drew closer, a gray inexorable wave. She lifted her eyes to where Simon stood, his legs already encased in the thick material, his body surrounded by twisted spines of reinforcing steel. He stared down at the mass about him in astonishment, in disbelief, in strange acceptance. He was quiet now, the screaming had stopped, and his face was curiously still.

Sally turned to see Albert, one leg useless, his breath ragged, his face covered with blood, clawing at the icy ground, trying to scramble from the falling wall. Sally stumbled to her feet. The cement had reached her now.

She stared at Simon, then turned to Albert. She made her decision. Very slowly, as if there was all the time she would ever need, as if urgency had ceased to exist, she went to the fallen policeman and helped him upright.

Albert looked at her in disbelief.

"Come on," she said, her arm about him. "We've got to get out of here."

She walked away, leaving the dream intact.

She would retain her love for the handsome youth she had salvaged in the heart of the night-bound city; she would keep the memory alive of the copper-gold hair and the fine-boned features she had rescued from the dark. It did not matter now what he had become, or even that there had been so little time to share. What they'd had was enough.

Without a backward glance Sally lifted the crippled policeman to his feet and put her arm about him.

"Let's go," she said in a voice once more under control. "It's time to leave."

Albert held her, and they began to climb upward toward the car, away from the tumbling wall, the sea of concrete, the Changeling bound with silver.

Once they stopped and turned together to look back at the rising tide of gray, liquid stone. They saw the creature in the corner bend and swing away from them. He seemed to begin to burrow into the sludge, to dig with his great, clawed hands into the rising tide of concrete, but whether in an attempt to escape or to return to the cavity whence he had sprung, neither of them would ever know.

"Why?" Albert asked from the safety of the higher ground.

"This is the accident. He had to stay."

"Why *me*?"

"I couldn't leave you."

Sally took Albert's arm and led him away.

Behind them the sea of concrete surged once, a sluggish wave rippled its surface, and then it was still. The clouds closed. The moon disappeared. The building site was vacant.

Closing

～Ж～

THE LAST SIX WEEKS in London were drawn out with
waiting and a welling sadness that at times overcame Sally Lawrence to the extent that her eyes
filled with a moisture finer than any tears she had
ever shed. It was like a film of melancholy that came
between her and the rest of the visible world, dimming and softening, blinding the hard edges of experience.

After the night in Tonbridge she had not returned
to her apartment near Victoria. Nothing would per-
suade her to go back to the significant rooms above
the tree-filled square; they were too full of recent
memory, too close to what she had done.

Albert Scot had arranged for her to go anony-
mously to a small hotel near Kings Cross station.
At first he wanted to send her somewhere in the
country where he thought she might achieve a greater
quiet, a more restful peace, but the idea of being
isolated and distinct alarmed her deeply. The busy

little Kings Cross hotel with its changing inhabitants, its noise, its clutter, and its new faces was what she wanted. There she began to forget the sharpness of her loss and to find herself again.

Albert organized the transfer of what she needed from her old apartment to the hotel; the remainder of her belongings he sent on to her parents in New York. Sally had wanted to go with them, but he'd persuaded her to stay. There were details he'd wanted to talk about, statements to be made.

Albert worked tirelessly, traveling between London, Dover, and Tonbridge, diminishing the curiosity about what had occurred. He was not so much concerned with covering over the events surrounding the deaths of the bulldozer driver, the van driver, and the ticket-seller as with diverting attention from them, keeping the media quiet, convincing his superiors that nothing was to be gained by disclosing too much of what, in the end, was unlikely to be believed by anyone. It would not be in the public interest to release anything at all.

He was leaner now, and walked with a limp. He held himself stiffly as if his ribs hurt him still; the hair was only just beginning to grow back thinly over the cut on the top of his head. He wore a suit and a tie when he called for Sally and took her walking slowly in the direction of Regent's Park where they would sometimes sit, talking or not talking, ending the knowledge they shared. On those occasions he looked like a fine ghost of his former self.

One day, while they stood in a patch of winter sunlight, waiting for traffic lights to change, Albert reached out and took Sally by the arm. It was a gesture that could have meant he wished to assist her over the road; it was an approach that could have been read quite differently. He felt, as his hand slipped beneath her arm, a renewal of the attraction he'd been so aware of the night he'd first seen her, sitting alone and desolate, in the canteen of the ferry building on the Dover pier.

When she felt the touch, Sally turned and glanced at Albert briefly. She saw concern in his clear eyes, she saw also the interest they held; but she looked away quickly and, when the pedestrian light turned to green, started across the roadway leaving him behind.

Albert caught up with her, understanding her decision; her grief was both too recent and too raw to hide. It was a pity, he reflected wryly, his mother would have approved greatly.

Something like a smile touched his lips, and he began to speak of other matters. He told her that the constructors of the car park at Tonbridge had decided to leave the fallen wall of wet cement where it lay. By the time they could have done anything about it, it was semi-solid; it was less expensive to let it remain as a further foundation to the car park to be built above.

A new wall was already in place.

Once an elderly policeman named Bates telephoned Sally and took her to lunch at Simpson's in the Strand. Not in the lower dining room, with its long, school-boy-like refectory tables which were reserved for male diners only, but upstairs in a Wedgwood-blue room where women were admitted. He was charming and gentle and spoke a lot about cricket, but between a reminiscence here or a tale of a day's batting in Australia there, he'd slipped in a quiet but acute question that she'd answered as best she could.

He seemed most interested in what Simon, as he called him at all times, had told her, and what she might have inferred about his past. Once he inquired obliquely about their relationship, but she'd said nothing. Finally, after a long tale about something called the Ashes, which she never quite understood, he led her down to a waiting taxi, which returned her to Kings Cross, and she did not hear from him again.

On another occasion she'd made a phone call to Cyril Fenick, or attempted to, not quite knowing what impelled her. Perhaps she would have told him not to be afraid. As the bearer of bad news he no longer had any reason to be concerned, but she was unable to speak to him. On hearing her name, his secretary had reacted sharply; his manner cooled, and he informed her that Cyril was not available. In fact, he added, Mr. Fenick had virtually retired and was no longer making appointments. He'd not been well, the secretary said, his voice quite tart, and was still convalescing.

It had not seemed important to Sally. She'd sat quietly after the call, seeing the fat man surrounded by cats, knowing he'd survived. Really, she concluded, that was the only reason for her calling, and it was comforting to be told he remained.

Finally the day arrived when Albert rang to say she was no longer needed, she could stay or go as she wished, but there was no official reason for her return to New York to be delayed if that is what she wanted to do.

Immediately Sally called an airline and made a reservation. The following day she left from Heathrow, driving out to the airport in the back of one of London's innumerable black taxis, watching the buildings become less crowded, seeing some of the green of the countryside intrude. She did not travel by the Underground; she could not have brought herself to descend its depths, to enter the tubes beneath the city.

The plane was not crowded. Sally took a window seat, and the one beside her remained unoccupied. She watched the other passengers settle, adjust themselves, wait with tense faces as the 747 lumbered into the lineup and then raced down the runway and lifted sharply into the air. She saw structures dwindle and become unreal, vehicles turn into toys on strips of black tape in the English green.

After a while a stewardess offered Sally a drink, but she declined. When the stewardess had gone, Sally undid her seat belt and made her way to one of the toilets at the back of the plane. There she examined herself, but there was no sign of anything.

On every other occasion that she'd flown since she could remember, the event had brought on her period. She'd waited, during the past few weeks of uncertainty, for this moment, knowing it would confirm what she had already accepted. She was pregnant; there was no doubt about it now. She'd not had a period since Simon had made love to her—she, who was always regular.

Sally looked at herself in the narrow mirror of the washroom. Her face had altered in a way she had not noticed before: her eyes possessed a new brightness; her lips were almost smiling.

Sally Lawrence returned slowly to her seat. She looked out the shining window with a mixture of awe and fascination; she could feel the beginning life within her, and it filled her with mystery.

Suspended between heaven and earth, in curiosity and amazement, she marveled at the clouds below: purple and saffron, pink with the rosiness of new flesh, they assumed shapes and postures she had never seen before.

She sighed deeply with a sense of great astonishment and wondered what they were trying to tell her.

A HORROR NOVEL
by
KENNETH McKENNEY

THE MOONCHILD 41483-X/$3.50 US /$4.50 CAN
Set in Europe at the turn of the century, The Moonchild
begins the chilling tale of Simon Blackstone, a young
boy struck by a mysterious illness, but at his death
his corpse does not succumb to rigor mortis. A series
of horrible murders follows, and with each, his corpse
grows more hideous.

THE CHANGELING   89686-9/$3.50 US /$4.50 CAN
The continuing terrifying tale of Simon Blackstone,
The Moonchild. Simon had been buried too long. And in
the peaceful, quiet English countryside, violent horror
was about to pierce the night. They broke the silver
clasp of his casket and perfectly preserved and handsome he had arisen—to love again, laugh again and
tear the flesh from a victim's body.

AVON Paperbacks